Enemies with Benefits

A Novel by Michelle Rabot

Chapter One- Dr Nick Willis

I sit nursing a cup of lukewarm coffee. It is ten to five in the morning and I have two hours and fifty minutes left on my twenty four hour shift. Surprisingly I don't need the caffeine, but after over six hours in my last surgery, it's nice not to be focused for a few minutes.

"Morning Nick," her voice calls out. Her sweet scent hits me as I turn to face my future wife. Well, one day to be my future wife.

"Good morning beautiful," I reply to the perfection that is Penelope. Her blonde hair is braided today and her lean long legs are encased in a grey pencil skirt.

"Just finishing up?" she asks whilst making her tea, Earl Grey, no milk or sugar.

"Not long left, "I'm back in ten,"

"I'm just about to start,"

"Of course five till five again?" I tease.

"Of course."

Her father is a board member and part founder of the hospital, as is mine. However I don't get the royal treatment like her. We grew up together. Our fathers have been trying to set us up for years. I'm all for it, she is perfection.

Penelope majored in paediatrics whilst I majored in surgery.

"What, or should I say who are you doing after work?" she asks as her shaped eyebrows rise.

"Just my usual, run and crash before heading back here."

"Kayley was raving about you,"

I grit my teeth, Kayley with her big tits and even bigger mouth.

"Just a bit of fun baby, you know it's all you for me," I say with a smile.

"I do not want a player Nick,"

"I will stop once you ask,"

"I highly doubt that."

I move my chair close to hers, her face only inches from mine.

"I'd give it all up for you Penny; be with me and I promise it will only ever be you," I say seriously.

I see her mouth escape a small smile. I know I'm getting to her. I know she wants me too.

"I cannot consider it while your penis has been inside half the female staff in this hospital."

Ouch! But fair.

She sips her tea and stands up.

"What can I do to change your mind?" I ask.

"Prove it," she replies, walking away, her heels clacking on the floor.

When she's gone I groan at having a semi, having being so close to her. Penelope Sinclaire is the only woman to say no to me. She is the only one that matters, so hell if it doesn't make me more determined. Another cold shower it is after work again. I do try my best to keep it in my pants, but damn I'm only a man. How long is she going to keep me waiting?

Chapter 2- Holly

I slip out of the staff coffee room unnoticed by Dr Willis. He is such an arrogant dickhead laying it on thick for the hospital princess. Honestly, the two of them should just get it on so he can leave the female staff free of his STD's.

Yes he is hot, with his muscular build and sexy dark eyes, but it doesn't appeal to me when he is such an asshole to mere nurses like me. It's like we are scum because in his eyes we are not important.

I change in the locker room, zipping up my hoodie as I finish for the day. Night shifts are hell but it's safer to be working when the monsters come out to play.

"Night Phoebe" I call out, when I pass my best friend in the hall.

"Morning Hol, still on for film night tomorrow?"

"Absolutely." I smile.

We have been best friends since nursing college six years ago. She is bubbly and sassy, just like I used to be.

I walk the three miles to my crappy bedsit down town. I feel relief as I see my apartment complex. I reach to open the door, when Martin stands in my sight. Relief turns to dread.

"Holly baby," he mutters his hands slide to my waist.

"I don't get paid till Friday you know that." I snap.

The door opens and he follows me inside. Sighing I allow him into my bedsit, knowing that protesting being indiscreet would be bad.

"What do you want?" I ask, hating the shakiness in my voice that comes through.

"Ten thousand, five hundred and thirty six pounds."

I wince as he tells me the full outstanding debt Robbie left me with.

"You can have a grand on Friday,"

"Fifteen hundred," Martin replies coldly.

"I can't afford it and you know it,"

"Your pay cheque states otherwise."

I automatically look around, to find my papers everywhere, my minimal furniture disarrayed. I've been ransacked.

"I take it this is you?" I fume.

"Harry and Tom had a nose earlier, yeah,"

"You have trashed my home." I shout out without thinking.

I see his hand before I feel the sting across my cheek
bone.

"You scummy bitch, you lied to me," Martin roars, as I
stumbled back onto my cluttered bed.

He grabs a slip of paper from his pocket. I see it's my
payslip.

"Eighteen hundred, fifty six pounds and seventeen
pence." he quotes.

"Yeah and I need to pay for rent, utilities, food? I scrape
by giving you over half my earnings,"

"I want it back faster. I am sick of being here, being
owed,"

"I understand but it is working, please ten months from
now and we are done, it takes time." I beg him.

Martin stroked his sallow, drug abused face.

"Imagine the problems it will cause when the hospital
finds out what kind of man you are married to, every
missing tablet, will have those fingers pointing." he
whispers.

My skin grows cold despite the fact that this isn't the first
time he has threatened me with this, but it works every
time.

"Give me fifteen thousand on Friday. There I do compromise,"

"But my rent…"

"Fifteen hundred or I will send the boys round to collect it and allow them to fuck you until you piss blood." he snarls before heading out.

Life was not always like this. Eight years ago I was simply Holly Turner; a trainee nurse desperate to impress my impossible to please parents. I just wanted to make them finally notices me, or maybe even make them proud.

Then I met Robbie at the local student pub. He was a bartender there, and was a gorgeous bad boy. I fell, and I fell hard. The bad boy that I thought would change through love. I was stupid and so naive.

My parents had nothing to do with me after I married Robbie, yet even then I didn't give up on him. When he left me two years ago, broken and battered, he also left me with his debt from the drug dealers he was using, leaving me to repay his addiction bills.

With a sob, I throw all the clutter off my bed to the floor and get into bed and cry myself into an uneasy sleep.

Chapter 3- Nick

Sweat pours off me as I jog back to my apartment. I feel the bitter sweet burn through my legs as my body finally starts to tire.

I love my apartment. I moved here three years ago to be closer to the hospital. It is less than a twenty minute walk. It is perfect, especially as it came fully furnished and decorated; it's spacious, modern, and neutral.

As soon as I get inside, I jog straight into the bathroom and into my gigantic shower. It can fit four comfortably, and I know that as a fact.

The hot water cascades all over my aching body and I think about Penny again. That conversation we had over a week ago is fresh in my mind. She may not want my reputation to tarnish her perfect one, but she wants me. To be fair most women do. Some may call me arrogant, which I agree with but it is also the truth. I've never had to try to get laid, even in my younger years. It's the face, the body which I spend a lot of time maintaining and if that wasn't enough, I have a fat bank account thanks to my trust funds and salary as lead consultant in general surgery.

Since our conversation, I have given up the one night stands, the flings and the quickies in hotel. I want Penny to take me seriously, she has to. She is everything I want in a wife: the brains, the looks, and the social status. She is just like me, she lives in my world, professionally and socially. We are a perfect fit.

I climb into my massive bed enough for perhaps six? But I don't know this to be a fact. I am not that bad or good, depending on how you want to look at it.

My hand automatically slides into my boxers. This will have to do, again.

The alarm wakes me from an empty sleep at six pm, another night shift again in two hours. This is my last one this week, and then finally two days off. I make myself a strong coffee and some granola before looking properly at my phone.

Kayley: when shall we hook up again?

Cindy: R u 3 2nite?

Laura: I want you now! Call me xoxo

I delete them all before I am tempted. A week of celibacy and I'm already weakening.

Eight hours into my shift and my hands are inside a man with a gunshot wound to the stomach.

"Vitals are dropping Willis." Matt stresses as the monitors inform me of the same thing.

I quickly feel with my fingers for where the bullet is, giving up with equipment. My fingers locate it and with my other hand remove it carefully with forceps.

I stitch with speed and precision.

"Stabilizing." Matt says calmer.

As I finish up I take a deep breath. I love the adrenaline rush of surgery. Every stitch I make is art; every incision I make is calculated. The responsibility of saving lives is a rush and I crave that rush. The chase, it's like sex. It's about reaching the result even more than the result itself, that's the pleasurable part.

"Good job," Matt says as I finish my final stitch.

"Thanks." I tell him, removing my gloves.

Samantha reads out the stats.

"Well done team," I announce to the room.

"Be out in fifteen to talk to Mrs Collins." Samantha calls.

I wash my hands repeatedly before heading to the changing rooms. At three twenty on a Wednesday morning, it is a grave yard shift. I pull my scrub top over my head and loosen the knots in my neck.

Then I hear singing.

"Burn, burn, burn, yeah, we're gonna let it burn." I hear a female voice gently through the air.

It's a male wash room, so what the fuck is a chick doing in here?

Curiously and perhaps indecently I walk towards the shower cubicles.

"They don't know what they heard," the voice continues, actually doing Ellie Goulding justice.

I see the steam billowing from one of the cubicles, and then notice two feet underneath, neat little toes with no varnish on.

She seems oblivious so I stand on the bench and stupidly decide to play 'peeping Tom' out of pure nosiness, not because I'm a horny, moody prick these days.

Glancing down I see thick, dark brown hair almost reaching a very nice bum; curvy and meaty without being overly generous. Day-umn! I feel my manhood alert in an instant.

Without thinking I groan quietly and the woman's eyes snap open.

I quickly duck my head. I could get my stupid perverted arse sued for sexual assault.

The shower turns off as I scramble down in a panic. She heard me, there is no doubt so I can both run, and hope she doesn't open the door in time, or I can face up to it.

The door opens so there's not much I can do except put a cocky smile on my face.

The woman stands in the cubicle fully covered by a towel now.

"Did you?..." she trails off.

I look at her properly. She is absolutely stunning. Huge hazel eyes framed by thick lashes dripping with water and lips that belonged to a make-up advert.

Seeing her faltering on what to say, I dive in.

"Did you know this was the men's changing room?"

She glances away, her cheeks pink.

"Yes, but no one comes in at this time," she mutters, chewing on her full lower lip.

The towel is starting to absorb with water and I can see the outlines of her curves. My hands clench to stop me from shoving her back in the cubicle with me.

"Well I did." I say hoarsely. Jesus, I feel the erection through my scrubs pulsating, she has to be new or something, there is no way I wouldn't have noticed her or slept with her before now.

"Well do you spy on your male colleagues as well? I know you're a whore but I didn't realise it swung both ways." she snaps, shocking the fuck out of me.

What the fuck? No one dared to speak to me like that. I feel my lust turns into anger. Bitch.

"Next time use the ladies" I spit out coldly.

The girl picks up her clothes and moves quickly into the cubicle to change.

"No problem," she says through the locked door. "I wouldn't want to be perved at"

"I didn't perv." I lie. I should leave before she makes a complaint against me. Obviously she hates me on reputation, yet my feet are frozen as I watch her feet beneath the cubicle.

She opens the door fully dressed into tatty, ripped jeans and a baggy hoodie hiding all that sexy body.

"Well you don't tell and I won't," she replies crossing her arms.

"Agreed."

It's more embarrassing for me than it would be for her, but works for me.

"Thank you Dr Willis." she says, her voice flooding with relief and slips out of the room.

I pull a clean scrub top on at long last.

Who the hell was she?

My cock aches again as I think of her naked bottom, how that long chocolate coloured hair fell against her creamy skin. I quickly jerk off in the toilets with the image in my head.

I am putting it down to my lack of sex. My body is reacting fiercely to the sight of a sexy naked body, that's all.

After sanitising heavily and cleaning up I go to see Mrs Collins, the wife of the patient that I had just performed surgery on. She is maybe in her late forties pacing the waiting room frantically.

"Mrs Collins?" I call out to her as her focus turns to me.

"Is he Ok?" the wife asks rushing over.

"I am Dr Willis, I operated on your husband. He had been shot in the stomach, but we are able to remove the bullet and repair the wound. He is stable," I inform her.

"Oh thank god, thank you doctor" she cries out. Her children, I presume, rush over to her.

"It's my job." I reply brightly.

The family are hugging and holding each other tightly. I am used to seeing affection but it still makes me uncomfortable so I leave quickly.

Chapter Four- Holly

My cheeks are still burning despite the cold weather as I walk home. I don't think Dr Willis saw anything, but the idea that he was close to me whilst I was naked in the male changing rooms is mortifying!

It's humiliating enough that I have been using the male wash room for the last few days. It's because I haven't been able to top up my gas or electricity meters since Martin took most of my wages. The rent is just about paid but it's left me with nothing to live on.

The women's changing rooms are always so crowded and I don't want anyone to gossip about me. Women always gossip or want to make small talk with me. Right now I don't want to talk to anyone, or explain why I am washing my hair at work.

On the plus side I am taking on extra shifts which mean more money for next month but the down side is that I have to be back at work in six hours, after finishing a twenty hour shift just now. Exhausted I make it home and collapse on my bed knowing I will be asleep within seconds.

My alarm buzzes five hours later and I groan, my heavy eye lids refusing to open. Half asleep I literally just roll out of bed and begin to walk back to the hospital still in the same clothes as earlier. Things were really hitting rock bottom again. I didn't think I would get back to that stage, yet here I am again, starving, exhausted and completely broke.

As I approach the hospital doors, Phoebe stands outside with two coffee take away cups.

"Morning," she chirps handing me a cup.

"Good morning, thank you," I say gratefully, she doesn't know how grateful I am, as I sip warm caffeine goodness.

"God Hol, you look a mess,"

"Extra hours,"

"Are you struggling this month?" Phoebe asks me quietly. She knows most of the truth, she knows about Robbie and the debts and she knows I am paying them off. She doesn't know about Martin hassling me constantly.

"Yeah but it's under control." I lie.

"You would tell me if you were struggling, I can lend you money if you let me," Phoebe grumbles.

"I'm fine, but thank you again."

We depart after changing into our scrubs; I set to work in Ward C whilst Phoebe heads to Ward B agreeing to meet up for lunch later as we have the same lunch break times today. The staff cafeteria provides free food and it's the only food I am eating now.

The day goes by busily as usual, checking charts, giving medication, taking bloods and temperature results the works. I love my job, it's busy, rewarding and I never get two days the same.

"Hi Mr Collins." I say brightly a few hours later.

Mr Collins was in surgery last night with a bullet wound to the stomach; some weekend hunting trek out in the country gone wrong apparently. Dr Willis performed his surgery it says on his charts.

"Hi." he replies in a croaky voice.

I get him some water immediately.

"How are you feeling?" I ask once he drinks a few sips.

"Ok I guess."

His next medication is due soon I read.

"Mr Collins, how are you?" a voice says from behind me.

Dr Willis, crap.

"Ok Doc," Mr Collins mutters.

"May I?" Dr Willis asks. It takes a second more than it should have to realise he is talking to me, wanting the chart that I am holding.

I give it to him quickly. His face flickers with recognition when he sees me.

Great, he remembers me.

"Everything is looking good here Mr Collins, I need to check over your incision and stitches"

I step aside to shut the curtains and go back to gently lift Mr Collin's gown.

Dr Willis snaps on his gloves.

I look at the incision. I admit Dr Willis is a jerk but he is fantastic surgeon. His stitches are always perfect and any infections are rare with him. I always feel relieved when I have his patients.

I watch him doing his careful checks, trying not to think of last night.

"You are healing well Mr Collins. If you carry on like this I think we should be able to discharge you in a day or two."

I put his gown back down.

"Um Miss…" Dr Willis says.

"Jones,"

"Miss Jones, sorry, could you get Mr Collins some anti-inflammatories with his medication?" he asks, his eyes lock on mine.

"Of course Doctor," I reply lowering my eyes.

"In fact, I can't remember the specific type. Can you come with me please?"

Damn it, I can't refuse a doctor.

I follow him to the medication store. He uses his card to access the room. It's deserted, unusually.

"What's your name?" Doctor Willis blurts out.

"Holly Jones."

He walks over to select the anti- inflammatories.

"What are you doing this evening Holly?" he asks.

"Working."

I turn away to get the rest of the tablets I need for Mr Collins. I feel him moving behind me, close. He is so close I can feel his breath on the back of my neck.

"When are you next off?" he mutters.

"Wednesday,"

"I finish at eight Wednesday; Can I pick you up at nine?"

I spin around shocked.

"No,"

"What? Why" he asks and steps back thankfully.

Christ, his ego is monstrous!

"Because I am not interested in spending time with you socially,"

Shock is written all over his handsome face. He looks at me, staring at me up and down with a heated gaze.

"You are," he whispers with a smile on his face.

"No I'm not,"

"Yeah okay, play hard to get, I'll see you at nine on Wednesday." he beams and walks out the room, leaving me stunned.

Egotistical arrogant prick!

I'm feeling both mad and confused when I take my lunch break at two pm. I load up my lunch tray with as much food as possible before it looks ridiculous. My stomach is growling noisily.

Phoebe is already seated and waves me over.

We chat about our day as usual but I decide to cave in, I have to tell someone.

"Doctor Willis asked me out," I blurt out quietly.

"What? No way!" she squeals.

Phoebe is weak when it comes to handsome men.

"Way, I said no,"

"You said no to Mr Ego? How did he take it?"

"I don't think he did, he believes it's happening," I groan.

"A man like that won't be used to being turned down,"

"Well he better get used to it, the pervert," I mutter darkly.

"Pervert?"

I move my chair closer to Phoebes.

 "I was in the male shower room last night showering," I start.

"Why were you in the men's?"

"Ladies was full," I lie.

"Ah,"

"So anyway, it was early morning hours, the place was empty. I was showering when I heard a groan,"

"A groan?"

"Yeah, so I turned off the shower in a panic and there he was outside my cubicle!"

"He saw you naked?" Phoebe shrieks.

"I don't know, I was in a towel but he was turned on, that was hard to miss," I blush.

"Then what happened?"

"Nothing, we agreed not to speak of it and I left. He didn't even know my name when we were with a patient earlier,"

"Jerk,"

"Then he makes me go with him to the medical storage room and asks me out,"

"Like on a date?"

"I don't think he was thinking dinner," I admit dryly.

"You think he was asking you for a shag date?" Phoebe asks, her high voice pitching higher.

"That's what he is known for, anyway I refused and he didn't accept it. What do I do?" I ask desperately.

"What do you want to do?"

"I want him to leave me alone. I don't even like him," I say honestly.

"Then tell him that, be straight with him." she tells me.

I smile brightly. Now that I have eaten my head is feeling much clearer.

"You're right. I thought I was direct but obviously he couldn't get it through his fat head. If he brings it up again, I'll be firm but polite."

I can't get involved with any one even if I wanted to. Not with Martin lurking around. It's a dangerous mess I'm in and no one can know.

I don't have to wait for long to tell Dr Willis. As I walk home at midnight that night I find a text waiting on my phone.

UNKNOWN: *Don't think about cancelling Wednesday, I will find you. Nick (Willis)*

Jeez! Stalker much!

Luckily I get free texts with my phone and I can charge it at work.

ME: *How did you get my number?*

NICK: *Personnel. Give me a night that's all.*

I sigh. He is such a player. I hate being out this late at night on my own but I can't afford the bus so I continue to walk. At least texting Nick will keep my mind off the monsters that lurk about this time of night.

ME: *Not a good idea, I don't even like you.*

NICK: *Ouch. What's like got to do with it?*

ME: *Believe it or not, I'm not that kind of girl.*

NICK: *That's what they all say.*

ME: *Maybe some do, but it's the truth in my case.*

NICK: *One night that's all I want, you can go back to hating me in the morning ;-)*

Did Dr Willis just wink at me?

I continue to walk home trying to compose how to be straight and blunt with him. I'm nearly home when I finish the text.

ME: *Look Dr Willis, I'm really flattered and confused by your interest in me. I really do not want to meet you. Wednesday was never on and now I am demanding that you leave me alone. Goodnight.*

Feeling relieved I put my phone back in my pocket and enter my bedsit. I haven't had a man chase me in a very long time, never a man as successful and handsome as Dr Willis, or Nick. But now I've knocked that on the head, life can carry on as it was before.

He didn't text me back.

Chapter 5- Nick

Today is Wednesday. Five days have passed since I asked Holly out. I can't get her out of my head though. I have done some digging on her. I know where she lives, in some cheap bedsit in the bad part of town. It appears I have worked with her for three years, yet I haven't ever noticed her and fuck knows how that has happened.
It could be that she is a brunette I originally thought, I usually go for blondes. Or that she hides her body under baggy oversized scrubs. Then the last few days I have watched her as she works. She acts like she is invisible. Colleagues walk by yet she never makes eye contact or speaks to them unless its work related. She is ridiculously quiet, but efficient, which is unlike our shower encounter with her sassy mouth. That Holly was never seen.
I move to check on Mrs Judd. She has bowel cancer. I removed most of it yesterday, but I couldn't remove all of it unfortunately. I have managed to buy her some more months but that is the most I could have done.
As I head over to her bed I notice Holly is talking to her softly. No one has seen me, so I wait behind the curtain.

"Elizabeth, you need to put on that brave face, your family will be here soon," she soothes to Mrs Judd who looks like she is having a weak moment.

"I look so awful Holly but I just haven't got the energy to look half decent,"

"Where's that big make up bag? Would you like me to help?" Holly offers kindly.

"You will do my hair and make-up?" Mrs Judd asks in delight.

"If you like,"

"Thank you dear, I would like that so much. My bag is over there."

I watch Holly retrieve the bag and carefully put make- up on Mrs Judd.

"I hope I'm doing this right, I don't do make-up much," Holly says shyly.

"You don't need it dear, you're naturally beautiful."

Damn right she is. I inspect Holly's face. Not a trace of make-up from what I can see and she still looks like that?

Matt clears his throat behind me. I turn to find he has an amused look on his face.

It startled the ladies.

"Sorry to interrupt. I came to check up on you Mrs Judd," I smooth over, walking to them.

"Can you give us five minutes gentlemen? Holly was just preparing me," Mrs Judd asks with a wink.

"Sure," I laugh. It's hard to believe she was sobbing moments ago.

I walk away and Matt follows.

"What?" I snap.

"What was that?" Matt asks.

"What?

"You staring at Holly Jones,"

"You know her?" I ask suspiciously, Matt's reputation is as bad as my own.

"Not like that dude, she isn't our type."

We check over Mr Green's head injury next, which looks good as well.

"What do you know about her then?" I ask as we walk back down the hall.

"Holly Jones? Not much, she doesn't wear a ring, unsociable, quiet, but the patients rave about her,"

"I can see that." I smile.

Holly seems to go that extra mile to make her patients happy, not just medically but emotionally as well. I am not built like that, but Holly is and I respect that.

We walk back to Mrs Judd, fully made up and beaming. Who knew a bit of lippy and a brush could cheer someone up so much?

"Mrs Judd, you look lovely," I beam, flashing her smile.

"All done doc, let's get me semi naked." Mrs Judd laughs.

Matt and I check her over while Holly assists.

"Looking good Mrs Judd," I say once I am satisfied.

"Visiting time will be here in ten minutes, knock your hubby's socks off," Matt tells her.

"Thank you Holly, you're an angel" Mrs Judd says to Holly.

Holly flushes and heads away.

"Just going to grab a coffee before the next surgery," I tell Matt and power walk after Holly.

"Uh-huh." is Matt's knowing reply.

Holly hears me too, and quickens her pace, it looks as if she is trying to shake me off. Just as I'm catching up with her, she slips into the ladies' toilets.

Shit.

I wait until no one else is coming in or out of the toilet before discreetly stepping inside the ladies toilets after her.

Holly is at the sink.

"This is the ladies," she protests.

"And you were in the mens," I argue.

Her cheeks flame up.

"What do you want?"

"You,"

"Not happening Dr Willis, stop harassing me."

Her long hair is wound up into a severe bun at the back of her head, how she usually wears it at work.

"I have issues with rejection," I try.

"Well get over it," she glares, putting her hands on her tiny waist. Fuck its hot.

"Can't,"

"Look I know your god's gift to women, I've seen the way you work around our female staff but I'm not interested. Even if I was, you're practically with Dr Sinclaire," she snaps.

"How do you know about that? Didn't take you as a gossip." I snap back.

Women are damn infuriating, this one is no exception.

"I have eyes and ears, you act like a player but around her you're all sweet and sickly."

Girl is observant, I'll give her that. I feel like a damn fool, here I am chasing a woman. I never chase women, yet here I am in the ladies' toilets getting rejected for a third time.

"Fine, it's your loss." I bite out and carefully leave the toilet.

Fucking woman, I don't need her.

After my shift ends I head home. I need to get over my funk. Fuck what Penelope says, I need to get laid. I grab my phone and scroll through my contacts. Each girl's name that comes up I have fucked casually and I try to select one for tonight. After ten minutes I put my phone down frustrated. Not one of them has my dick interested. I hit the shower and change, looks like I need to go hunting for one instead.

Forty minutes later I pull up close to Holly's crappy flat. The spot light is flickering. Paint peeling off the graffiti covered walls like sun burnt skin. I see a crowd of unsavoury characters by the buzzer.

"Open up Holly." one man yells.

Surprised, I open my window and kill the engine.

"Leave me alone Martin," I hear Holly's voice faintly.

"Let me in or I'll break in." he yells nastily.

The door opens and they storm into the first door on the left.

I jump out of my car and head to the bottom left hand window.

"Holly…. Money…. Now", I make out broken parts of the conversation.

"You have everything…. Five pence to last…" I hear her scared voice.

Part of me wants to play hero, but the more sensible part of me stays put, knowing the stupidity of messing with guys like them.

I hear a cry of pain from Holly.

"Next month I take every damn penny!" I hear a man yell.

I hide behind the wall as the men slink out the apartment block and down the street.

Before I think it through I stop the apartment doors from closing fully with my foot and step inside.

I have questions.

"Holly, it's Nick," I knock on her door gently.

I hear movement from inside.

"Go away please," Holly begs weakly.

"Not going to happen. Open up."

Holly finally opens the door.

"What do you want?"

"Can I come in please?" I ask.

She hesitates but eventually takes a step back, so I walk into her box of a home. There are no lights on, just a candle flickering miserably on a tiny table. It's very tidy and clean though.

"What did you see?" she whispers, her face is as pale as a sheet. No sassy spunk that I am used to.

"Enough to know you're in a fuck load of trouble." I reply.

She trembles and sinks onto her single bed. She is holding her wrist tightly.

"Are you hurt?"

Holly shakes her head but clutches at her wrist.

"May I?"

She sighs and let's go of her wrist. I take it carefully. It's not broken, just a nasty twist from the looks of it. That's a clever bastard.

"Hang on a minute, I'll get my kit."

I jog to my car and get my emergency kit out of the boot. I'm relieved that she automatically buzzes me back in.

She is rocking back and forth on the bed when I walk back in.

"What's going on Holly?" I ask gently.

She shakes her head.

"Talk to me,"

"They are drug dealers. Robbie owes them a lot of money, he ran off and the debt is now mine," she whispers as I bandage up her wrist.

"So you're not involved with drugs?" I ask carefully.

She shakes her head.

"Who's Robbie?"

"My husband."

I gasp, looking at her fingers. No band. I didn't think I saw a band, I don't do married woman.

"You're married?" I blurt out.

"Well technically yes, But once I find him I'll divorce him."

Shit, she looks too young to be a wife. She is only in her mid-twenties according to her file.

"How much does he owe them?"

"I'm not telling you that," she protests.

"I think you deserve to be honest with me here."

She doesn't say anything, so I finish up.

34

"Nine thousand and thirty six pounds." she mutters as I get up.

I could give her that. That wouldn't even make a noticeable scrape on my bank account. But why should I? I may save lives, but that doesn't make me a nice man. I push it to the back of my mind.

"You're all set, here is some pain relief," I say handing her some pain killers.

"Thank you Dr Willis, Please can I ask you keep this to yourself?" she begs.

I look at her properly then, her hair is loose and touching the duvet cover, it's that long. I touch her chin and tilt it up. She is just so beautiful, like a china doll.

"I won't tell anyone." I say as I draw my face closer to hers.

I kiss her lips, just a peck. But as soon as my lips touch her soft ones, bolts shoot through me.

She pushes me away quickly.

"Nick, good night." she says sternly. Her face is flushed though. Did she feel it too?

"Good night Holly."

I jump up and head out without looking back. If I looked back at her on that bed, I may actually jump on her.

I can't sleep. Tonight's events are swirling through my mind. Holly was scared and being bullied by drug dealing bastards. I want to help, but that's not me at all. It's making me uncomfortable that I even thought about helping her. She is nobody to me, I shouldn't care.

I am groaning into my pillow when my phone rings. I snatch it up to see it's Penny.

"Hey beautiful," I answer calmly, as if I haven't been having an inner fight with myself for the last hour.

"Hey, how are you?" her sweet voice fills up my ears.

"Great, what's up?"

"I've been thinking about us."

She pauses, but I don't speak. I don't want to fuck it up.

"I'm being so foolish. We would be good together wouldn't we?"

I sit up smiling. Reel her in Willis.

"Yes we would, we are a perfect match," I agree. I want to air punch or something ridiculous like that. I have been waiting for this for over a decade.

"It's just…"

My heart plummets.

"What? What can I do?"

"It's your reputation Nick. I hate being in the hospital knowing you've slept with so many of our co-workers." she admits.

Me and my damn dick! To think if I had played things differently, I might have been inside Holly right now, and not answered this call. Kind of lucky Holly rejected me.

"I can't change the past Penny but I have been without sex for over two weeks now,"

"Really?" her voice shows her shock.

"Yeah, listen, I am a bloke, and I have been a proper whore but I haven't bothered with relationships because if I am going to commit it's going to be to you okay?" I say, quite chuffed at how smooth I sound. Is it the truth? Not sure.

"I believe you Nick." she sighs, eating up my words. I imagine her in a silky pink nightie, sitting up in her princess bed.

"What if we gave it six months? You know put the distance between the old you and the new one who is ready for a committed relationship?" she suggests.

"Six months? Come on rumours are forgotten about in ten minutes," I protest.

"Four months? You slept with half my team Nick, be fair,"

"And I can't be with other women?" I ask, horrified. Four months? Two weeks is hurting me.

"I can't have any more women in the hospital bragging or bitching about you. Your reputation must be clean, because I won't tarnish mine." she trails on.

But that wasn't a no, that was a 'be discreet as fuck'.

This is why I will marry this woman.

A plan is forming. It is not a nice plan, but fuck it is a genius one.

"Agreed. In four months we go exclusive,"

"Yes," she breathes.

"Until then we remain unavailable,"

"Yes,"

"Done. Get your stamina up gorgeous; you are going to need it." I laugh.

She laughs quietly before hanging up. All of a sudden my future is looking absolutely fucking fantastic.

Chapter Six- Holly

Nick: *We need to talk, are you on a night shift tonight?*
He sent that text over an hour ago, yet I still haven't
replied. I am humiliated about last night and I don't want
to face him. He overheard the dark part in my life. The
side no one knows about, which I work so hard to hide. I
hide it well, no one knows until now. If he told his father
on anyone high up my career is done for.

Yet he took care of me so sweetly last night. I saw a
side to him I haven't seen, even at work he is so
practical about his patients. He has the coolest calmest
head I know, which is why I respect him so much as a
surgeon. He didn't pity and judge me like I thought he
would have. He helped me and then he kissed me.
Gosh that kiss, it was a hell of a kiss even though it
wasn't a full on one, just one simple peck created such a
heat it flooded through every part of me. It made me
dizzy. I don't think I can deny it even though I tried
originally. There was some serious chemistry between
us in that moment.

I am on the night shift and its seven pm now, with an
hour to go before I start. I finally drag my cold body to

the door. My wrist hurts more than I thought it would. I barely slept again and I am so hungry. A day off is a hungry day without the free staff food. But its only five hours or so until I get a food break.

I decide it's time to respond to Nick

ME: *Yes I am, 8-8*

He responds almost instantly.

NICK: *Great I'm on until 6. Can I meet you somewhere after?*

ME: *Why not at work?*

NICK: *I don't work to hear this conversation. There is a Costa not far from your's. Meet me there at 9am?*

My heart speeds up. He wants to talk about last night. I don't want to meet him, but after all he did for me last night, it wouldn't be right to refuse.

ME: *Ok, thank you again for last night.*

NICK: *Don't thank me yet*

My accelerated heart is going so fast it's making my head spin. He said he wouldn't tell anyone. Why would he say not to thank him? I wonder if he has already gone back on what he said. This is not good.

The night shift flies by ridiculously fast as usual, despite me trying to slow it down. But after it ends I drag my feet to the Costa to meet Nick. I spot him in a discrete back booth, away from the windows. It's very private.

As I join him I notice he has put a chocolate muffin and a cappuccino in front of me.

"Yours," He grunts whilst devouring his muffin.

"Thank you, this is very sweet of you." I say surprised.

He frowns at that compliment, not sure why but not sure I care, when I dive into my treats.

"So we need to talk," he says after he finishes every crumb of muffin.

"Please don't say anything Nick. I'm not into drugs. I haven't done anything wrong except get involved with the wrong guy. Please don't jeopardise my job, it's all I have now," I beg.

"Holly,"

"No wait. I'm grateful that you helped me, and Im sorry I can't give you what you want. At least you can see now why I can't,"

"Holly…"

"Please Dr Willis…"

"Holly, stop!" Nick says sternly.

I shut up immediately.

"You are not to blame. I have not reported anything. I'm here to make a deal with you."

A deal? Blackmail? My eyes narrow as suspicion runs through me.

"I want to help you. I don't think you will accept help, as I'm sure you wouldn't be in this mess if you did. I want to give you the money to pay off that creep and get him out of your life for good." Nick tells me seriously.

He wants to help me? Pay nine grand to a stranger? He didn't even know my name until the other day for goodness sake! He was an arsehole to me up until last night.

"Why?" I breathe.

"Because you don't deserve this. How much money do you actually have?"

My cheeks flame up big time.

"Nothing," I mutter humiliated.

"I noticed you had no lights on,"

"I can't put money on the meter." I avoid looking at him, if I see the pity; I think I may actually bolt.

"That's why you shower at work?" I don't need to look at him to hear the horror in his voice.

I nod stiffly. He could afford to pay off my debts I'm sure, but he wants a deal. I can do deals not charity but what's the price?

"Why do you want to pay it off? What do you want?" I ask suspiciously.

Nick leans in close to me.

"I want you to be my mistress." he whispers.

I splutter coffee all over the table.

"What?" I choke out.

"My life is complicated right now. I can't go into details until you agree and I have your absolute discretion." he says, whilst mopping up the table with some napkins. He is so calm and cool. I would giggle if I wasn't so confounded.

"I want to help you and I need help too, in a very different way I admit but it's still down to this: I can help you and you can help me," he continues patiently.

"I am not a prostitute," I gasp quietly in disgust.

"I never said you were. Look, this is a first for me too. I want you, but I can't do relationships or even dating, not that I would want to. It's just sex Holly, that's all I want from you for four months. If you agree I will treat you right and you will not be cold or hungry or feel afraid like you do now."

His hand touches mine. I feel a tingle as his skin covers mine. It wouldn't exactly be hard to have sex with this man, but under these circumstances?

"You're asking me to sleep with you for money?"

"Yes I suppose I am, but it is a win-win for you. You will get your life back, no more fear of debts, or the likes of Martin. You also get me for four months," the cocky bastard actually winks at me.

"You arrogant prick," I hiss yanking my hand from under his.

"Yes I am, but honestly Holly don't overthink this. It is not prostitution. It will be a very private fling. No one can know about this. No one" he says in earnest.

My head is spinning.

"I need to think about this,"

"Of course. It needs to be discussed in more detail. Can I ask one thing?"

"Yes,"

"That you do not tell anyone about this. Even if you tell me no, you can't discuss this with any one,"

I pause.

"Or I will reveal last night's events to the board," he hisses.

There's the ass hole I know.

"Fine," I grit my teeth.

"Go get some sleep, think it over. I want an answer by tomorrow night,"

"Got it."

He stands up, holding his hand out for me. I take it, but the prick yanks my hand so I fall into him. I gasp at his hard body against my back.

"Turn around," he whispers huskily.

I do and his lips crash on mine.

Shocked, I try to pull away, but his arms are ironclad. Stars are shooting across my eyes at the sensation and I return the kiss parting my lips. He tastes of chocolate and coffee and just deliciousness. I don't think I have felt such a sparks from a simple kiss. He is either so damn good or I want him as much as he seems to want me.

He does want me, as I feel his hardness pressing against my stomach.

I pull away flushed.

"Do you see how good his could be?" he moans.

I hurry away, my head and various body parts throbbing.

I am pulling another twenty hour shift so I don't have time to think. So after some much needed sleep I'm straight into work at eight pm. Nick is in surgery all night so I don't have to face him. It is a smooth shift, but busy so I don't even think about his proposal until my dinner break.

I'm alone, so as I eat, I weigh up the pros and cons of his offer.

Pros: Get rid of Martin; have my full wages, which is more than I have ever had before; sleep with a sexy man for four months.

Cons: Be a charity case; be a prostitute, and have no self-respect; let an arrogant blackmailing asshole use my body and be controlled by him. To make it worse who knows what kind of sick perverted kinky shit he may be into.

As if on cue, I find Nick sitting down with his surgical buddies. He sees me and his heated stare makes me skin warm. Frowning I look away.

I hate the idea of him giving me money and not being in control. Those are the worst two I think on my list. I could however try and compromise on this. We need to talk this over properly.

My phone buzzes; I know who it's going to be.

NICK: *I am waiting!*

I glance up to see him smirking at me. Asshole!

ME: *I have time*

He is chatting with his friends, I don't even see him text.

NICK: *Not much*

ME: *There are some issues that I have. I hope maybe we can compromise on? Can we discuss this further before a decision is made please?*

NICK: *I'm all ears*

I sigh as I see the time.

ME: *I don't have time right now; I have a set break time unlike his highness.*

NICK: *Ok Rag Doll, call you later x*

Rag Doll? How rude!

I rush back as I put my handbag in my locker I notice another text.

NICK: *By the way, your mouth tastes incredible. Can't wait to taste the rest of you :-P*

Well that has me flustered for the rest of my shift.

I have only ever been with Robbie and I am not used to Nick's crude language. That makes me worry even more. What if I'm rubbish in bed? Nick seems to be

47

interested but he hasn't seen me naked. He doesn't
know what my skills are, nor if I even have any. I just
don't understand what he sees in me. Why chase me so
much, or offer nine grand for sex with me?

I finish my shift and head back home, pushing my
aching legs home. The idea of being able to take a bus
or even a taxi if I take the deal is tempting.

When I reach my bedsit I stop dead. The window has
been smashed in. All I can see if shards of glass jagging
on the edges of the frame. All my stuff is there for
anyone to see or take. Then I see Dan my landlord
inside. I burst into tears. How the fuck can the last few
days get any more humiliating?

"What the hell is going on?" Dan asks as I step into my
bedsit.

"I don't know."

The entire flat is trashed again. Why does he keep doing
this? I am paying him and he knows he can't get any
more until pay day.

Dan is a really nice guy, he doesn't do credit checks and
is understanding when I have been late or short of rent
in the past.

"Come here." Dan says seeing my face.

I step over and he pulls me into a hug.

The unexpected contact breaks me and I cry uncontrollably.

"I can't afford to fix this Dan; I gave you every penny I have"

Dan stiffens and drops his arms.

"Are you in trouble?"

I look away.

"You are such a lovely girl. I don't understand what's going on. I can't afford trouble here anymore. The other tenants have been complaining about you and the unsavoury characters hanging about." he says gently.

He waits for me to say something, but I don't.

"I'll board this it up for now. I hate to say this Holly but enough is enough, any more trouble from you and you're out."

I understand. I really do understand and it's upsetting how pained Dan is to have to say it.

"There won't be Dan, I will sort it." I tell him seriously.

I've made up my mind in that instant, I'm selling my body and soul to the devil in scrubs.

I clear the broken glass as Dan patches a chip board panel over my window leaving no natural light. We are surrounded by a dark grey mist but Dan doesn't say anything.

"Shall I charge you a new window on top of the rent next month? I can get a window put in the next couple of days?" Dan offers like the kind generous man he is.

"Yes please Dan that is so kind of you," Tears still trickling down my face.

"Got a daughter your age. I hate to see such a good girl like you in a mess. I do mean it though, this is the last time." he tells me as he leaves.

After tidying and cleaning the mess completely, I roll into my bed and fall into a broken sleep.

When I wake up it is pitch black, then I remember the chipboard for a window. Pulling out my phone I see it twenty past nine at night.

ME: *Can we talk?*

I light a few candles then pour a glass of water and drink it thirstily. I'm hungry but I've found drinking glasses of water can help fight off the hunger pains. I don't even know his shift, is he working or just finished?

NICK: *Been waiting for you. When is your next shift?*

ME: *Doing a day tomorrow 8am-8pm you?*

NICK: *Day off tomorrow, just done twenty four hours. Sending a taxi to you, prepaid to mine, Apartment 9, see you in about half an hour.*

I was right to worry about control. Who said I wanted to go to his apartment? With a huff I get out of bed. Does that man ever sleep?

I brush my hair and tie it in it a pony tail and scrub my teeth.

Braving it, I strip off to have a wash. The water is freezing and my teeth chatter as I wash and shave my body.

Drying myself as quickly as possible, I dress in my usual tank top, baggy jeans and a hoodie. No point trying to look nice, there is a good chance it's all coming off any way, you slut.

By the time I've put on my worn out coat, a beep outside lets me know my taxi has arrived.

Nick's place is in the affluent part of town. As I see the building my jaw drops a bit. I'm confident one of those apartments to rent a month would be at least double my entire wages.

My hands shake as I press the intercom.

"Yeah," Nick's voice travels through.

"It's Holly." my voice is seriously squeaky with nerves.

Am I really going to do this?

The door opens and I head up the elevator to apartment nine, which is on the top floor.

My heart is banging through my chest as I knock the door.

Nick swings the door open.

"Come on in." he smiles at me.

I enter, taking in the beautiful surroundings.

"Wow what a gorgeous home,"

"Thanks."

I follow him to his huge living room, which is complete with a lit fireplace, an enormous sized TV and enough leather sofas to sit at least twelve people.

The coffee table is covered with boxes of various Chinese foods, smelling heavenly.

"I ordered dinner. I'm guessing that you're hungry"

My skin prickles. I really am his little charity case. But I am desperate and it smells so good that I swallow my pride and take off my coat.

"Thank you Nick, but you didn't have to order for me too." I say calmer than I feel.

Nick takes my coat and puts it on one of the sofas away
from us.

"Sit down Holly."

I sit down automatically like a dog.

"Look, you seem uncomfortable. Let's just chat, have a
glass of wine and eat some food, I'm fucking starving,"
he says gently, running his hands through his dark hair.

I relax slightly then, he is just trying to be nice.

Nick hands me a glass of red wine and a plate, so I help
myself to a variety of food and settle back on his comfy
sofa.

Nick is already tucking in heartily so I do the same.

"How was work?" I ask finally.

He seems startled as if he had forgotten I was here.

"Busy, open heart surgery, two tumours and
replacement gall bladder,"

"Just a normal day at the office," I joke.

"Exactly, I like that it doesn't put you off your food."

I laugh; the food is too delicious to put me off.

"That's a pretty sound." he says softly.

I can feel the atmosphere change as he looks at me.

"Eat up. I am actually knackered, so we better talk
soon."

I eat quickly and drink my wine far too fast.

"So what do you want to discuss or compromise on?" Nick opens up with.

Taking a deep breathe I begin with.

"First of all I don't feel comfortable about accepting that kind of money. How about you lend it to me instead and I'll pay it off in instalments?"

Nick shakes his head.

"No, a deal is a deal. I am paying for you to be my mistress."

He pauses looking at me darkly.

"It will be money well spent I believe," he adds.

"But Nick, I can't expect you just to give me nine grand," I argue.

"Holly it won't be a blip in my bank account, I am a wealthy man, trust me I can afford it." he rolls his eyes.

How people can be that wealthy that they won't miss that kind of money? It's infuriating.

"Okay fine, if it means nothing to you then thank you,"

"Besides, after four months I don't want any contact with you if I can help it." he continues bluntly.

I gulp. He sure has a way with words.

"When you say mistress, does that mean you have control over me? Where, when and dominatrix type of shit?" I blurt out.

Nick looks at me in shock then bursts out laughing.

"Oh Holly you are funny." he says between laughs.

I glare at him. I know I'm inexperienced but he doesn't know that and I don't know him.

"No heavy dominatrix shit, get your head out of Christian Grey's world. It's all very normal stuff don't worry,"

I let out a sigh of relief.

"But as for control, you will do as I please, you will be paid well enough for it, so if I want you, you will come running; if I want sex you will spread your legs. Oh and I will be changing your shifts to align better with mine," he says more seriously.

"Can I have a day off?"

"Sure I could do that, a work day though,"

"Agreed,"

"How will it work?" I ask.

"I'll text and tell you when I want you over. I'll give you a spare set of keys, when you're here make yourself at home. I'll let you know when it's time to leave,"

He gets up and moves to sit next me.

"Sounds fair,"

"It is. This is a mutual arrangement Holly, and you will benefit from this not only financially. I assure you I am not a selfish lover," he says quietly.

"So I have heard," I mutter dryly, as his thighs press against mine sending tingles through me.

"The most important rule you have to remember is simple. Do not tell anyone about us. This is between you and me. Nobody can know."

Is he ashamed of being with me?

"Holly it's not what you think. I must appear single and unavailable at all times. It's nothing personal" Nick says quickly, sensing my reaction.

"Is it Dr Sinclaire?" I ask thinking to the conversation I heard in the staff room.

His eye brows rise slightly.

"Yes, we are getting together in four months. It's important to let my lifestyle reputation die out of respect for her,"

That makes sense; the hospital princess and prince having a happily ever after.

"I see,"

"It's more to it than that, our families are interlinked. Both Penny and I are to be made board members next year, each gaining a ten percent share. Politically we can change votes with our parents. We need a united front." he explains.

Ah so it's a business match as well. Not knowing what else to say I nod in understanding.

"It's another reason I need your absolute discretion. I don't do blackmail, but don't cross me. I can ruin you in a blink of an eye and you know it."

He looks at me. His eyes are black and hard. It's actually scary, I believe him as the hairs prickle on the back of my neck in fear. But it still pisses me off.

"Nick you are saving my life, paying off Martin. I won't ever betray you, I'm not like that, and you can trust me there is no need for threats," I snap.

"Good, then we understand each other,"

"Completely, I will be your dirty little secret. You click your fingers and I fuck you, keep my gob shut and be discreet, Anything I've missed?" I say heatedly.

He stands up and kneels in front of me, nudging my legs apart and he moves right in between my thighs.

"That's about it. Will you accept my deal?" he says in a low voice.

Taking a few moments to think it through, I nod.

"Thank fuck." he mutters and pulls my neck towards him, kissing me hard.

Man that doctor sure can kiss. His tongue slides to part my lips and I let him, allowing his tongue to tease mine sending heat causing me to shiver.

His hands move down my neck and towards my chest. What if he uses me and doesn't pay up? Gets what he wants for a night and the rest of it is bullshit.

I freeze.

"Wait." I yell out as his hand touch my breasts. I almost groan aloud; it's been way to long since a man has touched me.

His eyes narrow and he takes his hands off me.

"You don't trust me do you?" he asks.

"No,"

"Fair enough, I don't trust you either," he replies.

"I'm sorry."

I am sorry truthfully in more ways than one. My body is not happy with me either.

Nick calmly hands me a piece of paper and a pen.

"No you're right, we should do this properly. Write down all your account details and I will transfer the money to you first thing, meet me back here tomorrow after you finish work. You can pay Martin off in your own time"

"Thank you." I say gratefully.

He smiles at me then, it's actually dazzling.

He puts his hand in his back pocket and hands me a generous wad of twenty pound notes.

"Nick... I can't," I protest.

"You're my mistress now; I will take care of you. It's for your taxi home, the taxi tomorrow and to get your meters on," He interrupts.

I look at the money in my hand.

"Thank you, I will be over tomorrow night about nine." I say and lean up to kiss his cheek as I move to leave.

He looks shocked as I look back on my way out.

I check my bank account the next evening after work. My account flashes up with a balance of ten thousand pounds and five pence. I gasp at the sheer amount, it's a grand over what we agreed and ready to withdraw. How has the fund cleared already?

I feel like I'm in a dream, this is too surreal to be true. Half tempted I grab my phone to call Martin, have that bastard out of my life once and for all. But then it's already gone eight and I should head to Nick's very soon.

I want to stay in my happy bubble a little longer. I still have well over a hundred pounds left from Nick's last night so I jump in a taxi and let myself be driven home. I stop at the shop and put twenty pounds on both my meters. Happily, I then go to Costa and buy a coffee and a bacon sandwich.

After I sort out the meters, I sit on my bed with the lights and heating on and enjoy my dinner with a stupid grin on my face.

I arrive at Nick's flat on time. He opens the door in a pair of tracksuit bottoms and nothing else. I can tell he keeps in shape, even when he is wearing scrubs, but I am not prepared for the sheer perfection of him. His muscles are ripped on his arms without being too huge, down to his defined stomach muscles and a sexy as hell 'v' disappearing into his low trousers.

I find that I am staring blatantly, mouth open at his naked flesh. Holy shit!

"Are you coming in?" he smirks, catching my eye.

I must be a shade of tomato red as I step past him to go in.

As the door closes, I turn around and look at his face this time.

"The funds cleared today, thank you so much, how did you get it done some fast?" I ramble.

"I have bank accounts in most banks, so I transferred it from the same bank as yours. It clears immediately,"

"Oh ok."

He moves closer to me, his chest touching mine. I can feel the heat from him.

"Can we continue last night's activities now?" he asks touching my arms.

"Wait, why did you transfer ten grand? I said I needed nine,"

"Because I can. You need to survive this month," he shrugs

I don't want to argue with him, because it is gratitude I feel. He didn't have to do any of this but the extra grand showed he cared, not that it was part of the deal.

"Thank you,"

"Show me you're grateful." he smirks lifting my chin up further.

I pause, my mouth inches away from his. I wait to feel dirty, feel like the prostitute I am about to become. But the only thing I feel is gratitude and I want to show him my gratitude.

His mouth descends on mine; I don't hesitate to wrap my arms around his neck, pulling him closer to me. It is not a gentle kiss, it's furious, hungry and rough and I love how it feels.

He tugs off my coat as he continues devouring my mouth.

"Always in baggy clothes Rag Doll." He whispers breaking the kiss finally.

I look down to my hoodie and jeans. I suppose I should have made an effort. It clicks then why he called me Rag Doll before. That's how he sees me; a bag of rags. I take off my hoodie and tank top quickly, as he watches with a heated stare.

"Fuck, look at what you're hiding." he hisses cupping my breasts through my plain bra.

Despite myself, I let out a quiet moan at his touch.

"Let me see you." he breathes unbuttoning my jeans.

I let him slide them off, so I am stood in his hallway in just my underwear, not exactly sexy ones either but at least they match both being plain black.

"You are beautiful Holly." he says staring at me.

I bite my lip embarrassed. I haven't been so exposed in over two years.

"Don't be shy with me."

He takes my hand and leads me the bedroom.

I see his bed, the pure size of it is intimidating enough, let alone what we will be doing on it.

"Lay down." he commands gently.

I do, propping my head up on the pillows.

I thought he would climb on top of me, but instead he sits next to me on the bed. He runs his hands over me. I'm trembling, I'm sure he can feel it.

"Nervous?" he asks his fingers touching the tops of my knickers.

I nod.

"It's been a long time." I admit.

He grins and slips a finger under my knickers. Just one stroke against me and I gasp.

"Fuck you're wet." he mutters and removes his finger.

Nick pulls my bra down and immediately puts his mouth around my nipple.

"Oh gosh," I moan as I feel it in my groin.

He continues to suck and cup me as I feel myself building.

Nick stops suddenly and removes the rest of our clothes.

His penis is long and thick. I have only seen one before and his is almost scary.

He slides a condom on and parts my thighs.

"Ready?"

I nod as he slides in slowly, stretching me almost painfully.

It feels amazing.

He is gentle at first, easing in and out of me slowly.

"You okay?" he asks hoarsely.

I nod; I am okay, more than okay actually.

He slams into me then hard and I gasp at the sudden change.

Nick smirks as he roughly moves fast, I can hear the moaning, and some of it is from me.

"Come for me Rag Doll," he groans and rubs his thumb over my clit.

I'm confused as hell as I explode, as I spasm over and over again.

"Fuck," he bites out as he finds his own release.

I've had sex before, but gosh that was something totally different.

"I knew you would be worth it." he says grinning.

Chapter 7- Nick

I jump into the shower as soon as Holly leaves. Damn that girl is really something; such a sweet shy girl, but so responsive in bed. That body of hers could make a weaker man weep and to think I would never had known it if I hadn't spied on her in the shower. She hides it well, I don't know why though.

My phone rings, so I step out the shower. Penny's beautiful face lights up my screen.

"Hello beautiful," I answer, wrapping a towel around my waist.

"Hey, what are you up to?"

"Just having a shower before heading to bed, what are you doing up so late?"

I glance at my watch it's nearly midnight.

"I noticed you're on a day shift the day after next and thought we could have coffee?" she asks.

Arranged coffee breaks with Penny? I smile.

"That would be lovely,"

"Great, text me when you can have a break and I'll sync it,"

"Will do,"

"Bye then,"

"Goodnight."

Damn I feel myself stirring, my earlier fucking awesome release is dwindling, I need Holly again.

It's not fair though to call her back again so soon, she is pulling eighteen hours tomorrow. Thinking of which, I call Mack.

"Bro," he chirps cheerfully.

"Hey Mack, I need a favour, a very discreet favour" I ask.

"Course bro, I'm your bitch, name it,"

I really like Mack. He is one of the staff who sorts the work rotas out. He is also very happy to be manipulated into bending shifts with a bit of cash. But he is trustworthy and is very inconspicuous when he tweaks the system.

"Nurse Holly Jones; is her rota done yet?"

I hear him clicking away.

"Yep, just needs to be finalised with her extra hours, girls a machine,"

"Cancel her extra hours and align her shifts to mine for the time being please,"

"Not cool, isn't she's married?" Mack protests mildly.

"Separated actually, oh and have her days off to match mine,"

"Gotcha."

He clicks for a few minutes, whilst I change into my boxers and slip into bed.

"Done," he sings out.

"Thanks Mack,"

"No problems,"

"Oh Mack, it is actually very important to keep your gob shut about it. I know you're always discrete but even more so this time, I'll pay you extra to ensure it," I tell him seriously.

"Sure thing, not your usual type though Willis,"

"Trust me, she's better," I laugh.

"Quiet ones are the wildcats bro," he laughs back.

"I'll bring cash tomorrow, thanks again Mack,"

"Laters." he says brightly before hanging up.

I lie down in bed, thinking again about what I did in here with Holly just a couple of hours ago. So good, life is good.

The next day I go to meet with my father for brunch at the Hilton. I spot him at our usual table and head over.

"Nicholas," he says as he sees me, and extends his hand like I am a business partner rather than his son. I shake his hand and sit opposite him. A pretty waitress immediately appears.

"Coffee, strong and white please," I ask.

"Scotch, double, best you have with a black coffee,"

"Certainly gentlemen." she smiles a flirty smile.

I ignore it, but see my father eyeing her.

She wanders off knowing he is watching her by the telling of her hips.

"What's up with you; all tapped out?" he teases.

"No, in fact I have made significant progress with Penelope," I inform him proudly.

"Excellent, knew that little prick tease wouldn't hold out much longer." he laughs.

He is a handsome man in his late fifties, with salt and pepper hair, once black like mine and dark eyes that I get from him.

"When do I announce the news to Lawrence?" he asks.

Lawrence is Penelope's father and my father's best friend.

"Not yet. She is giving me a little run around. Four months and we go exclusive."

The waitress comes back with our drinks.

"There you go Mr Willis, Doctor Willis." she says bending unnecessarily low to place our drinks, flashing her balloon like cleavage.

Dad looks though, such a pervert. What's worse is she is probably only in her late twenties at best; she will be in his bed tonight. No doubt about that one.

"I will take the eggs Florentine on wholemeal muffins thank you," I interrupt dad's eye fucking.

"Yes sir, and Mr Willis?"

"I'll have my usual thank you."

She nods, and walks away slowly.

"So why am I waiting four months then Nicholas?" he asks his attention back to me.

"She doesn't want to be seen with me seriously until my reputation has cooled down." I explain.

My father downs his whiskey.

"Seriously? What a load of horse shit. She better not rule you like this once you're wed boy," he snarls.

"I have fucked a lot of staff,"

"So? Woman like that should be proud to have a stallion of a lover in the sack. I am proud of you,"

"I'm just trying to do this right," I grumble.

"So what you are going to let your dick shrivel up like a carrot until the dick tease lets him out?"

"No actually, I have got a mistress," I say heatedly.

My father's face is one of shock, then pride.

"Ah, my boy, you are finally getting it," he laughs as the waitress brings him another whiskey.

"Thank you darling, what time do you get off work?"

"Around six"

"Meet me there in the bar after?"

She nods and walks away.

Jammy old git still has it. I'm not surprised. I'm used to it. He has been like it since my mother walked out when I was ten. I am exactly like him, he groomed me like that. However I won't make the mistake he made by completely falling in love and being owned by someone, like he did with my mother. I love Penny, but not that burning, consuming fire that he had with my mother. It made him weak, sacrificing his career, bending to her every wish. No, that's why Penny is perfect for me; she will be the perfect wife for me. Dad and Lawrence have pushed it since we were kids. This will happen and then when they retire the hospital will be mine.

Chapter 8- Holly

ME: *Martin, I have your money. If you're still up meet me at mine.*

I know its half past two in the morning but he always seems to be awake late.

I take a taxi home again. It's lazy but god it feels so nice not to walk home, I am sore all over from my encounter with Nick last night but fuck was that hot. I always believed that if you didn't care about the person you slept with the sex would be empty. Boy was I wrong. My phone buzzes twice.

NICK: *Meet me at mine in an hour*

Well that's how it's going to be then, no flirty winks anymore.

MARTIN*: Coming to yours now, be five minutes.*

I withdrew the nine thousand and fifty three pence on my break. It's dangerously in my backpack weighing me down like its gold, not paper.

ME: *Just meeting Martin, then I'm yours. Text you when I'm on my way.*

Four minutes later I see Martin approaching my bedsit smoking. I jump out and without talking let him follow me in.

"Well, what money do you have for me?" he slurs.

I hand him the large envelope crammed full.

He eyes are saucers as he empties in onto my bed, counting.

"Where the fuck did you get this?" he hisses.

"Bank loan, it's in my friend's name." I lie.

He looks furious for some unknown reason.

"You fucking lying to me bitch?"

"No, you wanted all the money now and I want you out of my life. It's all there as you can see, so you don't need to see me again." I say, relief flooding through me as the words hit the air.

He actually just looks angrier. What the hell was the matter with this man? It was what he wanted, and he still looks pissed.

I'm too busy looking at his ugly face, to see his hand has snaked around my arm until I am pulled right into his face.

"If this falls back on me I will gut you," he says icily.

"It won't. I'm free of all of this now, you and Robbie, and I am done." I shout.

His fingers dig into my arm painfully.

"It's very convenient Holly, suspicious too. Are you sure there is nothing you want to tell me?" his rancid breath tickles my face.

"No, I'm telling the truth let me go"

He drops my arm.

"Shame I was looking forward for another form of payment." his eyes roam my body.

I visibly gag, and I know he saw sees it.

"I hope I never see you again," I mutter as he stuffs the money messily back into the envelope.

"That's a shame baby, I look forward to the day our paths cross again." he smiles at me as he leaves.

I breathe in and out deeply for a minute or two. It's done, I'm free! No more drama or constantly being reminded of Robbie and the mistakes I made for him. No more Martin knocking on my window any time he pleases just to intimidate me. This is a fresh start for me; life is finally turning around thanks to Nick. I may have made a deal so I am not free yet I suppose, but in four months I will be Holly again; just Holly. Nobody's bitch or punching bag and besides dealing with Nick is a lot better than dealing with Martin. My body heats just thinking of how I deal with Nick.

I have a wash in hot water this time, change and head to Nick's.

As soon as his door closes, Nick slams me back against it, kissing me like a starving man.

"Well, hello to you too," I gasp pulling away finally.

"My room; strip off; take your hair down." he barks stalking off.

I stand stunned for a second.

"Go." he yells from the kitchen.

Well, no sweetness lost there then. I head to his room and do as he asks. I didn't feel like a prostitute last time, but now I do lying on his bed completely exposed.

It feels like an hour later when he finally comes in with two glasses of wine.

"Hi Nick, how was your day off?" I ask sarcastically.

He glares at me then.

"Shut up Holly."

Wow. There is the rude nasty Nick I remember.

"You look delicious." he mutters as his eyes trace my body.

I keep quiet; hating how my nipples harden, betraying me. My head wants out of here, but clearly my body has other plans.

Nick strips off showing me his magnificent body; he straddles me, leaning his face close to mine.

"Do you want me Holly?"

Pissed off by his rudeness I don't reply.

He seems amused by this as he trails kisses down my neck and chest, stopping just as he reaches my left breast.

"I said do you want me?"

I think I see his game, all about power with Dr Willis, but right now he won't get the satisfaction from me, so I ignore him again.

He chuckles at me, slipping his fingers into me. As good as it feels I don't make a sound. He slips his fingers out and into his mouth, sucking off my arousal. That is surely gross, but no, to me it looks so damn hot.

I look away.

I feel him shift then feel his breath on my clit. I open my eyes shocked, as his mouth touches me. I cry out, startled as his warm mouth sucks me. His mouth explores me, his tongue spearing me causing me to tremble. I have never experienced this before and it is just divine. My hands clutch at his hair as I moan loudly, shattering so hard I can see stars. Even as I'm coming down, Nick is still licking every drop of me.

I'm still in a wonderful haze as Nick flips me onto my front and onto my hands and knees. The crinkle of foil is heard before he slams into me from behind.

He groans loudly as he moves inside me, his balls slapping against me. I'm so sensitive right now from that orgasm, I am shocked to find myself climbing once more.

"God, you feel so good," he moans into my ear, he finds that spot inside me that has me moaning quietly too.

"One more time" he demands, holding himself against that spot, and I let go once again. He roars his release a second later.

He slips out of me and lies next to me, whilst we both pant with exertion.

"You liked me going down on you" he tells me amused.

I stiffen embarrassed. Was I loud?

He props himself up, looking at me.

"I've never experienced that before,"

"Seriously?"

I shake my head.

"How is that possible?"

"I've only been with one man, and he said he hated doing it." I explain with a shrug.

I am exhausted, mentally and especially physically. I haven't slept in nearly twenty fours. It's gone five am now.

"So I popped your oral cherry?" he laughs.

I nod as my eyes close.

"You can't sleep here" Nick says horrified, startling me. My eyes snap open.

"You're an asshole." I mutter mortified and jump out of his wonderfully soft bed. I grab my clothes aching. He says nothing as I head to the bathroom to change.

That's right, prostitute Holly; he got his end away and now he is telling you to leave.

"I've ordered you a taxi." he tells me as I step out the bathroom. He hands me a glass of wine which I drink in a few gulps.

"Thanks, I will wait outside,"

"No you won't; discretion remember?" he snaps.

I sigh and walk into his living room so I can see the taxi pull up from his window.

He doesn't follow. I can hear the shower running so he clearly isn't going to say goodbye; fine by me. No wonder the girls at work bitch about him so acutely with his 'fuck em and leave em' attitude. I feel dirty and desperate to wash his smell off me. At least I have been paid to feel like this, I actually feel sorry for Dr Sinclaire.

I start at eight, so I head straight to work. I know Nick doesn't start till four, so I can enjoy my shift without his glares and lusty gazes. My rota is back to normal hours now which I'm guessing Nick has something to do with; I guess I don't need the extra hours now, so when I'm not pissed with him any more I guess I'll thank him. I am so tired given I've had no sleep in over twenty four hours that I am actually thankful now.

 The day flies by checking and prepping patients for surgery, I'm so busy that I don't even hear Nick behind me.

"Get Mr Phillips prepped and do a final check on him, we head to surgery in one hour," he orders whilst I'm checking Mr Phillip's blood.

"Yes Doctor Willis."

No pleasantries, no manners.

"Oh and page cardio for me pronto." he calls as he is already rushing away.

Mr Phillips is in his thirties suffering with a gall bladder blockage, he had a heart attack two years ago so the surgery will be more risky.

"Is that my surgeon?" he asks me.

I nod.

"What an asshole,"

I laugh.

"Yes, he is but he is the best surgeon."

When I take a quick coffee break I notice Nick has texted me. Hoping it's an apology I open it.

NICK: *I am working late until 8am, be in my bed at 8.30am.*

My blood boils; he sure knows how to piss me off, and he also knows I need to sleep. I knew the deal, to be at his beck and call, but does he have to be so damn rude about it!

ME: *Are you forgetting I don't have a key? Unless you want to meet me after work?*

My phone buzzes again.

NICK: *No, discretion is everything. Where are you?*

I roll my eyes.

ME: *Coffee room*

The room is empty luckily. I haven't even put milk in my coffee when I feel him behind me.

"Holly," he mutters.

"Nick." I reply stirring my drink.

He glances around to see we are alone. He moves closer so my back is flush with his front.

"You smell good," he whispers in my ear leaving goose bumps down my body.

"Keys!" I snap impolitely, hating his effect on me.

He chuckles and slips them into my scrub trouser pocket, his fingers grazing me as he does.

"We are at work," I hiss quietly.

"Yeah," his fingers touch me through my trousers.

"Stop, Discretion is everything," I mock, trying to cover up how good his fingers are making me feel.

"Shut it." he hisses, as his fingers slide inside my knickers, stroking me. I feel a jolt running through me as he teases.

"I could make you come just by stroking that tasty little nub." he mutters into my ear.

I know it's true, I can feel it as he circles me faster, harder.

I hear voices close by and stiffen. Nicks fingers slip out and he leaves before I can even protest.

"Nick," Dr Sinclaire's voice floats through the room.

"Hey beautiful," he replies, grabbing a mug.

"Two coffee dates in one shift, aren't I the lucky one?" she purrs.

"The luck is all mine." Nick flirts back.

I move away unnoticed, it's like a de-ja-vu, the plain girl being part of the furniture by the glamorous couple. I move to the other side of the room to put my coffee in a take away cup. How can he be so sweet and gentlemanly with her, when the rest of us gets the rude prick. I slip out of the door quietly.

Dr Sinclaire is nicknamed the hospital princess; partly due to her father, but also because of her beautifully, perfected looks and snobby attitude, looking down on nurses and every one without a 'DR' status. She is not rude or unpleasant like Nick, but she just ignores us and avoids us if she can.

I see my place very clearly now. I am a mistress, just keeping Nick's dick warm until he gets his princess. Not that I want to be with Nick in that way; it's just the sheer pecking order that infuriates me and the fact that I'm left dumped, with wet knickers.

"Hey, do you fancy a few drinks after work?" Phoebe asks much later at our dinner break.
A few drinks would be very, very good indeed. I haven't been able to go out for months due to money but now I am richer than ever with a grand to my name and no bills to pay.
"Yes please." I chirp.
Phoebe's eyebrows rise.
"Seriously?" she asks in disbelief. I deserve it though, she asks weekly but she knows the situation so she knows I will say no, but it's so sweet of her that she always asks.
"I mean yes, I think my problems are over." I smile.
To my surprise she jumps out of her seat and hugs me.
"Oh honey I'm so glad to hear that," she says warmly.
"Me too,"
"Let's celebrate! Come to mine straight after work?"
 "Yeah okay,"
"Yah! I'm just so happy you're coming."
I smile back at her. I'm happy too I will be too.

"Cocktail happy hour." Phoebe cheers as we enter 'Blues' after work. I am working the night shift tomorrow night so I can allow myself a few to drink.

We go up to the bar to order a drink; men are looking at us in all directions. It's not me I'm sure, it's bound to be Phoebe with her green, shimmery vest that compliments her red flame coloured hair. I did make an effort though, keeping my jeans and flats but borrowing Phoebe's silky black vest top and I actually put on some makeup.

"Let's get on the woo woo train." she giggles as I grab our pitcher.

We find a table and pour a generous glass each.

"Woo woo!" she bellows like a train. We used to do that all the time at college. I laugh and join in as we down our drinks.

After drinking another couple of pitchers of the stuff we are giggling like school girls. I haven't been out in so long I have forgotten how much I enjoy letting my hair down, relaxing and just being with my friends.

"Let's dance." Phoebe announces as a song we both love comes on.

I follow her out to the floor and dance, men swarm around us Phoebe, but I'm part of the Phoebe package so they are around me too. I'm quite happy with that, I don't actually want any one coming on to me, or showing me that determination to get me in bed, as they do Phoebe. I hate the attention; attention only led to Robbie being jealous. When he got jealous, I got hurt or someone else did, or both of us did. Tonight though, I feel carefree and happy as some guy grinds against me. I am single enough and it's not as if I would go home with someone, even if I wanted to because of my deal with Nick.

"I'm Ryan," The guy shouts in my ear.

"Holly,"

"You sure can move girl,"

"Not so bad yourself,"

"Can I buy you a drink?"

Drink? Alarm bells ring.

"No but you can come with me to the bar."

He follows as I order another pitcher for me and Phoebe. She joins me automatically with some man attached to her.

"Holly this is Max, Max this is Holly" she yells indicating to the man behind her.

"Hi"

"Hey Holly, I see you met Ryan my buddy" Max says.

"Yep"

The men order a pitcher of beer, and join us at the table. It's nice to feel wanted, but I don't want Ryan. It is not that he isn't a good looking bloke, he is actually very good looking but I wouldn't want to take it any further. But still it's nice to be social and it feels good that Ryan is interested. We dance all night as a foursome and drink shots until we realise the club is closing. Damn its two am already?

"Can I get your number? I would really like to take you out for dinner." Ryan asks as we grab our things. I can see Phoebe is busy snogging Max.

I turn and smile at him.

"I'm really sorry Ryan, if I gave it to you, you would think I was available." I say gently.

His face looks a little crushed, and I feel sorry for him.

"It's not that I don't find you attractive or funny, you're both. I'm just not in a position to date right now."

He gives a sad smile.

"I see, well, no hard feelings, can't blame me for asking,"
"I am seriously flattered, and if I was available I would
be like them." I laugh pointing to Phoebe still tongue tied
to Max.

He laughs and drags his buddy away as their taxi
arrives.

"Maybe, if this continues, I'll be seeing more of you"
Ryan says as he puts Max in a taxi.

"Hope so."

Our taxi pulls up behind theirs and Phoebe and I get in.
Phoebe gives the address to the taxi driver as I look out
of the window. I gasp in horror. He is staring straight at
me; his ice blue eyes hold mine.

"Phoebe," I squeal as I point to him.

"Shit, fucking drive," Phoebe yells.

"Was that him?" I ask, my heart is hammering in my
chest as the taxi driver spins off.

"Maybe. It is dark; we have had a lot to drink. But yeah it
sure looked like him," Phoebe says panicking.

"It couldn't possibly be him, I haven't seen him in two
years Phoebs, he wouldn't dare show his face back in
public like that," I rationalise.

"No, you are right, if it really was him, he wouldn't have just looked would he?"

"No way."

We both let out a breath. It couldn't have been Robbie. I have had far too much to drink as my head sways, I am seeing things.

Phoebe lives with her sister and her family at the moment. She lived with a bunch of her nurse friends from college but they all got their own places eventually. She sleeps on the sofa downstairs. I don't like her sister at all, she treats Phoebe like a built in babysitter, but its only temporary until Phoebe can save up for a place of her own. The taxi driver stops at her sister's house.

"Are you okay?" she asks gently.

"Yep, the more I think about it, the less convinced I am that it was him," I lie.

"Okay, call me when you get home,"

"Will do."

She disappears inside. I know she wishes she could let me stay with her, but her sister won't allow Phoebe's guests to stay.

I sit back as the taxi driver pulls off. I am scared and I don't want to go home, what if Robbie knows where I live, it wouldn't exactly be hard to find me with Martin and his cronies around. What if it was him and he is waiting for me right now?

"Where next?" the driver asks.

I can't go home. But I could go to Nick's, I have keys. He won't like it but he wouldn't know since I'm supposed to be there before he gets back any way. So I reel off Nick's address.

As I enter his flat I suddenly feel guilt. He has been good to me; I shouldn't be here without his permission.

ME: *I hope you don't mind but I am at yours now, not feeling safe at home.*

Feeling a bit better I text Phoebe and turn on his shower, he did say I could make myself at home whilst I'm here. I just hope he meant it and I'm not overstepping the mark. I strip off and shower in his enormous cubicle, the water feels good against my skin. As I get out and slip into his bed, my phone rings. Panicking I glance at the screen, but its Nick.

"Hello,"

"Holly, are you okay?" he barks.

"Yes, is it okay for me to stay here just for tonight?"

"Sure, make yourself at home, use anything you like"

"Thank you,"

He pauses.

"Are you going to tell me what happened?"

"No its cool, just got spooked, thank you again,"

He huffs.

"Fine, go get some sleep, I'll be back by half eight."

He hangs up. His bed is so comfy I lie back and fall asleep instantly.

Chapter Nine- Nick

I step through my apartment, sweat soaking through my running gear, I need a shower.

I don't know why I agreed that Holly could stay, but it wasn't like I was there so what the hell. It was nice of me though, and I'm not known for being nice.

I step into my bedroom and see her in my bed. She looks so tiny curled up on the edge, the cream duvet covering up her skin, but her dark hair is spread out over the pillow. She is beautiful. That's why I let her stay, because she is on tap and I'm a lucky bastard. Lucky or just very clever, I choose to think the latter.

I get in my shower and have a wash quickly, I am absolutely shattered but I need to have her before I crash.

I climb into bed naked and nudge her.

She opens her eyes lazily.

"Good morning Rag Doll,"

"Morning." she mumbles. She even looks good first thing, and that's a rarity.

I pull her to me, she is already naked. Perfect.

I press a kiss to her shoulder and roll on top of her; she spreads her legs as I slip on a condom. She's already

ready for me as I inch myself into her, fucking hell she is so tight as I push through. It won't last long, as I fuck her, and with those sexy quiet moans she gives me is making it damn hard to last even a little bit.

I rub on her clit and feel her release, and with a grunt I come too. I am seriously going to lose my cred if I don't make it more than ten minutes.

She curls back up on the one side of the bed still half asleep. I should make her leave, this isn't how I do things, but hearing her soft breathing I realise she's already gone back to sleep. That's soft sounds actually sends me to sleep on the other side.

I wake up before my alarm to find the bed empty. I feel refreshed and have had a better sleep than I have had in a long time.

I get out of bed and wander around to find Holly has in fact gone. Shame; I could have done with a longer round two but good to know she knows her place. She shouldn't have stayed here at all. Wouldn't want her to think I wanted her to.

I go to get a coffee before I start work, and notice a brown paper bag next to the kettle with a napkin note.

Thanks for letting me stay. H.

Curiously I look in the bag to find a chocolate muffin and a fruit smoothie. I smile, that's a nice gesture. I sit at my breakfast bar with my 'breakfast' at six pm. It feels lonely all of a sudden.

On cue my phone rings.

Penny. Not who I was thinking of.

"Hello beautiful,"

"Hey Nick, I checked your rota, another night shift I see,"

"Yep," I reply, taking another bite of my muffin.

"What are you eating?" she asks.

"Chocolate muffin," I mumble, my mouth full.

"Oh naughty Nick, you shouldn't be eating those empty sugary calories," she tuts.

"I know but it's a nice treat,"

"Why are you treating yourself?"

I gulp it down.

"Because I'm taking you out to dinner," I say smoothly.

"Nick we said four months," she gasps.

"To be exclusive. We need to date to build up to it. Don't you think it will look a bit unusual, all of a sudden were a serious couple?"

I hear her high pitched sigh. Gotcha! That's going to be yes.

"Ok." she breathes. I wonder if she will be all light and high pitched when I fuck her from behind?

"But not yet, let's give it a month." she says.

I plummet. Always on her grounds, always on her terms, if she wasn't worth it I would tell her where to stick it. My father is right, she is a cock tease.

"Fine Penny, three weeks on Saturday, that's practically a month,"

"That's good with me Nick,"

"I'll book us some where nice and take the day off,"

"Fabulous,"

"Looking forward to it,"

"I'm looking forward to it too." she says and hangs up.

I fist pump the air, I have a proper date with Penny. Maybe I will be inside her satin panties before four months is up.

On Saturday afternoon I go for my usual jog, leaving Holly asleep in bed. Poor girl is exhausted after going three rounds with me after our night shift.

I admit life is pretty damn blissful this month. Penny and I are having coffee or lunch breaks most days and I have Holly giving me mind blowing sex each time I want it, which is always these days. I can't seem to get my fill of her. It's a novelty for me, as usually I get bored with the same woman after a few shags. As far a mistress is concerned, Holly ticks all the boxes and then some. She isn't clingy or needy, she never says no even when I know she exhausted. She leaves when she knows I'm done; I don't even need to ask. She just gets it and gets out of bed and slips out without hesitation, obediently. In fact it's kind of insulting that she never sticks around, she doesn't seem to want to. There hasn't been any repeat sleep overs either.

As I open the door to my apartment I hear the water running, Holly is in my shower. I know she uses it occasionally but I haven't actually seen her in it. I haven't seen her shower since that night in the male changing rooms.

Grinning I step into the bathroom quietly. She hasn't noticed me, and it's like de-ja-vu I can only see her thick dark hair that I like to knot in my hands as I fuck her. It's cascading to her bottom once again in wet locks.

"Turn around Holly." I ask.

She stiffens at my voice, but as always does what I ask.

I see the water dripping down her luscious large breasts and down her flat stomach. She continues to wash herself with her own sponge as if I'm not even there.

"Can I join you?" I ask my dick rock hard.

"I can't refuse you can I?" she teases.

No, she fucking can't.

I strip off and join her, pulling her to me, feeling her nipples on me.

"Suck me." I groan.

She doesn't hesitate as she sinks to her knees in the shower and takes me into her mouth.

"Shit." I moan as she sucks me like a damn hoover, even gagging ever now and again as she pushes me further into her throat to please me.

"Touch yourself." I whisper.

Her eyebrows raise, this is new to us, but I hate getting off without her.

I watch her fingers circle her pretty pussy.

It's enough to send me over the edge sooner than I thought as I release in her mouth with a shout.

She drains me then stands up with swollen lips.

"I just have to wash my hair then I'll be out of your way."
she says quietly, reaching for her shampoo.

No fucking way.

"I think you deserve a thank you."

I pull her to me, her back against my front.

"Put your arms around my neck." I whisper nipping at
her neck.

She does and I cup her breast, it does feel so good and
heavy in my big hand as I roll her nipple between my
fingers.

A little whimper escapes.

I move my hands lower and slip my fingers into her,
whilst circling her clit with the other.

"God." she moans leaning back

I kiss her hard, as I fuck her with my fingers.

"Nick." she groans as she shatters on my hand. I'm
already hardening up again, with me being a so much
taller than her, I got to watch her, she looks that good.

"You're fucking gorgeous," I mutter as she comes down.

I leave her to wash her hair in peace as I change into
my suit trousers and a white shirt. I should wear a tie to
'The Rose' it is a five star restaurant after all. I hate ties,

chocking at my neck. I grab a blue one and a silver one holding them up to my shirt.

"Blue," I hear Holly say, as she comes in wearing only a towel.

"Blue it is." I slip it on and knot it up.

I hear her tut as she approaches me.

"School boy error," she mocks and unties it.

"I hate these fucking things," I whinge.

"Let me?" she asks her hazel eyes looking up at me.

I nod, and she ties my tie perfectly.

"Thank you." I grin looking in the mirror. I do look good all suited even if it's uncomfortable.

"You're welcome." she smiles and moves to change in the bathroom. I don't understand that, it's not as if I haven't seen her naked; in fact I have seen her naked more than I have seen her dressed.

I laugh to myself as I do my hair and spray on some cologne. It's very wrong, my mistress doing my tie for me as I head out on a date. Come to think of it, she doesn't even know my plans for tonight. She has a day off too, yet she hasn't asked and I suspect she doesn't even cares that I'm going out.

What I don't expect even more is Holly coming out of the bathroom looking like that. She's wearing jeans but tight ones that mould her sexy backside and legs, with a low cut wrap around pink shirt.

"What's that?" I blurt.

"What's what?" she looks confused.

"Why are you wearing that?"

"Oh I'm going out with my friends from work tonight, we are going to 'Blues', mind if I do my hair and make-up here?" she asks plugging in the hair dryer.

I shrug and head to the living room and head out the door. Damn she looks hot, but not in any way slutty. Where are the baggy jeans? Where has my rag doll gone? Men will stare at her, they will dance and grope at her in that club. They will try and touch what's mine. Anger soars through me.

So I head back into the apartment silently, and I pace the living room angrily. I am being a possessive, selfish, dickhead and I know it. I also should have left by now. I am always early; it's the way of a gentleman. But I am here waiting to see how she looks when she is ready to go. I've never seen her with make-up on, she doesn't need it.

I hear high heels click. High heels really?

She stands out of the bedroom, her hair loose and swaying around her waist, her slim legs accentuated by the heels.

"Holly?"

She spins round. Fuck me.

"Sorry I thought you had left, I'm going now,"

Her eyes are highlighted by make-up and she has some gloss on her pink plump lips. She is edible.

I want her, I want to take her right now but I can't, I'm behind schedule. But damn if I don't remind her who's she is.

"Just a word of caution Holly, you're my mistress. I don't share," I snarl.

She looks startled.

"I wouldn't…"

"Just so we are clear, you fuck anyone else or so much as kiss any one, our agreement is void and I will make you pay back every penny, after I get you fired." I hiss out interrupting her.

Holly's lips part in a gasp. Yeah I mean that shit.

"Fuck you Nick. I wouldn't do that and there is no need to threaten me, you arrogant dick," she yells out.

"Glad that's clear then." I roar and storm past her.

I open the door.

"Oh and by the way be back here at midnight,"

"Why?" she asks confused.

"You heard me, midnight, here," I repeat angrily. She doesn't ask questions usually.

"But I thought you wouldn't want me after your date?"

Ah so she does know where I am going, perceptive little thing.

"Well maybe I do, maybe I don't. I still want you here." I bark as I shut the apartment door.

Chapter Ten- Holly

"Asshole," I mutter downing a tequila shot.

"Who's an asshole?" Phoebe asks pulling a face after her shot.

"Doctor Willis."

The other girls I have been hanging out with recently, Jenna and Lisa spin round at his name.

"Are you banging him?" Jenny asks her eyes wide.

Shit, I have had too much tequila.

"God no, I like having a STD free body thank you," I say laughing loudly.

"Then why are you slating him?"

"He just is an asshole, an arrogant demanding wanker that orders me around like I'm a slave because I'm a nurse." I snap out. Well it's true, I leave out that he is also like that because I am his paid mistress.

"Yeah but imagine how domineering he is in the bedroom." Lisa says lustfully.

That he is, I only have to breathe and he is asking me to spread my legs.

"Nah, I reckon he is just overcompensating for his lack of size," Phoebe chirps.

"I saw him with the princess yesterday; he was all over her like a rash," Jenny gossips.

"Yeah rumours are that the ice queen is thawing to the sleaze prince." Lisa says.

I snort. Sleaze prince! I love it!

"Enough about work, another round and lets hit the floor." I announce as I hand out yet another round of tequila slammers. I have been hanging out with Phoebe, Jenny and Lisa quite a lot this past month. It's been great getting out, drinking and socialising with the girls again.

"Hear, hear." Phoebe says and we all down our shots.

I feel the buzz creeping in as we make our way to the dance floor.

"I've said it before but I will say it again, I love this new look," Phoebe says to me as we dance.

"Thank you, I feel so much better now, like I'm free."

I do actually. I am happy right now, despite my spat with Nick. I have to put up with him being an asshole, but most of the time we are together we are having amazing sex, so it is bearable. Well more than bearable actually.

I never used to like sex much; I used to do with it with Robbie because it was what he wanted. But Nick has opened my eyes to the pleasure it brings and I am happy to keep learning.

"Only one more step to freedom." Phoebe says.

Yeah another three months.

"What's that then?"

"Men, you still turn men down all the time, why don't you move on fully?" she suggests.

I swallow; I can't exactly tell her I already am. Luckily The Killlers 'Brightside' comes on which changed the mood. This was our song back in college.

"Oh my god!" we squeal together and grab her hands, dancing and singing loudly to each other.

"Open up my eager eyes, cuz I'm Mr Brightside" I hear his voice in my ear. I spin around frantically, my body literally on all nerve ends.

He smiles openly at me, before drawing one of fingers to his lips signalling for me to shush.

"Fuck, is that?" I hear Phoebe say.

He blows me a kiss and then wanders through the crowds away from me. I should chase after him, demand a divorce, scream at him or just do something other than be frozen on the spot.

I see Robbie head out of the main doors and into the night.

"Shit honey, let's sit you down." Phoebe cries out.

Tears blur my sight as she leads me to a bar stool and sits my shaking body down. She wraps her arms around me, holding me as I tremble. It really was him that night a month or so ago. I managed to force my head to think I was being paranoid, that it wasn't really him, I was drunk and seeing things. But I wasn't at all.

"Robbie's back." I whimper.

A tumbler of whiskey is given to me by Jenny.

"Thanks," I say and sip it.

"Are you okay?" she asks concerned, Lisa by her side.

"Just shocked," I say lightly, it's a lie but I don't want to explain.

"I'm done with dancing, shall we go find a kebab shop and you can tell us all about it?" Lisa offers.

I glance at my watch it is twenty past eleven. I have a curfew.

"I think I just want to go home, Rain check?" I ask.

"Sure let's get a taxi," Phoebe offers standing up.

"No, you girls stay, don't let me ruin your night," I protest.

"I don't think you should be alone,"

"I am fine honestly, he doesn't know where I live, and its well secured I promise,"

"Okay let me wait until you get in a taxi then,"

"Deal." I smile at my friends. I am lucky to have Phoebe let alone two other terrific girls.

I get in a taxi and promised to text Phoebe when I get home and head straight to Nick's.

By the time I get to Nick's I'm a mess. Fear is crippling me. Robbie has managed to find me twice now; he was right behind me, in my ear!

Luckily Nick isn't here yet so I nose about and find a decent bottle of whiskey. I pour myself a large glass and drink it quickly. I sobered up the minute I saw Robbie, but the strong liquor helps my nerves.

I don't have nightwear here, and I don't want to be naked right now. So I search through Nick's wardrobe for a shirt to wear. I select one that looks less expensive than the others. After washing my make-up off and brushing my teeth I settle back down in the living room with another whiskey to wait for Nick. I need him. Well, no not him, but sex with him. It makes me lose myself, makes me forget everything except how good it feels.

I don't have to wait long, ten minutes later Nick walks through the door looking devastatingly sexy. I put my glass down and run to him.

"Hey are you alright?" he asks.

I don't reply, I just jump on him, wrapping my legs around his waist and kiss him.

I feel his surprise; I have never made the first move with him before. Never acted like I wanted it, he likes to be in control, and I don't like to let him know how much I want him. But tonight I don't care. He kisses me back so hard I think my lips will bruise, and I love it, returning his kisses just as hard. His hands tangle into my hair.

"Nice shirt." he mutters slipping his hands to my naked behind. I hear him groan as he finds my lack of knickers and lays me on the living room rug.

Quickly he takes off his clothes as I unbutton the shirt I'm in.

"You look damn good baby," he says stroking me with those miracle hands, in and out the hospital they work miracles. I smile; he has never called me 'baby' or any affectionate name, only ever Rag Doll.

He lowers himself down to me but I roll over and straddle him, pushing him flat on the floor.

"You wanna ride me?" he asks.

I nod.

"Go for it."

I sink down on him, taking him in slowly.

He groans as I rock him fully in. Then I move, fast and hard hitting my sweet spot every time.

"Fuck." he moans, clutching at my hips.

I've not done this with him before; I'm getting such a buzz being in control for once. I move faster as im climbing to what I know will be an epic explosion.

"Baby I'm not going to last" he says, slipping a hand up to cup my breast as they bounce.

"Come with me then." I moan.

I feel him swell even more, so I ride with everything I have. I can't hold back as I scream when I hit my orgasm. I hear Nick's animalistic cry as he releases, pumping into me.

"Fuck, just fuck." he cries out breathlessly.

Chapter Eleven- Nick

Holly has passed out on the living room floor completely spent. Not actually surprising, that was an epic fuck, I can't remember a better one. Guess Mack was right, the shy ones really are the wildcats.

I shouldn't leave her on the floor though, that would be rude. I should send her home but after that, I think that would also be rude. So I break my own rule by picking her up carefully, carry her to my bed and tuck her in. Stunning, she really is. How she has gone by unnoticed before now I just don't know.

Grabbing a quick shower before I head to bed, I think back on my night with Penny. It went really well, Penny looked mouth-watering in a low cut white dress. I see her dolled up at benefits and that, but I was proud that she was on my arm, on a date with me. We had a wonderful dinner, and I was allowed a kiss on the cheek as I dropped her home. We have arranged to go out next Friday again as tonight was such a success. I am on a day shift, but asking to leave at six should be fine, given I am always working overtime anyway.

I sink into bed, listening to Holly's peaceful breathing and like always it sends me off to dreamland.

The alarm wakes me up at six pm. Holly is gone as usual. Last night was unusual now I think back on it; fucking amazing but unusual. She never instigates sex, or kissing or anything sexual with me. I worry at times that she isn't interested in me at all; it's all just business to her. Then again she always gets into it as were doing it, she has lots of fun. I put it down to being a good thing, she's emotionally detached like that. She is like me, that it is just physical between us. But last night felt different, like she was feeling something. Not for me, but just emotional about something. Whatever it was it worked for me, she can move for sure. I bet she is sore today.

I text her, while I eat my breakfast.

ME: *R u sore?*

She texts me back, so I know she is awake.

HOLLY: *Maybe*

ME: *Last night was awesome, what brought that on?*

She doesn't text back straight away, so I finish up and get dressed. Finally I hear my phone bleep.

HOLLY: *Just fancied being in control for once. You never let me.*

I laugh aloud, she is right.

ME: *Well anytime you want to be in control like that, you just crook your pinkie. I won't complain.*

HOLLY: *I will bear that in mind, but maybe not just yet, I am hurting today.*

I like knowing that she is sore; it will remind her of last night throughout the day.

ME: *It's your night off from me tonight isn't it?*

HOLLY: *Yes thank goodness*

My grin turns into a scowl. That's not nice, in fact it's insulting. I don't like knowing she likes being away from me, which is ironic as I don't like her being out of my bed.

ME: *We are both on nights Monday morning so I expect you to be at mine by nine am, if not sooner on Tuesday morning.*

HOLLY: *Yes sir!!!!*

I put my phone away and jog to work. I want her already and now I have to wait over a day to have her. What plans can I make to keep me busy after I finish work? It's only for a couple of hours that you see her anyway, I scold myself. Jesus, she's like a frigging addiction. Maybe I can think of a way to keep her as my mistress when I go exclusive with Penny?

I'm in theatre for most of my shift with a viciously assaulted patient. We have lost her twice already, but luckily we keep bringing her back. A few broken bones, a bashed up face and stab wound to the neck. He is a nasty piece of work, the man who did this to her. He is with the police and will do time for this, that I am sure of. I hate jobs like this, unfortunately it happens more than it should.

"Janet Barker, 36 years old, surgery is successful, but further care and 'in house' treatment is needed." Samantha announces as we finish up.

I rip off my gloves and head off. It's been an emotional nine hours in that surgery. Now it is gone six am now and I'm desperate for a break.

"Taking a break, page me if I'm needed."

My team nod, as they also head out in different directions, leaving the clean-up crew to clean the operating room up.

I change my scrubs and head to the cafeteria, hungry. Grabbing a tray filled with food and a large coffee I plonk down on a nearby table, knackered.

Holly is sitting across the room with her usual friends. She hasn't noticed me, as she sips a coffee and giggling with the one she is always with, the red haired one. I need her after a shift like this one, but I promised her a day off. Well a hospital day off anyway.

"Knock, knock." a voice brings me out of my trance. Penny sits down opposite me with a bowl of fruit and her Earl Grey.

"Good morning," she says cheerfully.

"Hey," I say distracting as I try to find Holly behind her.

"You're grumpy,"

"Sorry, bad night, how are you?" I apologise.

"I'm good; hungry now, had to run extra hard this morning to work off all that food from last night."

I snort; the woman ate grilled chicken and vegetables, what's there to work off?

"You didn't eat anything to work off," I laugh.

"I'll have you know I am very strict with my food, you don't want a flabby girlfriend now do you?" she whispers.

Penelope couldn't be flabby if she tried. She has always been tall and lean.

"I'd make an exception for you."

She giggles at that.

"Did you have a good time last night?" I ask.

"Yes I really did, did you?"

I nod as my mouth is full of toast.

"You know the cancer research benefit is two weeks on Saturday, we should go," she says carefully.

"We always do,"

"No I mean together, as a date."

Wow. Penny is asking me out? Lovely jubley!

"What a wonderful idea, I'd love to be your date."

My pager bleeps.

OR 4

I look down at my barely touched breakfast. Damn it.

"Gotta go beautiful." I get up with my tray, as I pass her I kiss her cheek, before dumping my tray and power walk to OR4.

It's gone ten in the morning, the team and I have just finished a man involved in a car accident. It's been a team effort from us in general surgery, to neurology and cardio. You don't throw in your gloves just because your shift has finished. Never works like that when there is a trauma thrown your way.

"Man I'm beat", Matt yawns.

"Starving," Samantha grumbles.

"Fancy heading to Benny's any one? My treat." I offer. Benny's is a local café to the hospital and serves huge quantities of food.

Everyone cheers and heads to change.

An hour later we are tucking into gigantic hot breakfasts.

"So Nick, the rumour mill has dried up. What gives?" Samantha asks.

Samantha is essential to my team, and one of us in every way. She is also into women, which is why she is the only surgeon safe with us bunch of male whores that is my team, including me.

"Giving it up for now," I lie.

"Wow man, why?" Matt asks like he is in pain.

"I am dating Penelope."

A clatter of cutlery is heard.

"The princess? Fuck off" Liam snorts.

"True, you know we're close," I reply irritated.

"But she is the future wife," Samantha gasps.

"Man say it aint so! Old dog Willis hanging up his dick and having rich pretty babies," Matt says mournfully.

"Perfectly accessorized." Tom jokes.

I visibly shudder.

117

"We are just dating."

My appetite has vanished.

"Well I'm banging Tina from meds," Matt announces changing the subject.

Ah Tina with her plastic tits and bleached hair. She is a screamer that one, I know that as a fact.

"Hope you have soundproof walls," I laugh.

"Bitch,"

"I'm thinking Cindy from Obs next," Liam chips in.

"Sally from Cardio," Samantha joins in.

We all stare at her for that one.

"What? She is wasted on men with that dreamy mouth, I'll turn her," she argues.

"I want Holly." Tom says quietly.

My blood runs cold. Holly's mine.

"Holly who?" Liam asks.

"Holly Jones, long dark hair, real quiet and pretty, nurse that works mostly on the E.R and general floor." Tom explains, his eyes have a shine to them, I don't like. I grip the table tightly.

"Dude she's married," Samantha says.

"Nah, she's been separated for him for over two years now Jenny just told me. Apparently her husband was a complete jack ass; he was a druggie and beat the shit out of her a lot."

I grit my teeth. I didn't know this. I knew he was into drugs and left her with fuck loads of debt. But he hit her? He hurt her? That I didn't know and I'm furious.

"You don't fuck around with the damaged ones," Matt says, and I want to kiss him.

"No, I am thinking of dating her, I'm sick of meaningless fucks. I like her." Tom says a rose tinge appears on his face.

A groan echoes around the room, I keep quiet, I am too angry to speak, in fear of saying too much.

"Wow you like her? I think I need to look at Holly again with the marriage blinkers off." Liam laughs.

Samantha and Matt nod in agreement.

Great, my little secret is about to be noticed.

Chapter Twelve- Holly

I feel like shit, my head is banging, my body is aching and I'm beat. It's been a very busy day, and I attended to a patient that upset me. She had been badly beaten up by her boyfriend, she was recovering from surgery, Nick and his team had saved her life.

I do deal with abuse, doing the job that I do but it still makes me hurt when I see a woman hospitalised by the hands of another. She hasn't come round from the anaesthetic yet, but I set her up in her ward, got all the equipment set up and put medication in her fluids.

That was me two years ago. I try to avoid the abused patients and the addicts but I can't always avoid them, and it is part of my job. Besides two nurses are ill with the flu so we are short staffed. Then to top off my bad day I saw Nick kiss Penny in the cafeteria. I don't understand why it bothers me. I know what our relationship is and I'm fine with it. I think it's down the status thing again; I'm not good enough to be considered his girlfriend, just a sex toy. Those lips that gently touched the princess have been on every inch on my body, and not so gently.

I haven't made any plans with my time away from Nick in the morning. I think I just need to go home and catch up on some sleep. I'm actually looking forward to it, so much of my free time now belongs to Nick, and it will be nice just to be me, me on my own.

After I finally go home, I get changed into my pyjamas, climb into my bed and close my eyes with a contented sigh and pass out.

The buzzer interrupts my happy sleep.

I glance at my phone. 12.15pm.

"Hello?" I mumble groggily.

"It's Martin, open up,"

What the hell?

"Martin what are you doing here? Go away."

I hate how pathetic my voice is. I haven't seen him in over a month and it's been bliss.

"We need to talk, let me in or I will kick the window in again." he snarls.

I buzz him in. He slides in my door like the worm he is.

"What is this about?" I demand, regretting changing into pyjamas now.

Martin's nostrils flare, and before I can move, he charges at me and hits me right across the cheek.

God, it feels as if my eye ball has popped out, he has never punched me before.

"Did you know?" he yells.

"Know what?"

"That you beloved hubby is back in town?"

He knows. Robbie is putting me through hell again!

"I thought I saw him at Blues, but I was drinking, so I hoped it wasn't,"

"Lying bitch!" he roars in my face.

"I'm not lying, besides I have paid you back his debts. I am out of this and now thanks to me so is Robbie,"

"You think I would allow anyone to fuck me over?"

"This is between you and him, it has nothing to do with me anymore," I cry out.

"You think I believe that? You pay me nine fucking grand at the same time he starts crawling out of the woodwork again. Do you think I'm that fucking stupid?" he shouts, spit lands on my face but I'm too terrified to wipe it off.

"That was a bank loan in my friends name, I haven't spoken with him since he beat the shit out me, killing our baby in the process and fled. Do you think I would have anything to do with him?" I scream.

He smiles, as if he enjoys what I went through.

"I think you would, because you are weak and pathetic and he knows it. I think he gave you that money and I think you know where he is." he says and pulls me to his body. My back is against his front, as he holds me tightly with one hand. The other hand pulls out his phone.

"Billy, come in here" he barks, buzzing in a dangerous looking man. His eyes are bloodshot and dilated; another addict.

I pull away but Martin has both arms wrapped around me now. Panic is setting in as Billy comes closer menacingly.

"Hold her," he grunts to Billy and throws me into his arms.

"Martin please, I will help you, I will tell you if he comes to see me. I don't know where he is I swear." I begin to beg.

Martin takes off his jacket.

"I don't believe you,"

"Please Martin, I promise I don't know where he is." I cry out.

Billy pins my arms behind my back and I'm frozen as Martin punches me in the ribs. I cry out in agony but it's muffled as Billy puts a filthy hand over my mouth.

"Where is he Holly?" Martin roars.

"I don't know." I spit out.

He punches me over and over again, mostly my ribs but he gets a few in the stomach as well.

"Last time Holly, where is he?"

My head is spinning and I can't breathe properly.

"Don't know", I breathe.

"Boss, I really don't think she knows," I hear a voice say.

"Oh well, when he comes looking for her, he will know I'm looking for him." Martin says, his voice is really distant though, as if he is really far away.

The beatings stop, when I think it's finally over, I am dropped and I hit my head hard.

I hear them leave. I am going to pass out, I can't breathe without it feeling like I'm swallowing flames. I need help. I crawl painfully to my bag and grab my phone. I can't tell Phoebe, she would freak, and I can't go to hospital as that would involve the police. So it's Nick I text.

ME: *My place asap help*

It has to be Nick, he is the only one I trust and can help me.

I think it sends, as the dots blurring my vision become a sheet of black.

Chapter Thirteen- Nick

The alarm buzzes me awake. I was wiped out and crashed hard after 'Bennys'. One more night shift, then I get Holly back. I hope she is as well rested as me. I get up to switch it off.

HOLLY: *My place asap help*

Shit, that was sent over three hours ago. I change quickly and run to my car. I drive stupidly to Holly's place, cursing at the traffic; her place is right on the other side of town.

I buzz her flat, no one answers. It takes a full four minutes to finally be buzzed in by a neighbour. I bang on her door, calling out to her until she finally opens the door.

I gasp in horror as I see her swollen left cheek; she is sickly white in colour.

"Nick." she breathes weakly, and then pulls a face letting me know it hurts her talk.

I step into her bedsit.

"What the fuck happened?"

"Ribs... Can't go hospital." she staggers out painfully.

I pull up her pyjama top, her skin above her ribs are all inflamed. I can't tell if they are broken or not without touching her or using an x-ray machine.

"I have to get you to a hospital, if they are broken they could be penetrating a vital organ," I panic.

She shakes her head, tears running down her face.

"I have a full medical kit at mine," I say, my little first aid kit won't do much right now.

"Yours," she moans.

"Okay, but I have to carry you."

She nods, so I carefully pick her up but she still cries out.

"Shush baby I got you,"

I put her in the back of my car, laying her flat and fastening the seatbelt around her legs. Then I drive back to my apartment steadily. I hear her cry but then it's quiet, I pull over but she is breathing, but gritting her teeth to stop the noise, so I drive back home quicker and carry her up to my apartment, not caring who sees. I lay her on the bed and grab my large medical kit.

"You need to swallow these." I say, holding the strongest pain killers I have.

She tries to sit up but fails, so I head to the kitchen grind up the pain killers and put them in a glass of water with a straw.

"Suck the straw." I command putting the straw by her mouth.

She does, slowly; I put enough meds to knock her out whilst I examine her. She falls asleep within seconds of finishing the drink.

I sigh heavily as I use scissors to slice through her pyjama top; luckily she isn't wearing a bra. Using my hands I feel around her ribs. After triple checking, I can feel her ribs aren't broken luckily. They are severely bruised though and must hurt like hell. What is strange was although they aren't broken, they have been before, and I can feel where they have grown back as the bones haven't fully fused in places. She has other marks on her stomach which looks like they will also be bruised. Her head is bleeding but there is a lump that has come out, and she was acting fine, in pain but fine. So I don't think she needs any scans or anything. It's just a nasty blow.

"Fuck Holly what have they done to you?" I moan to her sleeping form. Who has done this to her? And why? I guess it would be Martin, but I can't see why, she paid back every penny of that bastard debt, at least that's what I thought.

I bandage her ribs up loosely, there's not much I can do for her, but dose her up heavily and let them heal on their own. I clean her head; it doesn't need stitches, so I put a plaster on her abrasion. On the one positive side she is incredibly lucky that she doesn't need to go to hospital at all. I place an ice pack on her stomach, and another one on her cheek I dial Dom, the chief of surgery.

"Dom its Nick,"

"Nick what's up?"

"I can't come in tonight, I'm sorry for the late notice, it's a personal matter. Can you arrange cover?"

"Sure, let me know if you need more time off, your owed it back from your overtime,"

"Thanks mate."

I hang up not wanting to chat. I have never called in for a personal matter before.

Luckily I grabbed Holly's phone at hers, so I text the absence line on her behalf, saying she has the flu and will be out a week or two. I know the nurses are coming down with it left right and centre so it's a very easy lie. She seems calmer and is breathing a bit better now. I leave her to sleep.

I head straight to my third bedroom, which is my mini gym area, and go to my punching bag and decide to beat my anger out.

I check on Holly after I have a shower; my body is aching after working out for two hours. She looks better in colour, her sides are turning a horrendous shade of purple, but that's a good thing.

Happier I go to the kitchen to hunt for food, I'm starving, and Holly needs food with the pain killers. There's not a lot in, there never is as I'm not around enough. That and I avoid cooking at all costs. I grab my large pile of take away menus. She isn't going to want greasy take out, then I notice Benny's menu has a delivery service. So I call them.

"Can I have two cartons of chicken soup, two BLT sandwiches and two pieces of chocolate cake please?" After giving all my details I hang up.

The buzzer goes as I'm watching a film in bed, lying next to Holly. She stirs, so I quickly fetch the food.

She is awake as I go back in the room.

"Hey how are you feeling?" I ask gently.

"Like hell, but luckily I have survived worse," she jokes, but I can hear the sadness in her tone.

"I got food, give me a minute," I say and head to kitchen. I put all the food and utensils on a tray and head back.

"Nick?"

"Yeah?"

"I know you like my breasts, but can you find me something to cover them, I'm freezing." she says pointing to her naked chest.

Laughing I toss her a clean shirt.

She sits up slowly, I can see it hurts by her face, but pulls it on and buttons a few buttons.

"Stay sat up, eat some food. It will help," I coax and place the tray down on her lap.

"Oh crap, work,"

"Taken care of, you have the flu; you won't be in for at least a week or two."

She relaxes.

"Thank you so much Nick, guess I owe you yet again,"

"Guess you'll have to let me claim your ass as payment," I joke.

Holly frowns.

"Joke,"

"We will see when I'm feeling better," she grumbles.

Jackpot!

"Eat, and then we will talk."

She takes a small spoonful of soup and swallows it.

"It's lovely, did you make this?"

"No, it's takeaway from Benny's, I don't have much food in, besides I'm a horrible cook."

"I love to cook, I just don't any more as I don't have a kitchen." she tells me.

We eat comfortably in bed. I end up eating her sandwich and most of her cake too as she isn't up for much.

"Why am I so tired again?" she moans as her eyelids droop.

"You're hurt; it's your body's form of defence,"

"Yeah. Can I stay tonight?" she asks in a quiet voice.

"You stay as long as you need."

I go to take the tray away, and when I come back she is out for the count.

I pull the duvet up to her chin and kiss her head.

Something stirs inside of me, warmth, and tightness in my chest. I don't like it.

Quickly I turn away and leave the room.

Chapter Fourteen- Holly

Three days later I finally feel better. Well better enough to function. For two days I have slept, taken pain killers and eaten soup Nick has brought. He has been so kind and attentive to me I am desperate to repay him.

I will go back home tomorrow. I can't keep staying here like a leach. But Nick is on a day shift today so I want to thank him before everything goes back to normal. He will be home in a few hours so I get up and start with a bath. I have not been in Nick's bath before, but it looks so big and deep that I am sure it will be worth the pain of getting up for.

I head to the bathroom once the bath is full, and slip off Nick's shirt. I un-wrap the bandages and stare at my naked body in the full length mirror. Damn I look like hell. Disgusting purple bruises are covering my torso and chest. My left cheek and eye are bruised too. Hell! There goes the gratitude fuck.

I lower my tender body into the bath. It is absolute heaven as the warm bubbles cascade over my skin. The last time I had a bath was back in the house I rented with Robbie. I take my time washing and shaving myself. By the time I finish I feel brand new.

My stomach growls, so I head to the kitchen to see if there is anything edible in there wearing Nick's towelling robe. If I can't thank Nick with sex, maybe food will be an alternative. I haven't cooked for a long time, but I can cook, well actually. Robbie always had friends over raving about my cooking skills. I glance through every cupboard to find virtually nothing. Cereal, breakfast bars, an out of date can of baked beans and a handful of penne left in its packet. The freezer has a bottle of vodka in it and ice cubes, and the fridge contains milk, beer and butter.

Frustrated I walk back to the bedroom to get changed. I will go shopping; I need to a walk any way even if I do look like a state. Bandaging my ribs proves difficult, strange how I can do it on patients without needing to think but on myself? Hard work! I finally manage to wind it into place and select one of Nick's hoodies and my jeans. No underwear as I haven't brought any. Never mind there is a Tesco Express round the corner.

I grab all the ingredients I want as I decide what I want to cook and ignore the stares of the young girl behind the till.

The bags feel like I'm carrying stones rather than food, the pressure weighs on my ribs but I hobble back very slowly. I drop the bags in the kitchen I smile proud of myself, and turn on the radio, happily I prepare dinner. Nick walks in, in his jogging gear just after half past eight.

"What's going on? You shouldn't be out of bed," he scolds coming into the kitchen.

"I'm feeling much better and thought I'd make us dinner." I tell him happily, I have had a wonderful, peaceful evening. I forgot how much I love cooking. Nick on the other hand looks startled.

"Why?" he asks confused.

"To say thank you."

His face scrunches up like he is angry. Shit. I've done the wrong thing. I'm acting like a house wife and he hates it. I've overstepped the mark. Maybe he wanted me out as soon as I could walk.

"You didn't have to do that Holly," he says carefully.

"I wanted too, I will be out of your hair in the morning, or even after I have cleared up."

He breathes heavily like he is trying to calm himself down.

"Or I could go now, I'm sorry I didn't mean to upset you or overstep." I stammer and try to head out the kitchen. He reaches out and holds my wrist gently, stopping me. "Sorry, I'm not used to this, please carry on."

I smile and head back to the oven to pull out the roast chicken.

"Wow," he mutters.

"Go freshen up if you want, whilst I dish up," I offer.

"Ok." he saunters away with a very confused look on his face.

I know he is a busy man and lives alone, but surely a home cooked meal shouldn't be *that* out of the ordinary, right? There is a lot more to Nick that I previously realised.

I went to town on this roast dinner and made every possibly trimming I could think of. I lay the table and put all the side dishes on the protective mats. I don't even know what Nick likes except chocolate cake, sandwiches and Chinese food. So I carve up the chicken and put some on our plates and leave everything else for him to help himself to. I look back at the table and frown, I put wine out and two glasses, it looks romantic. So I turn on the T.V to a football game and move the cutlery settings so he is facing the TV and I'm by the side instead of facing each other; much better.

Nick comes in looking more like him and less confused. He sits down and drinks some wine.

"Wow, I can't believe you cooked all of this," he mutters.

"I like to cook, it's been a while I think I went overboard," I laugh.

He helps himself to everything much to my delight and digs in.

"This is amazing," he says between mouthfuls.

"Thank you"

I'm eating like a starving person but luckily Nick is too. He can sure put it away I think as he helps himself to more of everything.

"Save room for pudding,"

"You made pudding too?" his eyes light up like a child's. It's damn cute.

I nod, feeling shy all of a sudden, he smiles at me and my heart thumps heavily in my chest. Alarm bells ring, Nick is not cute, he is just for sex. That's all.

But his beam continues as he polishes off every bit of food I prepared, and I made a ridiculous amount. I find that I am staring at him. It is just gratitude I chant silently to myself.

As I clear the plates, my hands shake.

"Are you okay?" he asks as he notices the chattering of the plates.

"Yeah."

I head back to the kitchen to clean up; I need to get a grip. I clean vigorously and take much longer than necessary. I can't develop actual feelings for Nick; I'm a paid sex toy to him, and nothing more. Maybe I'm even just a charity case to him and he is an emotionless asshole.

"Thank you Holly, I haven't had a home cooked meal in a very, very long time." he says startling me.

Come on, be the asshole I know you are. I need you to be.

"My pleasure, now would you like dessert now or later?"

"Later I am stuffed,"

"Me too,"

"We need to talk, come in the living room with me." Nick says taking my broom. It's not as if I haven't swept the floor three times anyhow.

Oh shit, he has seen right through me.

I follow nervously.

"Sit." he points to a chair.

I sit.

"You need to tell me what happened. I didn't ask whilst you were recovering, but now I am demanding that you tell me." he says seriously.

Not what I was expecting but slightly relieved weirdly.

"Martin and a thug," I shrug.

"Did you pay him off?"

Oh how dare he! There is the asshole.

"Of course I did." I hiss.

"I presumed you had, but why come after you and hurt you? It doesn't make sense,"

"It's Robbie, he is back and Martin thinks he gave me the money. He hurt me as he thinks I know where he is, or possibly to send a message to him." I tell him numbly. I'm just dragging Nick further into this, but I owe him the truth.

Nick's face is as hard as a stone, emotionless as usual.

"Look I'm so sorry, I didn't mean to keep getting you involved in all of this. I should go," I say standing up slowly.

"Sit down,"

142

"No Nick really, I feel like I'm taking advantage of your generosity,"

"Sit down,"

"No Nick I need to go,"

"You're fucking staying here, so sit your ass back down." Nick yells at me.

I sit down dazed.

"I don't want you hurt, and I sure as hell don't want this shit brought back to me. Stay with me temporarily until Martin and your husband deals with it and leaves you alone,"

"Nick I can't, it's too much you have been so generous already," I trail off.

"No you have earned and you will continue to, you can cook and clean on top of your other duties."

I smirk at that, 'duties' indeed.

"Don't forget you are my mistress, I take care of what's mine. You can't pay me dead now can you?"

I shouldn't accept it, but I find myself thanking him. I get to stay here in this palace away from Martin, Robbie and all that shit.

"There are rules though. You take the second bedroom, stay in there whilst I'm here; unless you're cooking, cleaning or fucking me. I don't want you under my feet or disturbing me. I don't share or play well with others, in case you haven't noticed," he grins at me.

"Agreed,"

"Nobody comes here; you continue to be discreet coming in and out of here. Tell no one that you are here, everyone must think you're still living at yours,"

"Agreed,"

"And when your ribs are better, we are kicking things up in the bedroom. I'm talking kinky shit may as well get my money's worth," he barks.

I can't resist, I clamber over to him, sit on his lap and hug him. It's like hugging a rock though, he is so still and hard, but I don't care.

"Agreed,"

"Don't get too comfortable. When one of those dickheads kill each other or in another three months you're gone, understand?" he says sternly.

"Yes sir," I mock.

"Don't mock me Rag Doll, or I'll take you now, fuck your ribs," he groans.

"Shall we indulge in chocolate fudge cake instead?"

"Damn that's my favourite!" he says excitedly.

"Mine too."

I climb off his lap feeling like I'm floating on cloud nine.

Chapter Fifteen- Nick

I am making idiotic mistakes. I have just agreed to a room-mate, shown emotion by sharing part of myself to Holly, and worse of all eaten three slices of fudge cake! I'm running now at a full sprint, punishing my sluggish body for its indulgence; it was one of the best chocolate fudge cakes I have ever eaten though, in fact the whole meal was. I was serious when I said I didn't cook. Once I was a keen cook but then my teacher who was also my mother took off when I was ten. Since then my father and I lived off take away meals and restaurant food. That was the first home cooked meal I have had in easily ten years. Very sad but true. My mother was a fantastic cook. She loved to cook and bake, I used to spend my evenings as a child icing a cake she would make for after dinner even cut up veggies for dinner. I don't like to think of her. It's still painful even after twenty four years.

My body protests and caves before I'm mentally ready so I jog slowly back home. The place is spotless and quiet. I walk into the bedroom to find it empty. The bed is made; my clothes have been put in the laundry bin.

She really thinks she is my slave.

I go the second bedroom and find her fast asleep in the bed. She looks peaceful, but I shut the door.

"Obedient as always." I mutter and head to my own vacant room.

The next day I text Holly from work

ME: *Don't go to your flat for anything. Go and buy everything you need, credit card is in my bedside draw.*

I really am starting to hate the situation she is in. I hope I never see Martin or that cunt of a husband in my life time. Her husband is starting to play on my mind. Her husband is back in town, how does she know that? Has she seen him? Does she still love him? It's been over two years; she could have divorced him by now if she really wanted to. Not that it matters to me, except if she is breaking the rules and being with both of us. No way do I want to catch anything her druggie husband will have.

"You still up for tonight?" Penny asks as she sits down next to me.

I glance up surprised; I hadn't even seen her come in.

"Tonight?" my mind is blank.

"Date night? The Golden Midas?"

Shit. How could I have forgotten that?

"Of course, I can't wait. Sorry my minds a bit all over the place,"

"Good." She kisses me cheek. I almost forget to take a breath. She kissed me! She has never kissed me before.

"You kissed me." I say stupidly.

She giggles that perfect feminine giggle.

"So I did. See you at nine." she wanders off swaying deliberately in her tight dress.

My phone buzzes.

HOLLY: *Thank you, I have my own money so won't use your card. Do you fancy anything for dinner?*

She was going to cook for me tonight; I told her I would be home. Shit. Oh well it's not as if I owe her anything.

ME: *Out with Penny, don't bother cooking.*

She can just have a night off; it's not as if she can fulfil any of her other duties anyway. It's selfish but that in itself is pissing me off. It's been nearly a week and I am in serious need. I've paid for a mistress and she is there constantly wearing nothing but my shirts with no fucking bra on and I'm getting nothing. It's unfair of me to be pissed off, it's not exactly her fault and I'm sure if I asked, she would do whatever I wanted. But I won't, even I'm not that nasty.

Hours later I am picking up Penny, I haven't seen Holly at all. I ran home, had a quick shower, changed and rushed back out, without Holly even saying hello.

Penny comes out of her family home, a very impressive, gigantic seven bedroomed house. The drive way is so long and far away from the road that no one would notice it's there, hidden amongst all the land they own.

We often giggle that like me she is thirty four years old and yet she still lives at home. Yet she argues very validly, that she has her own floor and her father's away so often it's like having her own place.

She is in red tonight. Very daring for her but she pulls it off like she does any outfit; the dress is like a second skin moulded to her body, and low cut, showcases her fantastic legs.

"Hello beautiful," I breathe as she closes the car door.

"Hey," She kisses my cheek for the second time this day.

"I've never seen you in red,"

"Do you like?"

"I love" I say looking her up and down. She's got heels on and her hair is down but is pinned to the slide with a sparkly hair slide. She really is a vision.

The Golden Midas is a high class Japanese restaurant. As we enter the restaurant with her arm tucked into mine, people stop to look at us. Penny and I are well known because of our fathers and the society we have been brought up in. It will change though one day if it all goes to plan.

I leave her to order the food as I ordered the wine, and they leave us to it.

"Nick I am so proud of you," she announces to me.

"Why?"

"You have done everything I have asked. Rumours of your man whore ways are vanishing. The girls are bitching, claiming you are off the market. You can finally be seen as the surgeon you are."

I bristle at this. I may go through women a bit but it never distracts from my skills. I am the best in that damn hospital and everyone knows it; hence my lead surgeon status in general.

"Huh." is all I can reply with. I am not going to lash out at her, anyone but her.

Penny doesn't pick up my vibes and carries on.

"I overheard a couple of the girls from radiology talking, they said you have turned down every one, and some of the surgeons have said you are off the market,"

"Huh,"

"It's all coming together Nick. We can announce we are a in a couple more months and then, maybe in six months, a short engagement,"

"What?" I blurt.

Our waiter serves us our sharing platter. I shudder discreetly at the raw fish. Not my thing at all, but Penny wanted this restaurant.

Penny beams at the waiter, who half stumbles back. He got the 'Penny Daze' as many people do.

She turns her attention back to me.

"Do you think six months is too long? Or shall we just announce our engagement when we come out that we are a couple?"

My head is literally pulsating.

"I didn't think we were thinking about marriage yet, I mean this is only our second date." I manage without squeaking.

She frowns.

"Come on Nick, we both know what we are in this for."

Clever, very clever, she always had been.

"What's that then? You know how I feel about you, and that has nothing to do with the board,"

"I know and I love you too Nick, but it's also to do with the board; joining forces with our fathers to make a deciding vote." she says practically.

I know all this; she obviously knows it too.

"Yeah I know, but it all seems very sudden." I mutter.

Penny selects a piece of sushi with her chop sticks like a pro, and eats it.

"I know, but we will be at the ball next week, so it will be seen as serious as it is, so why not? It's not as if everyone hasn't seen it coming."

I swallow most of my wine. Everything is falling into place exactly how I want it to, even faster than I hoped. I just thought we would enjoy dating for a while before we started talking marriage.

"You're on board right?" she smiles at me, the 'Penny daze' in full force.

Stop being a pussy, this is what you want and she is handing it to you!

"Yeah, I'm on board." I grin.

I swoop up a raw fish nugget and pop it into my mouth smiling.

As I pull up to Penny's front door, she turns to face me.

"I had a wonderful time tonight," she says leaning towards me.

"I did too."

She moves her inches from mine, so I lean to kiss her soft cheek.

To my surprise she kisses me on the mouth.

"Nick, kiss me." she breathes.

I cup her neck and kiss her gently.

She sighs against my lips, wraps her arms around my neck and pushes her lips harder against mine. I deepen the kiss parting her lips with my tongue. Her chest is pressed hard against mine; I can feel her nipples harden against my shirt.

"Wow I've been Nicked" she giggles breaking away.

I sit in shock as she gets out of the car swaying those hips. When she goes inside I drive away angrily.

I haven't got an erection, a semi, not even a fucking tingle. She used to get me hard just with one simple touch to the shoulder. I kissed her, our first kiss and nothing! No fireworks, no hungry, zilch!!!

What the fuck is happening to me? It was a nice kiss, a great kiss actually; Penny sure knows how to tease with that tongue. She gave that kiss everything, she wanted to impress me, turn me on, and make me want her. She was turned on, yet I'm as limp as a noodle.

I storm through the apartment door. All is quiet and spotless again.

I am starving, I couldn't eat another piece of sushi, and it took me a full five minutes to swallow the first piece. Luckily Penny didn't notice. I yank open the fridge hoping there is some cake left. I spot a couple of chicken salad sandwiches with a post-it on top.

Golden Midas called to confirm your res. Sushi! Gross! Made this in case you are still hungry after your fish eyeballs! H x

I laugh hard, she gets it.

I eat the sandwich along with the rest of the fudge cake.

154

With Holly, our kisses drive me insane with need. I'm hornier than a teenage school boy these days, it just doesn't make sense.

I change into my sweats and head to Holly's room, I am just not myself today. I'm stressed, and tired that's all. Maybe I'm freaked out about the engagement that's why he won't come out to play. It's rebelling against the ball and chain.

Holly is asleep but I touch her arm to wake her up.

"Hey." she says groggily.

I bend over carefully so I don't put any weigh on her chest and press my lips to hers. I can feel her shock as I kiss her how I kissed Penny, gently and sweet. Need over comes my senses, that spark that hits me so forcefully it scares me.

I yank back her covers. She is in an oversized nightie, with fucking teddy bears on; Unsexy as hell yet I'm as hard as granite.

"Nick," she whispers. It feels like a question.

"Night Holly, thanks for the sandwich." I mutter and hurry out of the bedroom throbbing.

Fucking hell!

Chapter Sixteen- Holly

I am finally back in work on Monday. Nick checked my ribs and told me I should be okay, just not to lift anything heavy and to take a regular rests. I'm taped up and excited to be working again. The bruise on my face has faded loads, so with some heavy make-up it's fully covered.

  It's been a strange couple of weeks that's for sure and I was going to go stir crazy if I had to sit in boredom for another day. Nick has ignored me pretty much all of last week. Since his date with Penny and that strange kiss he gave me. He has been out most nights and when he has been here. In fact he has only acknowledged me at meal times to say thank you. I don't question it, I think I know it's because I haven't been able to have sex with him, he quite simply doesn't know what to do with me. The week before that, he was a hot Florence Nightingale caring for me in a way no one ever has.

  It's so confusing his hot and cold flushes and attitudes. But at least it has cleared up my confusing feelings and I'm over it. It was just me being emotional, he was so sweet and he has helped me so much, I blurred gratitude into something more for a moment; a stupid moment that won't be repeated.

So I shoved it out of my mind, and with him being an asshole to me constantly last week. It has told me where I stand.

I go to our new arrival to get him all settled. My heart plummets when I see a boy, a young boy.

"Hello there I'm Holly, what's your name?" I ask cheerfully.

"Sam."

I check his charts; he is seven years old, such a cute little guy with blonde hair and big brown eyes. He has been sent from his local doctors with severe headaches, dizzy spells, vision problems and a big weight loss. Not good. He is coming in for a CT scan and a MRI during his stay.

I swallow hard.

"You must be Mr and Mrs Holmes" I say to his parents. They smile anxiously at me.

"Okay Sam let's get you all set up and settled, then you can play with your IPad."

I get him set up and check all his vitals which are not good.

"Alright Sam we will leave you to it, your first test will be after lunch, so enjoy, it's macaroni cheese today." I wink at him.

"Yum, I love mac and cheese." he says gleefully.

I hate children patients, we all do, but this little boy with his cute little face is tugging at my heart strings. Please don't let it be serious, I think to myself, but I know the signs well enough to know it's not good.

I take my dinner break with Phoebe today.

"How are you feeling babes? I don't know why I couldn't come and check on you," she huffs.

"I'm okay, sorry I think I slept for nearly two weeks," I laugh.

"Don't blame you; have you seen any more of Robbie?"

"Nope luckily, now how are you?" I change the subject.

Phoebe gushes on about the guy she has been seeing, that bloke from the club she met with me.

"You have to meet up with Ryan, we could double date," she pleads.

"Don't think so,"

"Come on, he asks about you. Just give it a try?"

Nick comes in with Dr Sinclaire, a pain hits my chest. It never used to bother me, it shouldn't do now. I know what I am to him. I push it aside angrily.

"Maybe," I mutter absently.

"Bloody hell, guess who's coming over?" Phoebe whispers.

"Who?"

"Dr Tom Westbury,"

That gains my interest.

"Why?"

"Hey Phoebe, Holly can I join you?" Dr Westbury asks a coffee cup in his hand.

"Sure." Phoebe says and she shuffles up.

He sits next to me.

"How are you feeling now Holly?" he asks kindly.

"Better now thank you."

This is surreal; Dr Westbury is sitting with us. He is gorgeous, and not an asshole. A rare combination when it comes to surgeons.

"So I noticed you're not working on Sunday, I was wondering if maybe you would like to go out for dinner with me?" Dr Westbury asks me.

Both mine and Phoebe's mouths drop. What the hell? I try my hardest to be invisible and it works usually and now I'm being asked out by the likes of surgeons?

"Um wow, I am so flattered you would ask, but um I have plan Sunday sorry." I mumble.

He looks crestfallen.

"Ok that's cool, would you mind if I had your number? so we can sort a date out another time?" he asks as if he believes I'm genuinely busy. Not surprising actually, not many single woman would turn him down. I wonder if I was available whether I would say yes.

Dazed and very confused I write it down, not wanting to seem rude and insult someone like him.

"Thanks Holly, I'll text you," he says and walks away with his untouched coffee.

"Damn girl, first Willis now Westbury?" Phoebe asks confused.

Not as confused as me. Nick wouldn't have said anything, would he?

"I have no idea what just happened there."

I feel angry eyes on me. I glance up to see Nick visibly seething, shooting daggers at me despite being opposite the princess, who is picking at her salad, not noticing her dinner partner looks like he wants to strangle me.

How can he be so jealous and possessive when he is sitting right there with her? He sucks!

I get to Nick's before him so I start on dinner, chopping up vegetables to sauté and put water on to boil for the pasta.

"Holly," he booms angrily as the door slams.

"In the kitchen."

He storms through.

"How are your ribs?"

"Better thank you,"

"Let me check," he is at my side and yanks up my top. Jeez! He unwinds the bandages and places his hands on my ribs. I feel a shiver from his touch.

"Doing well." he mutters and yanks my top off.

His eyes rake over my new bra.

"Dining room table, strip and lie on your back now." he snaps.

I do as he asks and place myself on the cool hard wood.

Despite how barbaric he sounded, I'm excited.

He strips off and slips a condom of his very proud looking erection.

"You look stunning." he moans and spreads my legs.

He is inside me in one hard thrust. I sigh as he stretches me.

"So fucking good." he groans and thrusts into me hard. We are usually rough, that's obviously the way he likes it, and I'm ashamed to admit I like it to, but this is so rough it's almost painful.

He slams his hips against me and I cry out.

"You. Are. Mine" he spits out between thrusts.

I wrap my legs around his waist, digging my heels into his toned bottom.

"Say it," he commands.

"I'm yours," I call out, im so close.

"Fuck, Holly,"

He moves so fast my vision blurs, dots form as I climax hard.

He roars his release; I can feel him coming inside me.

I'm jelly like as he peels off the condom and ties it up. I sit up and he stands in between my legs, his face right by mine.

"You are mine, we had a deal. So you do not date, or fuck or hand out your number to anyone else, especially not someone in my fucking team." he shouts at me, then storms off leaving me naked on his table.

After controlling my breathing, I get up calmly, re-dress and cook dinner.

"Nick? Do you want dinner?" I call out. I can hear him thumping around in his gym room.

He doesn't reply so I dish us both up a bowl full, clean and set up the now sanitized table; he just screwed my brains out on.

Nick comes out as I place the bowls down, he still looks angry as he sits down.

He doesn't talk to me, just eats.

"Why did you give Tom your number?" he barks making me jump.

"Because I turned him down,"

"He asked you on a date?"

I nod.

"Why?"

I stiffen. I may have asked myself the same question, but with him asking it hurts.

"I don't know, maybe you been telling him I'm an easy lay." I snap.

His eyebrows rise.

"I haven't told anyone about us, you know I wouldn't,"

"Yeah, because that would be humiliating wouldn't it? Dr Willis fucking a poor, ugly, loser like me," I shout.

"You're not ugly," he starts.

"I don't know why Dr Westbury asked me out. I gave him my number out of shock. I'm sure he is only interested in one thing, like you," I vent.

"You will not be dating him whilst you are tied to me," he yells back.

I stand up no longer hungry.

"No I won't; you have helped me more than you will ever know, with money, a safe place to stay I wouldn't dream of spitting in your face that way."

I walk into the kitchen fuming.

"Holly you are mine," he says quietly following me.

"Yes for two more months I am your dirty little secret. I am paid to fuck you, and I won't forget that." I bite out and head to my room.

He doesn't follow. Good job as I am actually ready to screw our deal and walk out. I need to calm down.

My phone has a message from a number not in my contacts. Panicking I open it.

Hey it's Tom Westbury. How was your day?

I ignore it and change into my nightie. Someone is actually asking me about my day, but I know what he really wants to know.

ME: *I'm not interested in being your fuck for the night. I'm flattered but it's not happening. Sorry.*

That should end that. I don't think I can cope with Nick's outburst if he realises I'm texting Tom, that I am actually for once breaking his iron clad rules.

TOM: *I know my rep so I deserve that. However I actually like you and want to get to know you better, honestly. This isn't me trying to get you in to bed.*

Yeah right. I am living with the man who could have invented the book of lines.

ME: *Yeah like I believe that, please delete my number. I shouldn't have given you it in the first place.*

TOM: *Can we be friends? I'm interested in you, not sex. I think you're a lovely person and a caring nurse. Don't freeze me and judge me. Just get to know me?*

I'm not a nasty person, and his comment about judgment stings. I get on my high horse about Nick

166

judging people, yet I am doing the same thing to someone who genuinely seems nice. Besides I could always use another friend, and Dr Westbury seems like a nice person, with a bad reputation.

ME: *I am not in any way in a position to date or be romantically involved. Friendship however is fine, but that is it.*

That should clear things up, I have set clear boundaries. Nick shouldn't be pissed off at that I hope.

TOM: *No problems, read you loud and clear. So again, how was your day?*

I smile as I slide into bed; this is the start of our friendship.

Chapter Seventeen- Nick

Tonight is the Cancer Research ball. It's a charity event for the rich and famous, consisting of everyone pays a ridiculous amount of money to attend. We do it every year alongside the board members.

I'm nearly ready to go; I just can't tie this damn bow tie! It crooked again, so I rip it off.

"Holly." I yell.

Things have been better the last two weeks, much more normal. We are just having sex and that's it. No conversations or cosy dinners. She still cooks like an angel but we are eating separately or at different times so we don't need this bullshit chatting. She clearly dislikes me outside the bedroom, which works for me; the damn girl was getting under my skin for a minute there. She is avoiding me thankfully.

She comes into my bedroom, her gorgeous hair loose the way I like it, dressed in a robe. Then I notice the killer fuck-me heels.

"Going out?" I ask casually. She has been going out a lot recently. She had better not be messing with someone else but she swears she isn't.

"Yep, need help before you kill that tie?" she teases.

I nod so she comes over and starts to tie it.

"Where?"

"'Steps' with a group from work, need me home by a certain time? I presume you're going to be late,"

"Not sure, I'll text you." I will be home very late, but she doesn't need to know that.

She leans up then, and I can see her cleavage. She is fully clothed but why is she hiding? What is she hiding?

"Take off the robe,"

"No," she replies and steps away.

"Why?" I glare.

"I don't want lecture thank you."

I pull her robe ties and let it drop to the floor whilst she protests. Underneath is a short, tight but simple black dress hugging her delicious curves. Teaming that up black heels, she looks smoking.

"Shit," I mutter running my hands over her.

"You will be late," she says neutrally, as if I'm not affecting her.

"Fuck it," I groan and unzip my trousers, freeing my hard on.

"No Nick, you have to meet your father in five minutes and I have to meet my friends in twenty." she protests.

I look at her in utter shock. Holly said no. She has never said no.

"Did you just refuse me?" I say darkly.

"No, sorry, we just have to be somewhere." She sinks to her knees and starts to suck me.

I moan and clutch fistfuls of her long hair.

I am angry at her, I know what she is doing and it's for speed, she doesn't want anything in return which means she doesn't want me. I am angry but as her hot mouth moves up and down my dick, I don't care.

I come quickly. She is still kneeling on the floor so I lift her up, loving seeing her with swollen red lips.

"You look sexy as hell Holly," I say quietly as I touch her cheek.

"Thank you, have a nice night." she says and hurries out.

I sit back down feeling pangs of disappointment. It appears Holly can't wait to get away from me fast enough.

I am in exceptionally bad mood as I meet my father.

"Looking good son." he says as I get in the limousine. A glass of scotch is thrust into my hand the minute I sit down.

I glare at him and down it in one; might as well get hammered.

"What's eating you?" my father barks.

"I kissed Penny, I keep kissing Penny but there is no spark," I blurt out.

"Who cares about that? Spark's burn," he replies bitterly.

"I know but after such a long chase, it feels disappointing,"

"It's not as bad as having your heart ripped out and stomped on."

True.

"She is perfect for you son."

I sigh as we pull into the Sinclaire driveway.

Penelope looks like the princess she has been nicknamed. She is wearing some kind of pink bridal style gown. Her hair is swept up with styled curls.

"You look pretty," I say pleasantly as she sits next to me.

"Pretty? Gee thanks." she replies dryly.

"Beautiful, stunning, a vision, is that better?"

"Much."

Penny talks to our fathers leaving me to drink, much to my happiness as I just keep the bottle of scotch with me. "Slow down Nick, what's the matter with you?" Penny snaps at me.

 I shrug, hoping it passes as an apology.

"Don't let her boss you around Nicky boy, if you let her now, imagine what it will be like when you are married." Lawrence, Penny's father laughs.

I scowl at him too.

Finally we are here; Penny tucks her arm into mine pressing herself close to me as the cameras click.

Great, this will be all over the hospital by the morning. Half way through the evening I am bored shitless. Even drinking heavily isn't helping; it's just making me more pissed off. Penny is annoying the fuck out of me. I don't even know why, she hasn't done anything wrong. It's just me and my black mood clouding what should be a highlight of the year for us.

Dinner has been and gone and the speeches have been made and now the band is playing. I wonder what Holly is doing at 'Steps'. Is she dancing in that tight little dress? Are men looking at her?

"Let's dance." Penny says standing up.

I smile and take her hand, twirling her around. We both know the classical moves, which is appropriate for this sort of occasion. No grinding here. We used to be dance partners in classes our fathers made us go to as teenagers.

Penny is smiling at me as we move, and despite my mood, I plaster a smile on my face. This is all I have ever wanted since I was eighteen; Penny and me as a couple, the respect of both of fathers and the board members. I have it all right now in this moment, but it just doesn't feel like I thought it would.

"I want you Nick." Penny whispers in my ear.

I freeze.

"I thought you wanted to wait,"

"I will wait, but I don't think I can wait for too long," she says huskily.

"Me neither."

Is that a lie? Or is it the truth? Maybe that's what's fucking up my head so much. If I sleep with Penny, then life goes back into balance. Holly is giving me something Penny isn't. I've been waiting years to put myself in Penny's perfect body.

A slow song comes on and I feel her melt into my arms, she fits seamlessly, just the right height to snuggle into my neck. This is my future. I kiss the top of Penny's head. She is perfect for me.

As the song finishes, I notice our fathers clapping. Looks like I have sealed the deal.

Penny blushes prettily as we sit back down.

"Champagne!" Lawrence roars to a nearby waiter; looks like we are about to toast to our perfect future.

I'm stupidly drunk by the time we drop Lawrence and Penny home. I text Holly as soon as Penny gets out the limousine; but she doesn't reply.

I wobble into my apartment and search for her. To my annoyance she isn't there. Not obeying my orders for the second time this evening.

I yank off my bow tie and suit jacket. If she doesn't want to do as I asked, I'll just go and drag her ass back here. She is not getting away with it. I may withhold her from an orgasm until I have at least twice as punishment.

I grab a taxi to Steps and head inside. It's smoky, crowded and so damn hot in here. I hate clubs. I avoid them if I can. Yet I still work my way to the crowds and order a beer. I scan the dance floor looking for her. It dawns on me then, I shouldn't actually be here. No one can see us together. I am such a stupid drunken idiot.

I finish my drink, giving up on Holly and am about to head back out when I spot Tom. He is certainly moving well. None of this twirling baloney that I was doing earlier; he throws his head back in laughter as his head shifts I see her. She is in front of him dancing way too close.

Red blurs my vision as I watch her move with him.

She gracefully steps off the floor and is heading to the toilets on the other side of the club.

I follow furiously and intercept her as she rounds the corner in front of the ladies.

"What the hell are you doing?" I yell.

"Dancing? What are you doing here?" she yells back over the noise. Her eyes look alight, her cheeks are all red and a big happy smile is on her face. She was having fun. It hits me hard. I haven't seen Holly like this.

"With Tom? I said no dates," I snarl backing her up against the wall.

"It's not a date, there is a group of us, and we are just friends."

Damn, she did say she was with a group.

"I texted you an hour ago," I try another tactic.

Her face pales.

"Oh I'm sorry I didn't expect you would be back so soon, I didn't check my phone." she says apologetically.

Now I feel like a dick.

"I'll come back with you now." she mutters.

I try to nod but I just stand there, feeling like a bully.

"Or you could come and join us? Just you know hang out, have a laugh as long as you keep your hands off" she suggests.

She doesn't want to come home. When was the last time I had a laugh?

"Don't know about keeping my hands off," I say and run my hand up her silky thigh.

"I dare you."

I like this Holly, she seems so carefree and young.

I smile my first genuine smile of the night.

"Fine, let's try delayed gratification." I mumble.

She laughs happily and goes into the toilets.

I head to the bar; I may need something stronger to play along with this. I find Tom at the bar and join him.

"Hey buddy what are you doing here?" Tom asks shocked.

"Letting my hair down,"

"Not your usual scene?" he questions. It's true. When me and the lads go out it's usually to a nice bar or to a poker night at the casino or something classier than a loud drunken club.

I shrug and Tom places a shot in front of me.

As soon as he holds a tray of shots, his group joins him. I recognise most of them, a real mix of hospital staff, doctors and nurses even the techies are in the mix.

Holly joins us. I see Tom looking at her, a look I know well. No chance of that buddy.

We down the shots together, and head to the floor. Holly can move. I can't stop glancing at her as she is dancing to Christina Aguilera's 'Dirty'. It's killing me. I hear Tom groan to himself and he moves up to her, grinding with her. I have to admit they look good together, happy. I'm dancing with some blonde but my eyes can't keep away from Holly.

The song finishes and another sexually charged song comes on, I discreetly slide away from the blonde and reach for Holly before Tom does.

Her face flashes with shock, but its hides it well as I pull her to me, her back against my front and move with her.

She wriggles her hips, her ass brushing against my groin. I place my hands around her waist as we dance pinning her to me to hide my obvious erection.

"You move like you do in bed," I whisper in her ear.

"And you are just as controlling." she whispers back.

I spin her around and move my head to kiss her.

She pulls away glancing away.

I frown then realise in my drunken haze what I almost did. I'm not the only one as I notice our group watching.

"Drink?" I laugh nervously.

She laughs too, helping the situation.

"I'll go get a round in." I say loudly. Our group heads to the bar eagerly, but as I follow a hand clamps around my bicep. I turn to see Tom as he pulls me back.

"Don't do that again buddy, you know you're my friend but she's mine okay?" he says almost desperate in his tone. It's not threatening or nasty in any way.

"Are you fucking her?" I ask carefully.

"No, but I really like her, please don't fuck it up for me." he begs now.

It's actually pathetic.

"I'm sorry bro, I didn't realise. It won't happen again. I've just never seen her out of scrubs, I got carried away," I lie.

"Yeah I know what you mean. I knew she was beautiful, but outside the scrubs she's a fucking wet dream."

I laugh. This I already know as a fact and she is mine.

I text her as he heads to the bar.

ME: *Meet me at home, you have thirty minutes.*

I can see she is checking her phone as I say good bye to the group.

"Do you want to take me with you?" the blonde I was dancing with earlier says.

"Thanks, but no thanks babe." I reply and leave.

After I stumble back into my apartment I realise how wasted I actually am, everything is spinning like I'm on a funfair ride. I don't get drunk often. I don't like being out of control.

My phone is bleeping as I begin to strip off my best trousers, which now stink of smoke and cheap booze.

PENNY: *I had such a wonderful time tonight Nick.*

I grin, I bet she did.

NICK: *Me too, you felt so good in my arms.*

PENNY: *I want to be naked in your arms.*

I puff up like a peacock. Penny is being naughty.

NICK: *I want you to be naked in my arms, on my bed, or just about anywhere as long as you're naked.*

PENNY: *Like the sound of that.*

NICK: *Shall I come over? Or shall we meet at a hotel?*

It's not the best idea actually, I am so drunk I am squinting at the screen, but if my future wife has an itch to scratch, I should be the one to do it.

I wait for her text, but she doesn't text back. Fucking cock tease.

The front door bangs. I get up despite the fact that my trousers still are unzipped and hanging by my hips ,and my erection is jutting out in front of me and slip my phone into my pocket.

Holly goes straight to the kitchen ignoring me completely.

"Hey." I slur.

She pours two pints of water.

"Hey." I repeat standing behind her, jutting into her back.

She moves away, turning round.

"Hello Nick, drink this," she says handing me water. Why do I want water?

"Um not quite what I want," I mutter and squeeze her right tit. She still has those fucking heels on.

"You had quite a lot to drink didn't you?" she frowns.

"Yeah so, you're the one saying let's have a laugh at the club,"

"Yeah well you fucking nearly blew our cover, you idiot." she snaps.

Yeah, I kind of did.

I down the water in a few gulps.

"It's alright, no one noticed,"

"No one noticed? Yeah sure, keep thinking that way Nick. Everyone asked about it,"

"Shit, I hope this doesn't ruin my reputation." I groan.

Holly's eyes blaze.

"I'm sure the reputation in question is mine,"

"What the fuck is that supposed to mean?"

"Holly being hit on by the man slut, god how stupid is she, she must be so fucking desperate or easy to catch the Sleaze Prince's eyes." she shouts back.

The Sleaze Prince? That's my fucking nickname? Is that how people see me? Fucking the desperate or the easy, she is bull shitting, she must be.

"That's a low, shitty blow Holly."

181

She shrugs and storms off.

I pace the kitchen angrily for a minute. Is that how she sees me? Is Penny right? Do my co-workers only see me as this male slut? Not as the seriously fucking fantastic surgeon that I am? I going to be a member of the hospital board and have a percentage ownership of the hospital and that's my fucking nickname?

I march into Holly's room and slam the door shut. She is there in nothing but her black knickers her nightie in her hand.

"Who calls me that?" I ask quietly.

"No one, it was me being a bitch." she lies. I can tell she is lying as she isn't looking at me.

"Lies."

She goes to put on her nightie, but I take it out of her hands.

"Just some girls at works, don't worry about it." she mutters.

I breathe hard.

"Do you see me like that?" I ask, as my fingers trace her collar bone.

I can feel her skin heating up.

"It doesn't matter what I think, I'm paid to sleep with you."

Not quite the answer I was looking for, but it will do.

"Do you want me now?" I ask as my finger strokes lower in between her perfect breasts.

"Doesn't matter either way, you will have me." she grits out.

I frown at that, but the monster inside me comes out.

"Damn fucking right I will." as I push her roughly on the bed.

She already sticks her ass out getting on all fours. It's actually disturbing that she is already in the position I want her in. But her shapely ass is on show, including the pink lips of her pussy teasingly coming into view.

I snatch a condom out of her draw and slide it on, before slamming myself into her.

"Jesus." I hiss as she closes around me like a vice.

I fuck her so hard, I think I can her whimpering in pleasure or pain, I'm not sure nor do I care as I am climbing.

I hear her cry out as she tightens around me, she is close and I'm about to blow.

My phone rings loudly.

"Fucking hell." I yell as I slip out of her, and grab my phone. Penny's face flashes up.

In a panic, I answer it.

"Hey," I say trying to sound chilled.

"Nick, you're out of breath," Penny says suspiciously.

"Just on my treadmill, what's up?" I lie, cradling my phone between my shoulder and cheek.

Holly tries to move away. I look at her all bent over, and I hold my hands on either sides of her hips pinning her in position.

Like the good girl she is, she stays like it, not making a sound.

"I'm sorry about not replying, I panicked,"

"It's cool, I'm far too drunk to be driving any way," I admit.

"You did certainly put it away, what was up with you?"

"Oh just my dad pissing me off as usual, it was nothing to do with you,"

"I get it, so I was wondering if we should have another date," she says.

"Sounds good to me, shall I book us dinner somewhere?"

"We could but.." she trails off

"But what?"

"I was thinking maybe we could go to your place? Or mine?" she suggests nervously.

Bam! Horny little minx does want me.

"I would like that very much, I got tomorrow off or Tuesday next week?"

"Shall we do Tuesday?"

"Great."

"At mine or yours?" she breathes.

I glance down at Holly, still unmoving.

"Yours, is Daddy going to be home?"

"No he is going away Monday, on a golfing holiday,"

"Good good,"

"Looking forward to seeing that side of you," she flirts.

"Oh you will see him alright, and you'll be screaming my name before the night is out,"

"Oh I do hope so,"

"That's a promise."

She laughs.

"Ok well we can sort out details later; I'll let you get back to the treadmill."

I glance down at my treadmill, every silky inch of her.

"Ok talk to you soon,"

"Bye, bye baby," she croons.

"Laters." I hang up.

Holly is stiff as a board.

"Where were we?" I mutter.

I move my hands to stoke her back, but she flips over.

"Seriously Nick?" she spits out.

"What?"

"I have cramp in my fucking back and legs, and you honestly think I'm going to continue this, whilst you have just made a date to hook up with your precious Penny?"

Well yes I kind of was actually.

"You know what this is, don't go getting jealous on me now," I say coldly.

"Jealous? Jealous? That's a joke." she hisses and snatches up her nightie.

She is jealous, isn't she? She just totally went on a jealous bend knowing I was discussing having sex with the woman I will be marrying.

"It sound like you are being jealous,"

"I'm not. It's just the mortifying situation. You holding me still like I'm a goddam sex slave, whilst you coo and flirt with her." she yells.

Yeah, maybe that was a dick move.

"Well you are my mistress not my girlfriend," I tell her.

"Yes, so I am aware. I wouldn't ever be your girlfriend because you are an absolute nasty, insensitive dickhead," she yells at me.

"You are paid to fuck me, so fuck me." I tell her crisply. I know I shouldn't have said it the second it leaves my mouth.

Her eyes widen in shock. I know I have gone too far, but I can't take back what I said. She needs to learn her place, she is my mistress and she owes me.

Silently she goes back on all fours and waits for me.

I don't want to do this, but my dick is still throbbing with need. And like the bastard I am, I take her. She doesn't moan, or gasp or even sigh. She is silent the entire time. I release but it's not fireworks; yet it doesn't feel bad at all, but it isn't the heights that I am used to with Holly.

As soon as I pull out, she scrambles into bed and pulls the duvet up to her chin.

"Look Hol.." I begin to say, feeling absolutely awful.

"Get the fuck out Nick." she screams.

Not knowing what else to do I turn on my heel, the condom in my hand and leave the room in disgrace.

Chapter Eighteen- Holly

It's just gone past four in the morning when the front door bangs.

"Holly!" he screams thumping up the stairs.

I squeeze my eyes closed and try my best to relax my position. It's difficult considering I'm shaking. I pretend to be in a deep sleep when he throws open the bedroom door.

I can feel him looking at me through my closed eyelids. I don't even need to look at him to know he will be high.

"Baby." he mutters into my ear, I can smell alcohol on him too. That I know is a terrible combination for him.

I ignore him, willing him to give up and go to sleep.

"HOLLY," he screams into my ear this time, and I sit up with a jump.

"Baby, there you are," he coos. His eyes are nearly completely red.

"Robbie you should sleep,"

"Nah baby, I want you," He removes the quilt from me. I shiver automatically, I wish only through cold.

"Robbie it's gone four, I have to be up for work in two hours."

His face goes from adoring, to pissed off in a split
second.

"Tough shit."

He rips off my t-shirt.

"Robbie." I protest.

His mouth latches on my breast, sucking so hard it is
painful.

His hands disappear into my knickers, feeling how dry I
am.

"You're fucking someone else aren't you?" he roars.

"What? No!"

His mouth returns to my breast, and bites me sharply.

"You're a lying whore," he snarls and pulls down my
knickers.

"I'm not cheating on you, I never have, never will," I sob.

"Bullshit, you're a whore and I will fuck you like one."

With that he drags me to the edge of the bed and
spreads my legs. When I automatically try to close them,
his fist collides with my nose. Blood pours into my eyes
as I'm pinned down, tied to each post of the bed with
something, it's pinching my skin but I am also
completely bare to him. He forces himself into my dry
centre and pounds into me over and over. I cry, I beg, I

189

protest but Robbie is lost into his own world and forgets
that I am a captive.
"You are so good baby, you love me so much," he
moans and groans as if he can't hear me crying.
When he finally done he literally passes out on top of
me.
I sob and sob with his heavy weigh on top of me, unable
to move.
How the hell am I going to get free and get to work
before he wants round two?

I gasp awake, sweat dripping through my nightie. I sit up
in bed, my heart is racing still at the nightmare which
was a real flashback from long ago. I didn't show up for
work that morning, I cried myself to sleep until Robbie
finally woke up ten hours later. He untied me with
remorse and then told me to "Get your stupid lazy ass to
work," which I did, pretending I was though I was on a
night shift; another mark against my tarnished record.
Finally, once I have calmed down, I get out of bed and
head to the kitchen for some warm milk and honey. It
always helped me even as a child, my grandmother
always swore by it. I used to get nightmares and

flashbacks a lot, but these last few months they have calmed down, in fact this is the first I have had since being with Nick.

Nick. My anger rolls in my body. I didn't want to, and he didn't care. It's not like he forced me like Robbie did, I chose to carry on but only because I felt I had no choice. I chose to make the deal with Nick, I know I can't refuse him; it's what I have already been paid for.

The microwave bleeps and I take out my cup of hot milk. I sit at the kitchen breakfast bar.

"Hey." a voice startles me.

I spill my scolding milk over my thigh.

"Argh!" I cry out.

"Shit sorry," Nick says and places a cold tea cloth on my thigh.

"Don't touch me." I hiss out throwing his hand off me.

Nick backs away as I clean the milk up, it wasn't hot enough to do any damage, but it just stings a bit.

"Sorry," I mutter. I finally look at him, he looks exhausted.

"Are you okay?"

I nod, I shouldn't have snapped at him like that. I'm just spooked.

"Look Hol I'm…" Nick starts.

191

"Don't!"

Amazingly, he shuts up.

I clean up the table and taking my mug head back to bed. I can't deal with him right now; I have bigger monsters to deal with it; the ones in my head.

When I finally wake up again, it's gone three in the afternoon; warm milk and honey always works. Feeling much more refreshed I shower and change into some baggy tracksuit bottoms and a baggy top. I want to look as unsexy as possible. There is no way I want a repeat of last night. My legs are still aching.

 I step out of my room cautiously, the apartment is silent. Hoping Nick is out I tiptoe to the kitchen to get some coffee. I notice his mug is already used and left by the sink. He must have gone out. Feeling relieved I sit down. It's my day off, not back on until Monday night and I have no plans for my day whatsoever.

I need to get out of here though, and I reach for my phone, I need Phoebe.

ME: *Fancy a coffee?*

I didn't have to wait long for her to reply.

PHOEBE: *Yes please, on a night shift tonight. Where and when?*

I know she is on a night shift, she bitched about it all last night. I actually love the night shifts, but she hates them, but then again she loves her bed.

ME: *How about Benny's? That way you can go straight to work and we have more time to chat?*

PHOEBE: *Love that idea; meet me there in an hour?*

ME: *Perfect.*

I finish my coffee go to get ready.

I get to Benny's on time, and find Phoebe looking less than refreshed in a big booth.

"Good afternoon sunshine," I tease as I slide on the other side of her.

"I actually think I'm going to die." Phoebe moans.

I giggle at her as I scan the menu. I'm not hungry for food at all, but something sweet sounds good.

"You need a greasy fry up and cake," I suggest.

"Yes, and coffee, plenty of coffee,"

"How was the rest of your night?"

"It is blurry, very blurry. But I think the highlight was when Prince Sleaze tried to kiss you."

I feel colder, so it really was noticeable.

"I don't think..."

"Oh come on, you guys were all hot dancing and then he reaches," Phoebe argues.

"Do you think people saw?"

"Everyone saw honey, why did you pull back?"

"Because he is Prince Sleaze," I lie.

"True, but man, he looked edible,"

Luckily, waiter came over, interrupting our conversation. We ordered a Full English and a chocolate muffin for Phoebe and an ice cream sundae for me.

"Are you not eating?" Phoebe asks.

"No just need a sugar fix, I will cook later tonight,"

"What are you cooking a pot noodle?" She laughs.

Of course, I can't cook at the flat; I don't even have a microwave.

"Good point, maybe a take away pizza," I joke.

"So going back to Prince Sleaze, why do you think he came to that club? I thought it was way to beneath him," Phoebe asks.

"I have no idea, why are you so bothered?"

"Just curious, he seemed different last night, you know? More casual and loose and if I didn't know him from work I would have thought he was one of us,"

"He is one of us,"

"I meant one who isn't stuck up his own arse,"

"Maybe he just is that way at work, you don't know what people are like outside of it," I argue.

"Why are you defending him?" Phoebe asks curiously.

"I'm not, can we just change the subject from him, it is humiliating enough,"

"Okay, okay, let's talk about Tom," Phoebe chirps happily as our coffees arrive.

"Tom?" I groan.

"Yes he is totally hot for you, and he is really nice. You should go out with him,"

"I'm not ready."

"You keep saying that, but you so are, it's been over two years now," she says exasperated.

"I just don't want another relationship right now,"

"Really, I think you're…"

"Ladies." a voice interrupts us.

Tom is right there in the flesh, fuck, alongside a couple of lads Pete and Glen who were with us last night.

"Hi Tom," we mutter.

"May we join you? I'm hung-over to fuck right about now and need some grease,"

"Sure," Phoebe says and scoots over. I follow suit.

"Hey Holly, you look a lot healthier than the rest of us," Tom says.

"I headed out earlier than you,"

"True. It got messy after you left." Pete groaned.

The lads ordered their food with the waiter as he brought our food out.

"Ice cream?" Tom remarked.

"Ice cream." I reply and gleefully dive into my huge multi-coloured, creamy sugar fix.

This is a nice way to spend an afternoon, with friends and treats.

After the gang went to leave for work I scoop the sticky mess at the bottom of my sundae glass uninterested, trying to think of something else to do to avoid going back to Nick's. So I walk around Tesco's looking for more indulgent food. Something savoury for later, I decide on home-made pizza. Nick may need feeding. I haven't heard from him at all, which is good but also curious. What is he doing today? Shagging Penny? That man is insatiable; I'm still sore and aching.

As I enter the flat I can hear the TV. Nick is home. I step in quietly. He is sitting on his sofa watching sports; I don't think he has heard me, so I tiptoe into the kitchen with my bags.

"Holly?"

Damn.

"Hi," I mutter and start putting the shopping away.

"Where have you been?"

"'Benny's' with some friends,"

"Oh, well I went out for brunch with my father." he replies, as if I give a shit.

I nod and shut the fridge, looks like I'm watching a film in bed again. Thank god he has Netflix.

Nick comes into the kitchen in his jogging bottoms and a t-shirt.

"Holly, can we talk?"

"What's there to talk about?"

"Us, last night,"

"There is no 'us' Nick. I am your mistress that doesn't mean we are an 'us'." I snap.

His face drops and I feel a pang of guilt, annoyingly.

"I am so sorry; I treated you appallingly, like you were an object,"

"Aren't I?" I arch my brow.

"No. We may have an agreement, but I also agreed to take care of you. Instead I was the one that hurt you and I am truly sorry." he tells me apologetically. His face is a picture of shame and guilt. As much as I don't want to, I think I believe him.

"You did hurt me. You made me feel like a paid whore and I know that's what I am…"

"No you are not a whore Holly,"

"No, but you took me, when I didn't want to be taken." I cried out.

He looks as if I slapped him.

"I did, that will never ever happen again, I swear it." Nick says quietly.

Why is this sounding like a relationship? I have no right to let him swear that to me, If he wants it, I should be delivering it, whether I want it or not.

"I shouldn't be asking that of you,"

"You shouldn't have too."

I look up at him then and looking at his sincere apologetic eyes and I know I have forgiven him.

"Well don't expect anything tonight buddy, my body is frigging wrecked," I say lightly.

"Noted."

We stand silently in the kitchen for a bit.

"Are you hungry?" I ask to break the tension.

"Yeah, I could eat,"

"I was thinking of making pizza, but it takes some time, so I can get started now."

"Why? Don't you just stick it in the oven?"

"I'm making it from scratch."

He looks lost.

"Don't worry about it, but know it won't be ready for about a couple of hours."

He goes to walk out the kitchen, but pauses at the door.

"I guess I'll go watch the game then." he says sadly.

I don't have a clue what is up with him, first an emotional deep felt apology and now he is acting… lonely?

"Would you like to help?"

He spins around.

"I can't cook,"

"Well then you can watch and learn, maybe have a lesson for when I leave."

A small smile lights up his face.

"Okay"

I give a half smile as I get the ingredients to make the base.

"I need you to open the yeast and pour it into this water here." I say giving him a jug of warm water.

Nick obeys.

"Now stir it up well."

He does, using a fork. He seems very uncomfortable; his body is rigid as hell.

I weigh out the dry ingredients and place them into a bowl.

"Do I pour it in there?"

"Not yet give it five minutes or so, stick the kettle on."

He does as I ask; it shouldn't feel this good to be obeyed.

An hour later, we are working on the toppings.

"Slice the mushrooms like this," I instruct as I slice.

Nick looks like he is cutting into a person; his face is a mask of concentration. He is slicing each mushroom in perfectly equal slices.

I try not to snigger too loud.

"Done," he announces putting down his knife.

"Want to help me roll out the dough?" I offer.

"Yep."

I dust the surface of the breakfast bar, as Nick washes his hands vigorously.

"Okay, knead it again briefly and then roll it out into the tray."

Nick starts kneading the dough as I instruct; he is actually really good at it. He seems lost in the movement, like he is somewhere else.

"You're a natural," I praise.

"Me and my Mum used to make pastry all the time," he replies.

"You never mention your mum."

His trance suddenly vanishes.

"I don't talk about her." he says coldly.

I should shut up given his tone.

"Why?"

"Drop it."

I sigh and leave it. I have wondered about his relationship with her as he never talks about her. I don't even know if she is around, but just seeing how defensive he is about her, makes me even more curious.

"Well that's perfect, it needs to prove again for about half an hour, so we can finish whatever toppings you want," I change the subject.

"Sure, I love anything."

I slice peppers and chillies, whilst Nick slices onions and courgettes silently.

"My family isn't an easy subject either," I admit breaking the ice.

"I do wonder about them, you were in so much trouble and yet your parents were never brought into it,"

"They didn't want to be part of it,"

"How can parents do that? Just cut and run from their kids," Nick mutters angrily.

"I don't know, we never had the best relationship but I don't think I can forgive them for just exiling me because I made a bad decision,"

"Or a decision your husband made,"

"That's even worse,"

"At least I had one parent, do you have any siblings?" asks Nick.

"No, I am an only and unwanted child,"

"Me too, although my mum did want me, but not enough," he says sadly.

"Maybe that isn't true,"

"Well, she has had twenty four years to prove to me otherwise, yet she hasn't showed up with an apology," he shrugs.

"I think my parents are waiting for an apology from me, but that won't happen,"

"Why should you? Parents should be there for you no matter what, the good and the bad,"

"Exactly." I mutter.

I check the dough again.

"Okay time to decorate." I say as I spread sauce on the base. We pile the pizza high with toppings and Nick pops it the tray in the oven.

"So what happened with your parents then?" Nick asks after a pause.

I really don't like talking about it, but then again I don't need to hide from Nick. He knows my dark past, not in detail, but enough. Besides, if I share maybe he will too and I can understand more about him, he is such a mystery with a dickhead front.

"It's a long story," I sigh.

"Well I can't have sex with you, and I'm too knackered to go anywhere, so may as well be bored." he grins at me.

I open the fridge and fetch us a cold beer each.

"Well my father is a travel journalist, so he worked away all the time and my mother went with him," I start.

"Who took care of you?"

"I had a live in nannies until I was twelve and then I went to boarding school,"

"Sounds lonely,"

"I didn't know any different. When I went home we would have a family holiday somewhere but again the nannies would come, whilst they went off socialising."

Nick nodded drinking his beer.

"So yeah when I decided on nursing as a career my parents objected, saying that I should be a doctor with my grades etcetera, but I didn't want to. I didn't want my whole life to be based on my career like his was," I tell him.

"So they cut me off until I came to my senses, which I never did and enrolled in nursing school using my savings my grandparents left me in their will"

"So they cut you off then?"

"Yeah we still spoke every few months or so, but that was the beginning of the end. I rebelled big time and met Robbie, who they refused to meet or accept that I was involved with some loser like him"

"Not wrong there then," Nick says grimly.

"Nope not wrong about that, anyway I fell in love with Robbie and I know I changed. I rebelled, I partied hard, I just couldn't keep trying to be someone they wanted me to be. When I told them we were going to get married that was it. My father told me never to speak to him or my mother again until this fixation with Robbie had ended," I admit feeling sick just by saying it aloud.

"So you married Robbie, and then he left. Why didn't you call them then?" Nick probes.

"The hospital did when I got hurt but their contact details had changed,"

"You got hurt?"

"Yeah" It is all I reveal. I don't want him to know that part.

"So I went to see them after I got out, I needed somewhere to go. I was planning on grovelling and begging for help but when I got to our home, someone else lived in it. Apparently they moved out a year or so before, and retired abroad," I continue.

"So no one knows where they are?" he asks in wonder.

"No one I know. The only family I had and cared about was my Nan, but she passed away not long after I married Robbie. I didn't even know." I say bitterly.

I'm shocked to find Nick placing a hand on mine.

"I'm so sorry," he says softly.

"Yeah well I better get the pizza," I shrug him off and go to the oven.

"That smells amazing," Nick says as I place the pizza onto the board and start slicing it up.

"You're a very good sous chef."

We dive in and it's the best yet.

"So you have no clue where your parents are and no way to contact them?" Nick says ruining my mood.

"I could if I really wanted to. I could track them down. But I didn't have the time or money, besides after that I just didn't see why I should," I admit painfully.

"I get it I could track my mother down if I wanted to but I don't. My father loved her so much, and she just wanted more all the time, more money, more of his time. He nearly jacked in his career for her and she just takes off with some millionaire at the drop of a hat and forgot about us," Nick says his voice laced with anger.

"Did she try for an arrangement to see you?"

"Did she fuck," he spits out.

"But she obviously loved you. You seem to have such fond memories of her,"

"I thought she did, but then again my father thought she loved him as much as he did her. Turns out she was a selfish, lying, whore" he spits out angrily.

I can't say anything to that. I can't judge him or his mother.

"But you had your father. What was that like?"

"It was good. He worked a lot, but he always spent time with me when he could. He showed me how the world worked and what to do to succeed in it. He made me who I am today." Nick tells me.

I don't know what to say to that either. He is successful, ambitious and absolutely brilliant career wise, but as a person? Not sure how much his father had on that.

"I've never met your father," I say stupidly.

"And you never will." he replies lightly.

Of course not! Mistresses don't meet the parents. I forgot myself then, forgot my place. I suppose that's easily done when two people are having a heart to heart, eating pizza and drinking beer like they were friends.

"Are you done?" I ask, shaking it off.

"Yeah, thank you Rag Doll" Nick says standing up.

"I'm paid to cook for you." I reply.

I take the plates over to the sink, and find Nick right behind me.

"No I meant, thank you for helping me cook with you. I haven't cooked in so long, not since my mother left, you made it feel okay," he says and kisses the top of my head before stalking out into the lounge.

He kissed my head?

I wash up, feeling his lips burn through my hair.

"So what do you fancy? Rocky or The Godfather?" Nick yells from the sofa.

So we clearly aren't going to be having any more deep and meaningful conversations tonight, much to my relief.

Chapter Nineteen- Nick

My palm grazes something soft and curvy as I start to wake up. I'm pressed against it, warm and I'm completely entwined in it. I breathe out a contented sigh, snuggling up to my warm… Holly. My eyes snap open as my brain registers not what I am snuggling up to, but whom.

We are on the sofa. I am behind her, spooning her one hand is resting on her stomach, the other on her breast. Shit. I have never 'snuggled' in my life and yet here I am pressed into her every curve as if I am sewn to her.

I get up carefully, untangling myself from her and step over the back of the sofa, whilst she sleeps unaware of my panic and head to the bathroom. I feel ridiculously awake and refreshed as if I have slept for a day not mere hours. After I use the toilet I look at myself in the mirror, all bright eyed and bushy tailed. I pick a few strands of Holly's hair off my chest and take a deep breath.

Verbal diahorrea, that's what I had last night. I don't understand how stupidly I am behaving around Holly. It's like she switches the insanity switch inside me. I take an extra cold shower to rid my morning glory, no way do I want to be close to her in any way right now. My life is great; it's fucking perfect. All these emotions she is stirring up in me are going to fuck up everything I have worked so hard for.

The alarm rings loudly at six pm and I hear a squeal, followed by a thump.

I step out to find Holly sprawled on the floor, legs akimbo as she tries to find my phone.

"Shit, shit." she curses.

I don't bother to help or make myself known. Seeing her with wild bed hair and wearing my t-shirt is enough to make me *want* to help, so I step back and get changed for work.

I go back into the living room twenty minutes later. Holly is up, dressed that hair all pinned back into the nun like bun and cooking bacon.

"Want a bacon sandwich before work?" she asks over the sizzling pan.

My stomach growls in response. Even if I wasn't hungry, I love the smell of bacon, like most of the world.

She has placed a mug of coffee in my cup on the breakfast bar and has already put out the brown sauce next to my place, tomato ketchup next to hers. My blood grows cold as I see this very relationship like scene.

"No." I blurt out.

She turns around.

"Oh…" she begins

"I got to go." I step out of the kitchen and almost run out of the door, like the pathetic creature I am becoming.

Work is slow today, far too slow for my energetic mood. There is always drama working in a hospital, but there was no adrenaline rush, no problems. My surgeries were smooth, no hiccups, no surprises and all went successfully.

I sit down for an early break at midnight with a bacon sandwich and a large coffee. I scan the room for Holly, but she is nowhere to be seen. About right really, we usually don't take food breaks till at least two am or so, so I don't know why I feel alone.

Lonely? Me? I was brought up alone, I like being alone. It's the best way to be. Yet I enjoyed last night so much more than I thought was possible. Holly and I ended up watching a 'Rocky' marathon, laughing at the same bits, discussing the stereo-type that defines sports based intellect. No sex, no touching or even flirting yet I felt closer to her than when we are having sex. Holly actually has a lot more in common with me than I thought. Both having parental issues, both only children and as much as she pretends I am the closed up one, she keeps her cards close to her chest as well.

"Knock, knock." a voice sings through my thoughts. Penny sits by me.

"What are you doing here?" I ask in surprise.

"One of my patient's is in labour I have tried to keep to keep that baby in three times now, I sure hope it keeps that stubborn attitude once its born," she sighs sipping her tea.

"Oh I'm sorry. How far along is the baby?"

"24 weeks,"

Damn.

"Is there much hope?"

"Not a lot no, but that's what I love about my job. Babies are so much more resilient than we are. If anyone can pull through they can."

Her face lights up as she talks and I remember why I adore this woman so much. That fire, that passion it matches my own. I pull her closer to me and hold her in my arms.

"Nick!" Penny protests, and tries to pull away.

"Oh come on, the ball is over with and everyone thinks we are together any way." I shrug.

It's true, the rumour mill is sure going round and round again. I can hear whispers.

She shakes her head and moves away.

"We still on for tonight?" she asks lightly.

"Of course what time shall I come over? I finish at two this afternoon,"

"Come over at eight? Now I have had to come in I will finish up after the ten am rounds I will have time to get dinner ready"

"Are you cooking?" My eyes light up.

She gives a delicate snort.

"Hardly, I can prep a salad at best. But I know a wonderful French restaurant that delivers to me,"

"Sounds great." I lie, ashamed at comparing. Holly's home cooked meals are spoiling me.

"Excellent, well not long to go anyway,"

My pager goes.

The scans I have ordered for Samuel Holmes have come back. He hasn't left the hospital since the G.P referred him. He had a brain tumour. Neurology has managed to remove most of it. But it's just part of it. There is a secondary tumour growing all over his lungs that is spreading aggressively; as if it wasn't bad enough not one tumour at the age of seven? We have had to wait for neurology to do their part as that was the pressing matter and wait as long as we can to start our part. He is still terminal though, but their work won't help if I can't get to the lungs fast. It's just the risk factor; Can a seven year old cope with that kind of operation twice in a matter of weeks?

I get up, hoping these scans are showing the tumour is slowing down a bit, but I doubt it.

"It's Samuel Holmes, I have to see these scans" I mutter.

"I'll come too" Penny stands too. He isn't technically her patient as he a child not a baby, but she can take on children cases if she needs to.

"Okay"

We walk out together. I feel like leaning on her for support. No, no her, I actually want Holly. She has taken care of Sam like he was her own, sneaking him treats and playing games with him in his bed. She cares about him so much. It's a heart-breaking situation. She should be with me for this.

The scans are as I predicted. The tumour is growing daily. It's getting far too close to the airways. I need to operate as soon as possible.

"Fuck sake," I roar, cursing my bored mood earlier as I stare at them.

"Poor boy," Penny says shaking her head.

"We need him into theatre as soon as possible," I tell her.

"No,"

"What?" I spin, my eyes blazing.

"You need parental consent first Nick. Stop and think" she says calmly.

"What? You think they will say no?"

"I'm not saying that, but the bulk of the brain tumour has gone, he is still terminal but if you operate on him now there is a huge chance he will die in theatre," Penelope says practically.

"I know it is extremely risky, but if I remove it he will have months, maybe even a year,"

"If you get it,"

"I will get it." I inform her loudly.

"If anyone can, you can. It's not that I am worried about" she says gently.

"His body could fail with the stress but I have to take that chance, He is seven years old," I yell.

"It's the parents decision whether to take that chance Nick"

I know she is right, I know the rules and I know everything but if they say no, he will die very soon. Of that I am positive of.

"We will talk to them as soon as they wake up," I snap.

"I will do it,"

"No you won't this isn't your case. I'm the lead consultant on him,"

"Calm down and get it together Nick. I will help you as you seem very heated about this." Penny orders, her hands on her hips.

Again, she is right.

"Fine," I turn to a nurse passing through the halls.

"You. Get all the paperwork ready for Samuel Holmes. I want it in the next hour." I demand to the back of her. Holly turns round.

"Yes Doctor Willis." she says quietly and scurries off. Oh it had to be Holly didn't it? The volume of nurses in this place and I speak to her like she is a piece of shit. Just fucking perfect!

The parents are making a decision that would be impossible for any one, let alone making it for their seven year old son. Penelope is perfect, so professional and so clean about delivering the news. I let her do the hard bit; she is right as I can't stop sneaking glances at Sam. He looks tiny, all bandaged from his previous surgery. I pride myself on being cool at work, but Penelope trumps me today, especially as the baby she delivered three hours ago, died almost instantly. She changed her bloody scrubs, got another Earl Grey and came straight to me to plan Sam's options.

I launch into the technical side of his surgery, trying not to look at the boy who is playing with his toy cars on the hospital bedding.

"We need time Dr Willis," his father chokes out.

"I really do understand and sympathise Mr Holmes. But every day that passes, the riskier the operation is." I say slowly. I feel like such a prick just for saying it, but it is the truth.

"I know. We will let you know as soon as we can." he replies before rushing out of the door. He needs to let it out. He is one strong man holding it together for this long.

"Where's Daddy going?" Sam asks.

"Just to get some coffee mate," I reply for his mother, who is holding back the tears.

"Strange, Daddy hates coffee" he replies and continues back to his aeroplane.

I head out too, also needing to escape the kid.

I finally finish work at two pm. Eighteen hours on my feet and I am swaying back home. I want to tell Holly the situation with Sam, but I shouldn't really, not outside the hospital. It's bending the rules not exactly breaking them, but I don't bend any rules at work. I finally drag my tired ass up the stairs and force myself to go straight to my bed. Not Holly's. She must be fast asleep by now anyway. I should be back on a night shift, but given my date with Penny this evening I switched things around so I am back on at two am. Not quite as much time as I would like to be with Penny, but she of all people understands. I lie in bed and my eyes close instantly. The alarm wakes me at six pm as usual. My head is groggy as I force myself to get out of bed. Certainly a change from the last time I woke up. Four hours is not enough sleep, even for me. I consider a shower but decide on a rare bath instead. Running the water and bubble bath into the tub, I wander into the kitchen to make some much needed coffee.

"Evening," Holly mutters sleepily behind me.

"Hey," I reply not turning around. I start up my coffee machine. I grab me and Holly a mug as wait for the machine to finish brewing. Why did I decide on this contraption when I could have just had instant?

I feel her brush against me with naked thighs, her sweet scent filling my nostrils as she leans over me to switch on the kettle.

"I need caffeine now." she mutters.

I can't say anything as all my blood and senses go straight to one place. She's in yet another unsexy nightie but at least this one is shorter than usual and pale green in colour, which suits her skin tone.

The kettle switches off and we both grab for it. Fuck it, I will have a brewed cup next.

Automatically I drop my hands and spoon instant coffee into mugs whilst she pours the water into both, stirring mine first.

"Ta."

I take it gingerly over to the breakfast bar.

"I need this tonight," she moans as she joins me with milk in hers.

"Yeah,"

"I didn't hear you come in, did you stay later?"

"No I finished late at two,"

"Is it to do with Sam?" she asks.

"Yeah,"

She nods slowly. I'm grateful she is doesn't push for more, I am impressed. I know she cares about him and must want to know.

"So you have had like three, four hours sleep tops?"

"Yeah,"

"Don't burn yourself out,"

"Never do."

She pauses then as she finishes her coffee.

"Well I need to get ready," she says hopping down from the stool. Her nightie rides up as she jumps, showing me her knickers.

Damn. I can't have Holly. I will be with Penelope later. I need to save my boys for the big game.

"I'm on at two so I will see you later on."

She pauses.

"Oh yeah, see you." Holly says quickly and dashes off.

I pour a now ready brewed coffee into my mug and head off to my bath.

"Nick?" Holly asks stepping into the bathroom, while I'm bathing.

"Yeah?"

"Can I come in?"

I open my eyes to see her at the door.

"You already are."

She walks up and sits on the side of the bath fully clothed. She looks worried.

"Is he going to be okay?"

"Who?"

"Sam."

I sit up, sploshing water over the rim.

"I can't discuss that with you outside work and you know it," I tell her.

"I know that. I don't need the stats I just want to know." she says, her big eyes wide. I can see tears filling up in them, much to my dismay. I don't do tears and emotional women. It pisses me off big time and I have dealt with many crying woman as a result of me dumping them. I haven't seen her cry before. Not when she was hurt, not when she got spooked, not when I treated her like shit recently. Still I look at her face and know she won't let those tears fall for anything. She is concentrating hard.

"I am going to do all I can," I say honestly.

"Then it should be enough." she replies.

She looks so vulnerable sitting on the edge of my bath, despite all her situations; she has always been so strong and just dealt with it. Yet a single patient has her crumbling like a sandcastle. I lean over and kiss her lips. Holly jerks at the soft touch and moves away.

"I can't." she says panicking.

It wasn't about sex genuinely. It wasn't. For once it really wasn't about lust, I kissed her to comfort her and that's the gratitude I get?

"Fine, fuck off then." I shout.

She runs out of the door. I hear the flat door slam shut as well and I sink back into my bath, as if I would shag her an hour or so before shagging Penny. Honestly what does she think of me?

That you paid ten grand for her to be your paid sex slave? a voice nags me.

I actually kissed a woman and not because it's a motion before sex. I think that pissing me off more than her believing it was an act of lust, not me caring.

Caring? What a fucking notion, me caring and comforting another human being.

I laugh dryly to myself as I get out of the bath. I'm glad she ran now actually, it will give me chance to beat this ridiculous behaviour out of my system.

"How's the soup?" Penny asks two hours later.

I glance down at the French Onion soup in a porcelain soup bowl.

"Good." I reply taking another soup spoon full.

We are sitting at her dining table, which is big enough for a dozen people. At least she placed us at the top, opposite each other.

"Pierre's is the best. I love getting a take away from there when I'm feeling naughty" she replies.

As always Penny looks sensational, even dressed casually in a fitted cotton trousers and a blue blouse.

"Feeling naughty is a greasy pizza or a curry lovely, not soup." I laugh.

She screws her nose up at that.

"Hey I got Madeleine's for dessert." she says seriously.

I act shocked and gasp loudly.

She sticks her tongue out like a child.

"Are you finished with your soup?"

"Yes." I reply, watching her stand and clear the bowls. Her bottom is hugging every inch of bottom. I stare as she walks back into the kitchen. Her bum is small and toned, but nothing is happening.

I sigh in disappointment.

The evening has been pleasant; so civilised with a bottle of perfectly chilled white wine, as we make small talk. She is very easy to talk to, but then we have been friends for so long, it's natural and the conversation flows. Penny has made such an effort to make me feel welcome and wanted in her home.

She steps back in with dinner plates.

Penny bites her lips nervously as she places my plate in front of me; salad.

I burst into laughter as she eyes me, to challenge me to say anything.

"Oh do fuck off." she huffs in a haughty voice that makes me laugh harder.

My eyes are literally streaming as she sits on my lap.

The atmosphere changes instantly as she wraps her arms around my neck.

"Or we could just skip the main course altogether?" she breathes.

We could, if my dick would respond. I can feel her heat pooling onto my groin.

She leans towards me and presses her lips against mine.

Shit, she is going for it and I am on autopilot kissing her back. Panic is flooding through me. Can I do this? I don't feel like I can go through with it physically.

"Let's take this slowly" I mutter.

"Slowly?" she says amazement in her eyes.

"Slowly, I have been waiting a long time for this."

I unbutton her blouse, all fiddly buttons of course, but it slides off eventually.

"Oh Nick." she breathes as I kiss her collarbone gently. I'm thinking on my feet as I trail kisses along her skin. If I don't get hard, I could get her off. Make her feel good and it makes me look like a gentleman and shows I have changed. I grin as I get up carefully and she leads me to her bedroom.

I hold back a snort as I enter her bedroom; gold and white, very regal, very Penelope.

She doesn't notice though as she is unbuttoning my shirt.

Gently, I push her onto her immaculate bedding and unbutton her trousers.

"Nick I want you." she moans as I remove her underwear.

I stand back to look at her; absolutely perfect, like a model all trim, lean and golden. I grit my teeth as nothing at all happens in my boxers.

So I kneel between her legs and place my mouth on her, doing what I do second best.

A short while later Penny is giggling hysterically as she comes down from her high.

"Oh my gosh that was..." she trails off.

"Glad you approve, you have a whole life time to enjoy those," I say smugly.

"Sounds wonderful."

I stand up to button my shirt back up.

"Wait…" she asks confused.

"This was all about you princess,"

"But don't you?"

"I can wait." I reply with a wink.

She sits up and gets a robe.

"Wow Nick, you really have changed." she says shocked.

"Yep I really have, now let's go enjoy our naughty salad," I laugh.

Chapter 20- Holly

"Hey buddy, how are you doing?" I ask Sam as I approach his bed at seven am.

It has finally been confirmed. The dreaded 'c' word is threatening his life again. It is just so unfair; the boy has had major surgery to remove the majority of this brain tumour. Not all of it. He is going to die; I think I managed to swallow that bitter pill, and now this! Seven years old and he has to battle with two aggressive, murdering tumours. I actually went straight to the on call room and cried when I was informed.

His parents have opted for surgery. The chances of surviving it are low but without it he will die from the lung tumour in a few weeks tops. I thought over and over what I would do if it was my child. But I decided I would do what Sam's parents are doing, giving Sam a chance. If the surgery works, he could live with his remaining brain tumour for months, perhaps even years, there could be future operations to remove it entirely or reduce it down at the very least.

"I'm good." Sam replies smiling.

I start to prepare him for surgery, letting him amaze me with his jokes.

"I'm brave like Superman." he whispers to me.

My heart tugs; yes, yes he really is. It's our little saying between us. He loves the Marvel Superheroes, and we have many, many debates on who will beat who in a battle.

I hear a cry and see his mother sobbing in her husband's arms, silent tears running down his face as well.

"Here, I snuck this in for you." I say, drawing a mars bar out of my pocket.

Sam snatches it happily.

"Oh thanks Holly, I'm starving,"

"You can't eat it now, but you can eat it after your operation." I tell him.

He slips it under his pillow. I make a mental note to tell the surgical team to remove it discreetly.

"Okay little man, that's me all done. I will see you after surgery, be strong like Superman" I say touching his hand. With the rest of my strength I walk away casually, despite my heart hammering through my chest. He needs to see that we believe he will come out of the other side of this. He trusts me enough that I have been put as the main nurse on his case. His family trusts me, and I can't show my fear. As soon as I'm out of sight I hurry my pace and go straight to the staff room for a coffee. It's a strange shift. I'm supposed to have finished at eight this morning, my usual night shift, but I'm going to stay on until Sam comes out of surgery. I have to be there when he wakes up. I'll take nap or something in the on call room, something I hate doing.

 Tom is already there, he is part of the team about to operate on Sam. He sees my face and comes over holding out his arms.

"Come here Hol,"

I stand frozen as he pulls me into his strong arms. I concentrate on holding back the tears; I learned how to hold them back from Robbie, as it made him angrier if I cried. My body is shaking though as Tom holds me.

"Dr Willis is the best. He has the best chance with him," He soothes.

"Did I hear my name?" Nick says.

I spin round to see him walking in, Princess Penelope wrapped around his arm. Her body language says it all, they were together last night. The rumours have been going crazy all day about them but I have blocked them out. Sam is all that mattered.

In a cloud of emotions I reach for Nick and he comes to me, pulling me into the hug I need.

"Please, please save little Sam," I say chocked up.

He strokes my hair softly, sending comforting tingles through me.

"I will do everything I can Holly, I promise you,"

"I'm putting my faith in you, if anyone can save him you can,"

"He will do all he can Nurse Jones. Can you let him go now?" I hear her crisp voice. I shake my head in disbelief as I realise we are not alone.

Nicks hands drop automatically as I jerk away from him, my face blazing. Tom and Penelope are both staring at us.

"I'm s-o-o sorry, how unprof-fessional," I stammer moving well back.

"It's ok Holly, you're an exceptional nurse because of how much you care." Nick says in his most professional voice, the one he uses with patients. I can't read his eyes as he isn't looking at me whilst he says it.

"Good luck, Save my little superman please." I say before ducking out the door, my coffee forgotten about. I stand behind it breathing hard.

"Emotional fool." I hear Penelope bitching.

I seethe; my emotions make me who I am. I am exceptional, Nick told me himself. My emotions make me that way. Although in a personal sense, I am a wreck. I broke three rules in one stupid moment. I cried, I could have compromised mine and Nick's deal and worst of all I wanted comfort from him. It was as if he was the only one who could have calmed me down. Not a good move all round. I need to sleep. I tell my co-workers to page me when Sam is coming out of surgery and hit the on call room.

I hate not being able to lock the door here, anyone can come in. It's not protected but as I lie on a used bed and I find my eye lids closing.

Just over five hours later I rush out of the on call room. My pager has bleeped to say they are finished in surgery. I see Sam's parents with other people in the waiting room, so I wait too.

I see Nick approaching in his scrubs, his face is blank.

No! No! NO! I know what that means. I hope I'm wrong.

"Mr and Mrs Holmes, I am so sorry, Sam didn't make it." Nick says professionally, his eyes show me that he is feeling anything but professional.

The room begins to cry and I force back my own tears.

"We managed to remove the tumour from his lungs but then his body went into failure. We tried, we did everything we could to save him," he continued blankly.

"Trying doesn't bring our baby boy back!" Mr Holmes yells, sobbing.

"I'm so sorry for your loss, we tried so hard." Nick continued more to himself than anyone else.

He meets my eyes.

"I tried," he repeats to me.

"I know you did,"

"My boy!" Mrs Holmes wails.

Nick storms out leaving me with the broken family.

I finish up finally at two am; I don't go back to Nicks, there's no point with having to be back on in six hours so I just work through and into my night shift. I don't see Nick again during that shift. I heard he left already, left early. It's always hard losing a patient, devastating when it's a child. But Nick just faces it with the cool professionalism he was born with. Not this time.

As I walk into the apartment I find Nick slumped in an armchair, a whiskey bottle in his hand.

"Nick?" I ask looking at his red blank eyes.

"Holly," He looks at me and to my shock starts to cry. "Oh Holly, I couldn't save him. I failed."

I wrap my arms around his shaking body, but he cries even harder.

"I was in there, screaming at the team. I was pumping his heart with my hand, begging for him to live for an hour. They gave up and tried to call it but I refused and carried on until Tom pulled me off. I killed him."

I pull him against my chest, stroking his hair. It comforted me when he did it to me, not so long ago.

"He was going to die. You were trying to save his life. You went beyond what anyone else would have done." I tell him.

"But it went wrong. He could have had a few more weeks to be with his family, die feeling loved and not on an operating table," he starts to yell.

"You tried…"

"Trying didn't SAVE HIM!" he shouts.

I give up talking to him and just hold him to my chest rocking him. My heart is breaking for him. I don't know how long we stayed like that for, me on my knees cradling him like a child. His sobs die down and I can feel his body calming down. His mouth nuzzles into my neck and he begins to kiss my throat.

"Holly." he breathes and reaches up to kiss me. He kisses me so gently, so softly, his lips lazily exploring me. Nicks fingers stoke my face. It takes my breath away at how sweet he is being with me. He cups my face and leaves little kisses all over my face, my eyes, my nose, my cheeks making me feel dizzy. It's not lust that is driving him this time. He never kisses me like this. He stands up and holds his hand out to me. I take it holding his hand as he leads me into his bedroom. Nick takes out my hair bobble, running his hands through my locks.

"You are amazing." he whispers and pulls off my top slowly. I do the same to him, pressing kisses on his chest and neck. This isn't something we do, this is something entirely different.

His hands unclip my bra and his mouth comes down on my breast, sucking gently on me. I go to unbutton his jeans but he stops me moving me onto the bed. He spends time lavishing attention on both my breasts and then moves to kiss a trail down to my jeans. He takes them off and puts his mouth on me. There is no urgency as he devours me, it's like he is savouring me. I come far too soon.

"It is you that is perfect." he mutters and slides inside me slowly.

I wait for him to slam into me, pace and speed is what I'm used to. But it doesn't happen. He is moving slowly, beautifully. He is making love to me.

I feel myself building up and take the chance to kiss him in a way I never have, lovingly, as we explode again together what feels like in rainbow and stars.

I go to move away after we calm down but Nick tucks me up with him, cuddling up to me. I should panic. I should go as I'm sure he will be pissed about this tomorrow but I can't. I pass out more contented and safe than I have ever felt before, in Nick's arms.

The next morning I wake up alone.

I search the apartment but Nick is gone.

It's been two weeks and Nick hasn't laid a hand on me. He has barely spoke to me and is rarely home. At work he is like a machine, surgery after surgery. Then when he isn't working he is with Penelope. The rumours are well and truly founded. People are saying they are together now. They take breaks together constantly, if they are on shift together. I had to put up with seeing them all laughing and fucking each other with their eyes more than one occasion. I now avoid the cafeteria when she is on shift.

It hurts, it hurts so fucking bad. It's like everything is cannonballing on me. Nick changed everything the night Sam died. That one night he made love to me I realised that I have fallen in love with him. I don't know if it was a gradual thing or whether that night just made me realise it with pure clarity. I am in love with him and he doesn't love me back. He refuses to talk about that night, like it is something he is ashamed of, maybe he saw straight through me, maybe he was so drunk that he doesn't even remember it. I don't know, all I know is that I woke up alone and he ran straight to Penelope the woman he does want.

I don't even know why I am still living here. He hasn't asked me to go but what's the point if he doesn't seem to want to touch me. I am there as his mistress until he and Penelope become a serious item. It seems like it's they are on their way and she has taken my duties away. I should feel relief. I am not being used any more but I long for him.

To make it even worse, I have been assigned to the babies ward for a while as a reward for my work with Sam. As if it is a reward to be put with more sick children that pull at my heart strings and as if I want to work under Penelope. I should be flattered; there is only an elite team of nurses Penelope trusts to work in this department. But I just feel jealously and hating myself for respecting the 'other woman'.

"Holly can you check on Kimberly's vitals and change Lewis's catheter please?" she calls to me.

"Sure."

I do everything she says and double check my work as usual.

"I'm starving, I'm heading for a lunch break" she calls out as I finish injecting some more painkillers into little Suzie's IV.

I don't bother replying. I have been here for eight hours and yet to be released for a break. She walks away in her high heels and yet another figure hugging dress. Yes, I am jealous of that too; she is so super slim no doubt any fat would literally melt off her. I am not exactly fat but my boobs, hips and bum are at least double her size if not triple. Curvy is what I used to call myself, but now I just think I am chubby.

Let her go off and eat her fruit salad or lemon grass smoothie. I'll just finish up here and go home and eat ice cream again.

I'm checking on Freddie's stitches when she floats back over again. Freddie is a one year boy who thinks he is Peter Pan and decided to fly off his brother's bunk bed and fall into the TV cabinet and split his cheek completely open. Luckily aside from a huge scar he is absolutely perfect.

"Oh my Gosh I totally over ate at lunch, I'm supposed to be going out for dinner with Nick later as well." she gushes at me.

That's the one of the many reasons I don't like Penelope. She talks about herself and her personal life far too much.

"What, did you have like four strawberries?" I mock gently.

"Very funny, no actually I caved and had a white bread roll with my salad," she says horrified.

"Oh no, white?"

"Yep, going to take off and head to the gym for a bit,"

"Okay,"

"Although I'm sure I can persuade Nick to burn it off with me." she giggles.

I think I just vomited in my mouth.

"See you later Holly,"

"Where is the medication report?" I ask.

"Over on the desk and make sure you hand over correctly to Suzanna,"

"Yes Dr Sinclaire,"

"Page me if you need me,"

"Will do."

She spins on her heel, and I am about to let out a breath of relief when she spins back around to face me.

"Holly?"

"Yes?"

"You don't talk much do you?" she asks me amused.

"I keep to myself,"

"Yeah well, you should go out some time. I heard Tom Westbury has a thing for you,"

"I don't mix personal and work together." I lie.

She rolls her eyes at me; even then she manages to make it damn graceful.

"Think about it, you could double date with me and Nick."

I *think* I want to shove the medical report down her skinny throat.

I shake my head politely and walk away before she can suggest anything else that may twist the knife further into my open wound.

My mood is black as I finish work and storm up to Nick's apartment. I get in and grab Nick's gym bag and begin packing up my things. I blast some Evanescence from his laptop and let myself drown in the sad but beautiful vocals of Amy Lee.

I don't even hear him until he taps my shoulder.

I spin around gasping in shock.

"What are you doing?" he asks, his hands are on his bare hips. He must have been for a run judging by his jogging bottoms and a sweaty t-shirt bunched in his hand. I feel my body respond to his glistening muscular torso, which further angers me.

"Packing,"

He turns the sound down on the laptop.

"I can see that," he says rolling his eyes. What is with people rolling their eyes at me today?

"Then why ask?" I snap and continue to fold up a hoodie.

He clutches at my shoulders forcing me to face him.

"Are you going somewhere?" he asks coolly.

"I think I should go home."

His eyes widen. Those eyes I once thought were cold and hard. Now I just see the beauty of them, so dark like the black coffee he drinks, almost hypnotic.

"Has your loser boyfriend been thrown in prison or been murdered by the bastard Martin?" he asks.

"I don't know." I admit in a small voice. I didn't think of that with my mood.

"Then, until you know, you stay the fuck here until I tell you otherwise."

I sigh. He is trying to protect me, as much as he pretends he is an indifferent asshole he cares about my safety. He is right, it isn't safe.

244

"I just feel like a leach now, it's not as if I am doing anything for you in return."

Nick moves closer to me, his chest against mine. My nipples harden instantly.

"That's my choice, not yours."

Don't I know it? I can feel his heartbeat quicken. He is affected.

"What's wrong Holly, why are you trying to run away?"

He asks sitting on my bed and pulling me with him. He is too close.

"Penelope asked me to go on a double date with you and Tom," I blurt out.

His eyebrows rise.

"You and Penny are talking?"

"I don't want to, but she keeps talking to me,"

"Shit, yeah I forgot you have been moved onto the babies ward for a bit."

"Didn't think you noticed,"

"I'll make a call. I don't want you two working so close together." he frowns.

Of course not! How awful for him, his girlfriend and mistress working together.

"I like being on the babies ward" I protest.

"I don't like you working so closely to Penny. I don't need you dropping us in it," he hisses.

"Like I would,"

"You never know. Your emotions get the better of you,"

"And you don't show any emotions at all, unless you're drunk" I spit back.

His eyes blaze with anger.

"What are you referring too?"

"Forget it,"

"No I won't. What do you mean by that?"

"The night Sam died, it was different. Since then you have been ignoring me."

He gets up quickly, as if he doesn't want to think about it.

"I've got to go. You are not leaving," he barks at me.

"Fine, but I'm going out in a bit" I yell back.

He spins back round.

"I need you here,"

"No you don't. You don't need me here at all,"

"Are going to see Tom?" he asks briskly.

Oh no way.

"So what if I am. I only have five weeks left, may as well get the next one lined up" I say stupidly. Great, now I'm acting like the whore I am paid to be.

He is back in my face in an instant.

"You are mine Holly,"

"Not for much longer."

We are literally panting in each other's face waiting for one of us to back down.

I grab his head and pull him down to my lips. They smash together ferociously. In this moment, I don't care that he is taken, he was mine first.

My hands wraps around his neck as he lifts me up, wrapping my legs around his waist. His tongue plunges into my mouth hungrily and I moan loudly. I need this, I need him. His hands wander up my back underneath my vest top, causing my skin to hum under his touch. My top is pulled off as I run my hands through his hair tugging on it.

"Nick." I breathe, looking into his eyes.

Please see me, just see me.

He looks at me and I can see pain flicker through them.

He lowers me onto the bed and takes a step back.

"I can't." he says painfully.

I watch him walk away; each step crushes my heart even further.

Vodka and plenty of it is my new friend as I go out dancing. I should be sleeping. But right now I don't want to be alone. Phoebe and a bunch of us are all together, forgetting the world. I throw my hands up in the air, and grind my body to the beat of the night club.

Tom is my new favourite dance partner as well, as we get all sticky him grinding against me. Maybe I should punish Nick and go on this double date? Just to see him sweat it out as I make false girlie talk with Penelope. Tom is actually gorgeous and can move that sexy body of his well. He wouldn't be ashamed of me, he wouldn't hide me away. He moves closer to whisper in my ear.

"We move so goddam well,"

"We do,"

"SHOTS!" Phoebe calls out, coming towards us with a tray.

I down mine instantly, I can't even taste it, I am that trashed.

"Holly, are you okay?" Phoebe asks.

"I'm wonderful." I slur.

She eyes me carefully. I know why; she knows I don't get trashed. I have to be alert always. But tonight I need to forget him. He left without another word to me; I know where he is and what he is doing. Worst still, I know how I feel about it.

Tom's hands wrap around my waist again and I smile at Phoebe as I get pulled into another dance.

He pulls me even closer, his body flush against my back.

Tom has been getting more and more physical as we dance. I should stop him. It's not as if I can do anything with him even if I want to. It's selfish and I am leading him on. Yet if Nick wasn't in the picture he would be perfect. Nick and I are coming to an end. I will be alone all over again. I have a perfect man who couldn't be sweeter or kinder and he likes me.

He stops dancing, staring at me. I know what he is going to do and my head spins at how to deal with this.

"Tom you need to dance with me." Phoebe squeals cutting in thankfully.

Being the gent that he is, he smiles and whisks her off. I meet her eyes in gratitude and head off to get another round in.

"Holly, can we talk?" Tom asks behind me.

Drat.

"Yeah let's go in that booth," I reply leading him to a slightly quieter area of the club.

"Holly, I know we agreed to be friends, but I need to tell you how I feel," he begins, fiddling with his glass.

"Tom, I'm sorry, I feel like I'm leading you on,"

"You haven't, I have been pushing you for more,"

"I just can't, I'm not ready."

Tom moves closer to me and touches my face carefully, like I matter.

"I know, I see you." he says sadly.

Those words echo through my fuzzy brain as he cradles my face.

He is going to kiss me I think stupidly as his lips brush mine.

I'm frozen as he kisses me gently but all I can see is Nick.

I pull away.

"I'm so sorry." Is all I can say.

He sighs and runs his hand through his hair.

"No, I'm sorry Holly; you keep saying no and I just keep pushing,"

"You are such a wonderful man. If circumstances were different…" I trail off.

"That kiss told me everything Hol. You don't feel the same," he tells me rightly.

I stick out my hand.

"Friends?"

He shakes it grinning.

"Friends."

I stumble back through Nick's apartment and drink two pints of water. Nick isn't back yet. I don't want to see him anyway. I scrub my teeth and climb into bed. All I can see is him as my eyelids close.

In my groggy state I can feel myself being carried, yet I can't open my eyelids. I can smell him, but I still don't want to see him.

Nick lays me into his bed and then climbs in next to me. To my astonishment he pulls me into his arms.

"I do need you Holly." he whispers in my ear.

I don't want to wake up fully. I don't want the complications of facing the real world. I feel his lips on my shoulder and he snuggles into my back. I let myself drift back off to sleep with a smile on my face.

251

"Nick." A female voice shrills through the apartment. I'm wrapped up in Nicks arms so peacefully that it doesn't click for a moment.

"Nick?" she shrills again.

Panicking I break out of Nicks arms, waking him up. He blinks sleepily as he hears her footsteps.

"Hide!" he hisses, fully awake now.

I run to the walk in wardrobe and close the door behind me.

"Nick, there you are," Penelope says as I hear her come into the room.

"How did you get in?"

"You were supposed to be in a meeting an hour ago Nick, your dad gave me a key to come and get you,"

"Shit what time is it?"

"Ten past three,"

"Oh fuck, I forgot,"

"I figured. I know you don't want to face the lawyer about Samuel Holmes but sleeping in isn't the answer," she says gently.

"I wasn't,"

"It wasn't your fault Nick."

"I know it wasn't my fucking fault" he roars.

252

"Nick, calm down, what can I do?" she asks with a purr. I can't help myself as I look through the crack of the door. I see her kneeling in between his naked legs. He only has the duvet covering his groin.

"Nothing, I better change.." he says quickly.

"Are you sure?"

Her head disappears under the duvet.

Fuck no! I bite my lip to keep me silent.

"Penny, don't," he protests. His eyes go straight to the wardrobe.

"You're so big, come and play," she mumbles.

"No Penny, fuck," he says trying to pull her off.

"No, Nick, its time," she shushes him.

I see his hand relax as her head bobs up and down under the duvet. I look away in horror. He is letting her. I hear him groan and I start crying silently, wrapped up between his suits.

I hear him moan as he releases, hear her breathy sighs. I can't shut it off. I can't make myself not hear this. I am stuck hearing him find pleasure with another woman.

"Let's go face that meeting," she says smugly.

"Okay,"

"I hope that cheered you up,"

"Yeah."

I can see that he changes into the clothes he was wearing last night. Why not open the wardrobe? He has clearly forgotten about me being in here.

They leave but I can't move. The dams burst and I am crying my heart out.

Chapter Twenty One- Nick

There is no bigger cunt than me right now. I go into the meeting to report what happened with Sam. Nothing will come of it. Mr and Mrs Holmes have no leg to stand on trying to sue me. They are just hurting and lashing out over their son's death. I take their abuse and the accusations because I deserve it.

Penny stays with me the whole time, her hand on my thigh for moral support. I actually feel sick. I let her blow me whilst Holly was in my wardrobe. If I hadn't carried her to my bed last night, she wouldn't have known, wouldn't have heard. Instead she witnessed it close up; I'm a selfish twisted fuck.

When the meeting's over I throw myself into work. I see Holly twice but each time she doesn't even meet my eyes. She just ducks her head down.

I know I have hurt her a lot over the last couple of weeks. What happened after Sam's death has me reeling. Holly was right last night. When we had sex it was different. For the first time in my life I made love. I care about her way too much. It's as if she is chipping away at the ice block of my emotions. The way that she comforted me when I broke down was beautiful. The last time someone held me while I cried was my mother. No one has ever been there for me since. The first time a patient died on me, I drunk myself stupid and then returned back to work with a hell of a hangover and locked it up in my head. I have had children die on my table, many times. This time it was different only because of Holly. Holly adored that boy, she put her faith in me to save him and I let her down. I failed him, his parents and most of all I failed her.

I see her head towards the staff room and I follow her. As I get in there I see Holly heading to a table where Phoebe is sitting.

Balls! I make myself a coffee in a takeaway cup and head back out. She doesn't even look up.

Then I text her,

ME: *Medical supply room now*

As I jog down there I get a reply.

HOLLY: *no*

I stop in my tracks. Excuse me?

ME: *That wasn't a question.*

HOLLY: *Fuck off asshole.*

Wow. I know I deserve that and then some, but fuck am I going to admit that to her.

ME: *Medical room NOW or I WILL come and drag your ass there!!!*

HOLLY: *Doubt you would do that, lots of people here, Penelope will hear about it.*

I curse. She is damn right she would. She's got me. I fume as I punch in my next text.

ME: *Fine, but we will be having a chat later at home.*

HOLLY: *Not my home and no we won't be. I'm not going back to yours.*

Fucking hell, I need to explain, I need to apologise. I just need her.

ME: *Please Holly, we need to talk.*

I wait for ages, my coffee is long gone. But she doesn't reply. I have to go into surgery, an appendix rupture, but my head is only thinking about her.

She didn't come back home that night, or any day that following week. She ignores my calls and texts and avoids me at all costs during work. All her stuff has gone and she has left her key.

The first couple of days I figured I would give her some space. She is hurting and she deserves to get her head straight before she comes back. I worry about her safety, but I check to make sure she arrived for work on time each day. It's all I can do.

After those days, I hate being in the apartment without her. It is like she breathed life into my place, and now it is just dull and boring. Like before. I go out with Penny a lot as I need to get my head back in the game. Penny is what matters. Technically we are a couple now, everyone knows it, and we only had a month to go before we made it official. I can't cheat on Penny with Holly now anyway. It should be a good thing she is gone. Yet I sleep in her bed, smelling her sweet smell on the sheets.

But it isn't the sex I miss the most. It's her: talking with her, laughing with her, eating her food with her, even watching a film on opposite ends of the sofa is better than doing it alone. I still haven't slept with Penny. She thinks it's because I'm waiting until we are official and thinks it's noble and sweet. That blow job was a one off and the only reason I think I was hard was because it was pressed up against Holly all night.

Maybe subconsciously that's why I let Penny do it. I needed to get over this fixation that Holly is the only one who can do it for me now. Holly was getting too close and maybe if she saw me for the bastard that I am she would pull away. That's exactly what she did and at times I miss her so much I can barely breathe.

 I snap by day nine of pacing the floors of my apartment and grab my keys. It's our day off and I tell myself I am just checking up on her, making sure she is safe inside that shit tip of a bedsit. She has been paying for it still, so I assume that is where she will be.

I can see her shadow behind the curtain, so I press the buzzer.

"Hello?"

"It's me, can you let me in?"

"Go away,"

"No damn it we need to talk."

She doesn't respond so I tap on her window for a solid ten minutes.

She finally buzzes me in and I go in with sore knuckles.

She opens her door and I am horrified to see her eyes. They are so swollen and red, black rings surrounding them.

"Fuck Holly, are you hurt?"

"No,"

"But your eyes…"

"What do you want Nick?" she snaps.

I want to hold her, smell her, just have her body against mine. But I lock down.

"In case you have forgotten, you are in my debt. You owe me. Now I know I was a very stupid and thoughtless prick and I am truly sorry. But you knew what you signed up for. You are my mistress for another four weeks" I yell at her, the past week has been building up.

"So, what now? You expect me just to go back with you? Allow you to own me and my body and not mention this again?"

"Yes,"

"I can't do that Nick. I know what we agreed and I am sorry that I am backing out on my promise,"

"You can't…"

"I am so grateful for all you have done for me, but I just can't do this anymore," she says exhausted sitting on her little bed.

"Are you with Tom? People are talking about it at work."

I fume. I have heard rumours that Tom is attached to

her, that they experienced a 'moment' in 'Steps'. But I refused to believe it. Holly knows that she is mine.

"No. We are friends,"

"Bloody better be. You are mine," I snarl.

"Please don't make me come back to you, I will pay you every penny back." she begs.

I gasp what the hell? She hates me that much?

"Do I repulse you that much?" I yell, kneeling in front of her so she has to look at me.

"I wish that was the case,"

"Then why?"

"Because I am in love with you." she whispers.

No. Fuck. No. My head spins.

"No, no you don't, don't say that," I beg horrified.

"I am so sorry. I know you don't see me like that. I understand. But I can't go back feeling how I do now. I can't go back to meaningless sex with you."

I look at her in dismay as I watch tears pouring down her beautiful face and it wrenches my heart.

I grab her and suddenly we are kissing desperately. The world blurs as I clutch her face and kiss her like it's the end of the world.

I can't do this. I can't allow myself to love her back. It will ruin everything. It's that burning love my father warned me about. It will crush me like it did him. It will consume me and Holly may not know this, but she has the power to destroy me.

I break off the kiss and stand up. I turn around to compose myself. With the mask firmly on I turn around to face her.

"You're right. We can't continue like this now. It's over. Forget about me and the money. We go our separate ways right now." I say emotionlessly.

I'm anything but emotionless right now but the mask holds it all in.

Holly nods through her tears.

"Thank you for everything Nick."

I lean over and kiss her head tenderly.

"Thank you Holly."

I walk out without looking back.

Chapter Twenty Two- Holly (One month later)

Today is the day I have been dreading for two months. I didn't expect it so soon, but given the rumours I wasn't entirely surprised.

"Can you believe Dr Willis and Dr Sinclaire are together?" Lisa squeals.

Unfortunately, yes I can.

I shrug neutrally.

"It's like a match made in heaven. Like the Bragelina of the hospital world" she sighs.

I continue filling up the paper cups with various medication hoping she takes the hint I am not interested in this conversation.

"Oh my god. Think of how beautiful their children will be." Lisa continues gushing.

I feel a knot twist in my stomach, hot tears fill my eyes but I blink them away furiously.

"How's Mr Phillips doing this morning?" I ask hoping to change the subject.

"Grumpy, like you, but out of the woods,"

"He is due his meds, I'll head there now."

I go over to Mr Phillips. He fell off a ladder whilst fixing a loose tile on his roof. It was touch and go for a bit but Nick pulled him through it.

"Hey Mr Phillips," I say to the elderly, bandaged up old man.

"Hey Holly, I told you to call me John,"

"Sorry John, here is your pain relief,"

"You diamond." he winks at me.

I help him sit up and hold a glass of water as he swallows his tablets.

"How are you feeling?"

"Alright me duck, much better in about twenty minutes I'm sure."

I smile at him. He is such a rude man to most staff, but to me he is a total sweetheart.

"Mr Phillips, time to check your head of steel." Nick says behind us.

I stiffen at his voice but step aside whilst Nick comes over to the bed.

"Holly,"

"Dr Willis,"

"How are you?"

"Fine thank you,"

"Good."

He carefully looks over Mr Phillips and performs some routine checks on him.

"Looking good Mr Phillips, you are healing very well" Nick says as he writes up his notes.

Mr Phillips narrows his eyes at him.

"Great, now get outta here. My girl and I are having a chat," he growls at Nick.

"Sure thing Mr Phillips," Nick says looking amused.

"Holly,"

"Dr Willis,"

Then he is gone.

It's been that way between us ever since we ended our arrangement; cold, formal and very distant. I know it's for the best but every time he speaks to me it cuts just as deeply a month later.

I continue through my duties, watching the time zoom by. When Two o'clock hit, it is time already.

I wandered over to the blood test results counter, awaiting my fate. The night me and Nick made love for the first and last time was also the night he went without a condom. With the events that followed I didn't remember until I skipped my period. It's not unheard of given my stress level, but giving the way I haven't been able to hold food down, and being late, I got myself checked out and now its show time.

"Holly Jones." I whisper quietly to the older woman behind the counter.

She scrambles around and finds my report.

"There you go honey." she smiles at me.

I smile shakily back and try not to run out of the hospital doors. I settle for a power walk.

Outside on the bench I read my fate.

"Pregnant 3-4 weeks."

I crumple up the paper in my fists. My heart is racing so fast I felt dizzy. Like the news of Nick's official relationship I knew, I expected it, yet seeing if confirmed sent my head spinning.

I am pregnant with Nick's child.

Fuck!

"Hey," Phoebe says as she approaches. I quickly put the paper in my pocket.

"What are you doing out here?" I snap.

"Jeez sorry, I was looking for you,"

"Sorry Phoebs,"

"Forgiven, however now you are on cooking duty tonight," she teases.

"I'm always on cooking duty"

"Not true, just I always get take away." she sticks her tongue out at me.

I moved out of my bedsit a week after Nick and I ended it. I had so much money saved up thanks to Nick so I put down a deposit on a two bedroomed flat, not far from the hospital and invited Phoebe to be my roommate, with her paying half the rent. I knew how hard it was for her to save up for her own place and needed to get away from the cow of a sister's sofa. She agreed instantly and it's wonderful to have company and a fresh start. It was so good to be away from the memories of Martin and his cronies, away from the bad stuff and the memories of Nick and our painful goodbye. I have changed so much since meeting Nick. I can always be thankful for him for that at least. I am finally free. Well I was.

"Fine,"

I need a friend. I need to tell her everything tonight.

"Let's go grab some lunch, we are wasting chow time out here." she moans.

I head back into the cafeteria with her and select some soup from the hot counter and a bottle of water.

"Still feeling crappy?"

"Yeah, it will pass." I say not lying.

My breath catches in my throat as I see Nick walk in laughing with his team. His eyes scan the room, and I look away. I know who he is looking for.

"Nick." I hear her voice even on the other side of the room.

I see him walking over to her, before pecking her mouth softly. I hate feeling like this, so jealous it burns me from the inside. I shouldn't be jealous. I have no right to be jealous. He was always hers and never mine.

He sits next to her and she scoots closer to him as they chat to each other, looking very much like a couple in love.

I spin away and forget about the soup.

"I've gotta go," I say to Phoebe getting up.

"But..."

"I'll see you tonight." I mutter before rushing out.

I run to the toilet and throw up before bursting into tears.

This baby will not have a father. My baby was created from his mother being a whore and father who used me for my body.

I glance down at my stomach.

"But you will always have me." I whisper to it.

When Phoebe and I arrive home I sink straight on the sofa exhausted.

"What are you cooking then? Oh, can you make pasta with that mushroom sauce?" Phoebe asks.

"Can you call for pizza instead? We need to talk."

Phoebe sees my face and sits down.

"You ready to open up finally?"

I nod and burst into tears for the second time that day.

Alarmed she runs over to me and puts her arms around me.

"Talk to me Hol," she begs.

"I'm pregnant."

Phoebe's arms stiffen.

"Pregnant?"

I nod.

"How can you be you pregnant?" she asks dazed.

"I had unprotected sex," I snap.

"Obviously! But who with?"

I take a deep breath. I know the risks in telling her, but if I was going to risk it, it would be her.

"Nick,"

"Nick who?"

"Nick Willis."

Her gasp literally could have been a scream it's that loud.

"Right hold on." she says pinching her nose. She storms across to the phone.

"What are you doing? Phoebe you can't tell a soul," I scream at her.

She rolls her eyes and speaks into the phone.

"I need an extra-large mushroom pizza and a tub of Ben and Jerry's…. No I don't care what flavour just bring it," she barks before reeling off her details.

"Right, how the hell have you been sleeping with Dr Willis and for how long?" she demands returning to the sofa.

"I had been sleeping with him for three months. It ended a month ago,"

"Why didn't you tell me?"

"I couldn't. It was a very private and discreet fling. It wasn't a relationship. It was an agreement," I try to explain.

"An agreement, like an enemy with benefits type of agreement?" she laughs bitterly.

"Kind of, listen, I haven't been completely honest with you about how deep I was in with Robbie's debt,"

"What do you mean?"

"I mean I had a lot of problems, Robbie left debt and also left me with Martin, his drug dealer."

Phoebe gasps again.

"Martin made me pay him half of my wages every month,"

"That why you were so broke all the time? He made you pay half of your wages?"

"Yeah and then it turned worse about three and a half months ago when he decided he was taking it all"

"You mean your entire wages?"

"Yes,"

"Why didn't you go to the police?" she asks stupidly.

"You don't go to the police with those kinds of guys, I would be dead before I made it back home." I say

271

slowly. Well that's what they threatened me enough time for me to believe it.

"Shit Hol! But what has that got to do with Dr Willis?"

"Nick saw an incident between us and paid off Martin for me,"

"He did what? He is the most selfish, arrogant prick of all time. Why?"

"It was a deal."

"A deal, you mean?" her eyes go like saucers as she twigs.

"Yep, I was paid to sleep with him for four months with the utmost discretion" I said mocking his voice at the end.

"You were his prostitute?"

I wince at the word despite using it so many times to myself.

"His mistress,"

"Why would he pay? Wait, wait a minute, has this got something to do with Dr Sinclaire?" she asks.

I nod.

"They are planning on being a proper couple and she wouldn't be seen with him until his reputation from his as being a slut was clear?"

"Oh my god it's making sense now. So when all the staff were bitching that he wasn't sleeping around anymore, he was sleeping with you?"

I nod again.

"Shit, Hol I don't know what to make of all of this. You have been my best friend for years and now it feels like I don't even know you," she says gently.

"I know, I am so sorry, I have hidden so much from you and I am sorry. I just didn't want you to worry or change your view of me." I say, my voice breaking again.

The buzzer goes and Phoebe disappears, leaving me to get it together.

She comes back with the pizza order dumping it onto the coffee table.

"You are a survivor Holly, I just wish you didn't always insist on doing it alone," she says quietly.

"I won't, I promise you Phoebe I will never keep anything from you again." I promise. I mean it too. I just can't do it on my own any longer. Nick has made me weak. When I was with him, I talked to him, confided in him, opened up to him. I can't be without that now. But if I can't have Nick it damn well feels good to talk to Phoebe. She won't turn her back on me.

I open the pizza box and take a slice of pizza, suddenly ravenous.

"So you have been sleeping with Dr Willis but you are out of debt and free from scary, murdering drug dealers correct?"

"Yep," I reply with my mouth full.

"Okay, I can deal with that. You aren't in danger any more so it's all good,"

"Except now my very discreet affair has resulted in me being knocked up" I moan.

"What has Nick said?"

I gulped down my pizza.

"He doesn't know and I am not going to tell him," I explain.

"He has a right to know,"

"Maybe, but his reputation is everything to him. He will not be happy about it at all. It won't change anything, it will make everything worse,"

"Will it?"

"Of course, he doesn't like me. I was just a sex slave to him. He doesn't want a child with me, he needs to marry Penelope and have her babies," I shout.

"Ok, okay chill. Sex slave really?" her eyebrows rise.

"Yeah" I blush a little.

She puts another slice of pizza on my napkin.

"Do spill."

I laugh a little as I relax and divulge some of the naughty details.

Half an hour later, Phoebe is fanning herself with her greasy napkin.

"Phew, you little minx you." she laughs dramatically.

I giggle as well, as if a weight has been thrown off my shoulders.

"Now you know, Dr Willis does live up to his name and more,"

"Wow, I need to get laid. I'm gutted to be single again now."

Yes, her latest man got dumped just like all the rest. I don't know why she is so fussy. She finds one thing about a bloke she doesn't like and runs for the hills.

"Is there anything else you need to tell me, before my head explodes?" Phoebe asks picking up the pizza box.

I look at her clear in the eye.

"I am in love with him."

The box is dropped.

Robbie slams through the front door, so hard the wall must have cracked again. I'm in the kitchen cooking a cheap dinner of spaghetti and tomato sauce. His temper has been worse than ever the last few days. I know it is because we are absolutely broke. I literally haven't got a penny in my purse or bank account. It's nine days until pay day but Robbie withdrew the rest of my wages a week ago. I can scrape together a few cheap meals from the cupboard staples, but he can't afford a drink, or any form of drugs. It's rough on him, but rough on me too. I have the bruises to prove it.

"HOLLY!" he shouts.

"In the kitchen," I put the wooden spoon down shakily.

"I need money. Give me your bank card," he hisses from behind me.

"There is no money in there Robbie,"

"Fuck that, there has to be,"

"Not since you withdrew my last hundred."

His hands are shaking. His pale blue eyes are darting around everywhere in his green tinged face.

"No! No! NO!" he roars, clutching at his head.

"I'm sorry," I say returning to my pan.

"Fucking liar!" he hisses next to me.

276

I flinch, waiting for his hand, but his hands go to the pasta pan.

I breathe a sigh of relief.

"Hungry?" I ask.

Suddenly the pan of pasta is flung at me; boiling water covers me, my clothes enveloping the starchy water in fiery heat. All I can see is steam; which is why I don't see him coming.

In an instant I am on the floor, his fists pounding into my face.

"Robbie." I cry out, blood filling my mouth. My hands automatically go to my stomach to protect our baby. Sixteen weeks, but I survived the twelve week period with Robbie's beatings, so I pray he or she hangs on another assault.

"Fucking food. Is that all you think about? Feeding this bastard child?" he spits out.

I quickly roll out of the way in anger. He can insult me all he wants, but not my baby.

"Bastard child? This is our baby." I shout back at him.

I don't know what possesses me to speak out like that. I know better than that.

Robbie's eyes fill with fury and with a scream I flee out of the other side of the kitchen and towards the stairs. I can hear his footsteps behind me but I push myself faster to the bedroom and lock the door frantically.

"Open the fuck up," he roars, banging on the door.

I can't do it. I should, it will be far worst if I don't. But I grab my emergency overnight bag and unlock the window.

It's a long way down but there is a ladder to the side, the one I put there again in case of an emergency. I have never used it before, despite his vicious assaults, but something snapped when he talked about our child like that. I don't know why but I thought that once the baby comes, he would settle down, become the father and husband I have always wanted. When there was a child dependent on us, Drugs will not be first priority. He promised me he loved this baby, he wanted this baby and for us to be family. But with that one comment I see it now. I see it clearly. Nothing will change at all, except a child will suffer as well.

I open the window quickly and reach for the ladder. The door is splintering. My heart is racing uncontrollably as I lean out to try and grab it from under the ivy.

The door bursts open as I grab the ladder.

*"WHERE THE FUCK ARE YOU GOING?" Robbie
screams behind me.*

I don't answer as I move the ladder against the wall.

Robbie runs to my side and pulls me into his arms.

"You're a stupid, ungrateful bitch!"

"Stop!" I protest as he grips me painfully.

"You want to leave?"

"Yes Robbie, please let me go."

His arms loosen around me.

I step out of them.

*"You're leaving me?" his face breaks and he is breathing
hard.*

"I have to protect our child Robbie."

His body crumples. Tears roll down his face.

My heart breaks, but I have to go. I must go now.

*His body is blocking the door so I decide to go through
the window, before he snaps back to anger again.*

I move back across to the window with my bag.

*Maybe one day I will come back, maybe this is the major
thing he needs to sober up.*

*I didn't even hear him stand up, but the next thing I
knew he was carrying me bridal style in his arms.*

"IT'S ALWAYSTHE FUCKING BABY! NEVER ME!
FUCK YOU AND THAT BASTARD THEN." he roar.
Suddenly I feel his hands grab me, and I am being
thrown through the window onto the street, falling in a
broken heap on the pavement.

I jerk awake, my face wet as I wake from my worst
nightmare: the one where Robbie kills my baby. I had
broken many bones from that. I miscarried almost
instantly. By the time the neighbours called the police
and an ambulance, Robbie had vanished.
I remember waking up in the hospital I worked at, casted
up and in pain. But was nothing in comparison of being
informed that I had lost the baby. In his anger and
desperation for drugs, he destroyed everything. He
threw me out of a window because I couldn't give him
money. An innocent life was taken, for such a pathetic
reason.

This is the third time this same memory has haunted my
dreams since I found out I was pregnant two weeks ago.
I don't know if it is pregnancy hormones or the fear of
losing another child. I only have four more weeks to go

until I have my first scan. I hope it puts my fears to rest, that there is in fact a baby and it is healthy and happy. My stomach churns, as I head to the toilet. No need for an alarm clock with morning sickness, or late afternoon sickness like this one, depending on which shift I have. I always need to throw up before I even need my first wee these days.

I get up quickly, strip my sweat soaked clothes off and jump in the shower. I scrub myself vigorously, trying to wash the negative thoughts away before heading into the kitchen for a decaffeinated coffee. I make Phoebe a regular one, inhaling the scent of coffee.

I was going to inform Nick after the scan proves everything. But after my nightmare, I am having second thoughts. He will hate me for putting him in such a precarious position. What if he wants me to have an abortion? I had a miscarriage with my first baby and I will not allow anything to harm this baby.

I knock on her door and place the coffee by her bed.

"Afternoon gorgeous," I mock as I see her hair sprawled all over her face.

"Afternoon." she mumbles back.

I love Phoebe. I always have, but since I told her about Nick and the baby, she has become more than my best friend. She is my rock, my family. She is all I have. Phoebe has been amazing, dealing with my morning sickness, helping me carry stuff I shouldn't be carrying and just being someone to talk to, a shoulder to lean on especially when I see Nick. The best part about her is that she doesn't judge, she doesn't try to talk me into anything. She lets make my own choices and supports me throughout it all.

"How are you feeling?" she asks me sitting up.

"I had the nightmare again."

She winces.

"You okay?"

"I've decided I am not going to tell Nick about the baby. I can't risk it."

She nods her head.

"Whatever you want to do, I'm here. But you don't think he will guess?"

"Don't care. If he asks I will deny it. He will want to hear that any way." I say bitterly.

She smiles sadly.

"Your baby, your choice,"

"Exactly, my baby." I mutter and leave Phoebe to get out of bed.

I go back to the kitchen and reach for my manila envelope. I know the divorce paperwork back and front from reading it so many times now. But it is like a comfort blanket for me. I finally am getting divorced. I used some of the money I had left over from Nick to pay for the divorce proceedings. The lawyer has got copies of my medical history to prove Robbie's abuse. I explained the situation to the lawyer and he has managed to bypass Robbie in being involved completely due to the circumstances and the fact that no one can find him. The forms are at his parents, leaving it to them to find him, not that they would be able to or care to. They haven't been a part of his life since he was eighteen. I haven't ever met them. In about four more months from now I will be divorced. I will not be a Jones when this baby is born. My baby will not have that name. He or she won't be a Willis like they should be either. But knowing they will have my maiden name of Turner is good enough.

As I get to work I see Nick pull up in his Porsche. He looks so handsome in his jeans and crisp grey shirt it almost takes my breath away. Then I see him open the passenger's side and her long slim legs slip out in designer heels.

Phoebe rubs at my arm as they pass us, hand in hand. Nick doesn't even notice me; I am as invisible as I once was to him. Why would he when he has someone like her on her arm?

Chapter Twenty Three- Nick

I finish up my shift at eight and jog back to my flat, I don't bother going anywhere except my gym where I pound away at my punch bag angrily. Nothing has gone wrong. Everything is just how it was before. Work, work out, sleep repeat. Oh and see my perfect girlfriend who I have always wanted. Yet I am completely miserable and angry.

This is my mood and it continues to darken in the weeks since Holly left. I try not to think about her, I don't talk to her unless I absolutely have to. I hate seeing the pain in her eyes whenever I look at her. It's more than I can bear knowing, that I am the one to have put that pain there. Her life has enough blackness in it without what happened between us as well.

At first I thought wasn't my fault that she fell for me. She knew what this was and I never led her on to think it meant more than what it was. Then the more I tried to defend myself, the more it dawned on me how I let this happen. It was my fault. I was like a knight in armour to someone like her. I got rid of the bad guys for her, fixed her up when she was hurt. I even gave her a place to stay, like the good guy. Things got so blurred at the end, it wasn't just sex. I knew it at the time and I understand it even more now in hindsight. Just because I didn't tell her things had changed, doesn't mean she didn't feel it. Fuck I felt it, and it threw me entirely.

"Nick?" Penny's voice floats through the room, as I am continue to assault the bag.

I really want to ask for the key, I never gave her, back.

"Hey," I mutter.

"Look at that bod," she breathes as she comes into view.

Yeah, I know I'm a stud, but I am busy stud.

"To what do I owe this unexpected visit?" I say sweetly. She stands before me dressed immaculately.

"I thought I would pop in with some dinner before you crash." she smiles. That radiant smile can't even cut through my mood tonight.

"Oh that's nice of you,"

"I know I am nice. Go and grab a quick shower while I plate up."

Numbly I remove my gloves, obeying her every command as usual.

We have been together officially for about six weeks, but it feels so much longer than that. Making that deal over since six months ago was the starting point for us. We still haven't slept together though strangely. I just keep playing the 'let's make is special' card. I know I need to get it together and get him to keep it together; it won't be long before Penny sees through my bullshit, if she doesn't see it already.

After a quick shower, I join Penny at the dining room table.

Dinner tonight is some kind of weird looking purple risotto.

"Thanks, what is this?"

"Beetroot and kale risotto,"

"Oh cool." I take a bite, it's not too bad. The rice has a weird texture though. I have lost all the weight and more that I gained whilst living with Holly.

"So Nick, I have been thinking" Penny begins.

I pause, a spoonful of the purple, grainy stuff half way to my mouth.

"This rice tastes different,"

"It is pearl barley that's why. No empty white starch,"

"Oh,"

"So Nick, things have been going well for us, since we became official," she continues.

"Really well," I agree. It has as well, aside from the physical side of things. She is, as I predicted, a good partner to me. We agree on everything and fit perfectly in each other's world. We are even having 'family' brunches at the Hilton now on a weekly basis with Lawrence and my father.

"I think we shouldn't mess about with the courting any more. Let's just bypass it and get engaged" she says. My heart accelerates as I pick up my wine glass, gulping heavily.

"You want to get engaged?"

"We both know it's where it will be heading soon any way."

True. I know this is what we planned, but it just feels so soon. I prefer the idea of us dating for a bit longer you know? I love the thrill of the chase, but now I have caught her, she wants to lock me down fast.

"Is that what you want?" I ask.

"Well, the board meeting review is going to be late November next year. I want the wedding and everything to be done and be old news before we become members so no one can accuse us of marrying for a vote" she says practically.

This indeed is very true. I'm sure people will still gossip but then again everyone knows it was always meant to be, Penny and me.

"Is that what you want though Penny?" I ask reaching for her hand.

"Of course it is. Isn't it what you want?" she replies, holding my outstretched hand.

I look at her. It was all I ever wanted, before some curvaceous little nurse came into my life.

"Yes, it is." I say seriously.

Fuck Holly, fuck everything except the dream. This is everything I have been working towards since I was sixteen.

She beams at me.

"Wow, okay then. Its official, were engaged," she breathes.

"Not official. I am still a man after all. We can go ring shopping, and then we announce it"

She deserves the best and, to be honest, this matter of fact discussion isn't exactly romantic or how she deserves a proposal.

"Well then," she winks and gets up from the table.

"Well what?"

She reaches for her zipper and unzips her suit dress. It falls by her heels as she stands in front of me in sinful underwear. I can see every inch of her through the sheer material.

"Wow."

Penny smiles shyly and pulls her hair out of its clip.

"Pulling out the big guns Pen?" I tease.

She winks at me and heads to my room.

I stay for a few seconds in despair as nothing is happening yet again. Fucking hell, she looks like a fucking porn star in that underwear and yet it still refuses to work.

I rub myself through my jeans as I follow her.

Penny is waiting on my bed.

"You wanted special, I'm giving you special." she says and leans up to kiss me.

I need this, I want this with her. She deserves it.

I kiss her back how I know she likes it.

She moans as her nipples harden against my chest.

"Tell me what you want Nick."

I need to deliver. I must follow through tonight. I can get myself hard. What gets my rocks off is being in control. I can work with that.

"I want to watch you." I mutter.

She looks a little surprised but smiles.

"You're such a naughty boy,"

I strip off and lie on the bed.

"Get up and show me that perfect body."

She stands up slowly, still in her heels and stands in front of me.

"Touch yourself." I say, as I take myself in my hand.

She spreads her hands across her body as I move my hand back and forth across my shaft.

Penny is very good at teasing; I shouldn't have been surprised at this, as her hands cup her breasts.

"Take it off." I groan, as my dick is finally hard.

She slips her underwear off and slides her fingers inside herself.

"Oh Nick," she groans as I hear her wetness.

"Get over here."

She almost sprints to me and sits on my lap, rubbing against me. I run my hands over her. She's so thin her breasts literally take up a fraction of my hand. Not like

Holly's, her breasts literally over fill my hands. Holly is no way fat, but her curves just feel like silk under my hands. Penny's skin isn't like that; I can feel her delicate bones.

That's when my dick starts to soften.

Panicking I spin Penny around so she is on all fours on my bed.

"Nice" I lie, as I tug at myself frantically.

"Give it to me Nick. It's time" she moans.

I squeeze my eyes shut, and block everything out, as I reach for a condom.

"Give it to me Nick." Holly says her dark hair spread against the cream duvet.

Slipping the condom on, I push into her, and she groans.

"Oh yes baby." she roars.

I grab at her curvy hips and push in and out.

"Shit."

Holly is moaning and clutching at the sheets, making her sweet gasps.

My hand slips between her thighs.

"Come on Rag Doll" I mutter and rub the spot I know so damn well.

"Oh Nick, Nick," she cries out, as she spasms on my fingers.

"Yes." I hiss as I release, pumping into her.

I breathe hard as I come down.

"Oh my god, that was just incredible," Penny says rolling onto her back.

"Yes it was,"

"Why did you call me Rag Doll?" she giggles.

"You're just so beautiful, like a perfect doll." I lie, horrified she heard me.

I take the condom off and tie it in a knot.

"I'll just put this in the bin." I say and leave a naked Penny to it.

I am an absolute fucked up, evil bastard. I can't believe I just did that!

I return to the bedroom calmer and more collected.

Penny is already in my bed on my side.

"Coming to bed handsome? We have to meet the Daddies at midday tomorrow. We can go ring shopping in the morning" she coos.

I slip into Holly's side, hating that I still think of it like that.

"Sure." I yawn and roll onto my side, not facing her.

Her hands slip around my chest as she snuggles into me.

I pretend to drift off, until I hear her high pitched breathing, telling me she is asleep and slip out from her. Great, Penny likes to snuggle.

We walked into the Hilton at one pm precisely. I am surprised we are not earlier considering the ring shopping took all of an hour. I should be relieved, I hate shopping. Penny knew exactly what ring she wanted and we headed straight out to Tiffany's. She had obviously done her research and knew her ring size. I couldn't help but snort to myself. What if I had said no? Not that I would have, but still it feels a little bitter knowing, she knew I would have said yes and knew it would have been last night. It took ten minutes, then fifty minutes to have adjusted to her size using my black credit card as leverage.

She wears her ring proudly on her finger as we approach Lawrence and my father.

"Princess, what have we here?" Lawrence says, clocking the ring instantly. It's not exactly hard to spot, that bling cost me big time.

294

"Nick and I decided we didn't want to mess about any longer." she says sitting prettily next to her father.

"Congratulations to the both of you," my father says signalling over a waiter.

"Thank you so much Michael," Penny says warmly.

"Come and give your soon to be Dad a hug."

Penny wriggles over in her dress and bends over to hug him.

He is totally checking out her breasts as she hugs him.

He really has no shame.

I roll my eyes at him but he winks back.

Lawrence stands up and shakes my hand.

"Good to have you on board son,"

"Likewise,"

"Champagne cocktails all round." Father orders to the waiting staff.

And so it begins.

The night shift couldn't come soon enough. I rush straight to work, leaving Penny to sleep on her drunken state in her bed. She had six of the champagne cocktails and was one of those giggling, loud drunks that couldn't stop touching me. She tried to give me a hand job under the table with our fathers present for Christ sake! At least Penny was happy though, which is more than could be said for me unfortunately. I am exhausted and grumpy thanks to an agonising four hours with my father, who is exasperating, Lawrence who I don't care about and a drunken silly fiancé.

I recall a conversation with my father when we headed to have a cigar outside.

"Are you happy with all of this son?" he asks through thick, swirling smoke.

"Why wouldn't I be?"

"I don't know, you just seem moody,"

I actually broke a bit at that. I should be deliriously happy but I'm not.

"It's the bedroom," I sigh.

"What is she shit in bed? Won't play dirty?" he asks intrigued.

"No actually, she is fine,"

"Fine?"

"I want my mistress back." I whisper to him.

My father looks like he is going to burst with laughter.

"Why is she gone?" he asks tightly.

"I don't want to cheat on Penny, but fuck Dad my mistress was just…"

"Untouchable," he nods in understanding.

"Exactly, I have to think about her to get off with Penny." I admit shamefully.

My father lets it out then, howling.

I scowl at him, I shouldn't have said anything. I bet nothing stands in the way of his fucking.

"You are such a softie baby," he teases.

"Fuck off."

"Pull your tampon out and get your mistress back,"

"I can't cheat on Penny," I gasp.

"It's not really cheating son. A lot of men have mistresses, of which their wives are grateful. Do you really think Penny wants to suck your dick night and day?"

I remember going back inside in outrage, but his immoral thoughts have already planted seeds within me.

I want Holly. Last night knowing I was mentally having sex with her, whilst with my fiancé is a sign that I need her back in my life. I can't keep imaging her in the bedroom. It's fucking up my head. I don't quite know how I am going to do it, but fuck it. I'm Nick Fucking Willis, I will make it happen.

Throwing myself into work, I battle through a case of appendicitis, a burst spleen, and a man who claimed he stabbed himself in the stomach. It's nearly two am when I catch a break. I know Holly will be taking a break soon so I go and grab a sandwich and a coffee and wait in the cafeteria for her.

Holly doesn't let me down as she heads in not long after I have finished my food. She doesn't see me, as she pays for a cake and coffee. I know she will check her phone soon. Surely enough as soon as she sits down, she reaches for her phone.

ME: *On call room, ward 6, meet me there asap.*

I can't see her face but I notice she slips her phone straight back in her pocket.

After a few minutes I notice she is not exactly rushing to head out. Angrily I text her again.

ME: *I am right behind you, don't make me come over. On call room, ward 6.*

Holly reaches for her phone and I see her glance behind to look at me. Her eyes look sad as she shakes her head at me.

For fuck sake! I'm sick of this game already. I get up and head over. She is alone luckily.

"Holly,"

"Nick,"

I can smell her already that sweet scent of her hair washes over me.

"We need to talk,"

"No we don't. I don't owe you anything Nick. We are done remember?"

"I just need to see you, please?"

"No, I am busy and have to head back to work." she replies and stands up, her cake half eaten.

"Holly, please," I am almost begging now.

"No." she replies as she hurries away.

I grit my teeth and head back too; I need to be back in surgery in ten minutes any way. Fuck her.

I am just about to finish work when my pager goes off. The man who had 'apparently' stabbed himself is kicking off, security is on their way but I go down any way.

I find Holly by the man who is hurling abuse at her and the other staff nearby.

"Get me the hell out of here!" he is roaring.

"Please Mr Smith, you are not stable enough to be discharged." Holly says quietly, as she re hooks his oxygen mask.

"I am just fine, seriously," he protests.

"Mr Smith, you are not ready to be discharged until..." One of the other nurses cuts in.

"I DON'T GIVE A SHIT!" he yells.

I step into the cubicle and place a hand on Holly's shoulder.

"Nurse Jones, let me take over." I say smoothly, she nods and steps aside.

I grab his chart.

"Mr Smith. I am Dr Willis. I performed your surgery a few hours ago." I say coolly.

"Dr Willis, thank god. Tell me I'm okay so I can get the fuck out of here." Mr Smith says.

I look through his charts.

"It is not in your best interest to be discharged, due to the surgery I performed. I want you in here at least eighteen hours, twenty four would be best just to check for any complications to the surgery or to the medication we used," I reel off.

"I'm fine Doc."

I ignore him and study at his charts.

"Well now that you have been mobile and trying to force your way out of bed, I am going to have to check the incision for any disruption."

He groans as Holly pulls the curtain across.

"Is this really necessary" he moans, as I pull up his gown.

"Well no Mr Smith, it isn't, I wouldn't have had to do this if you stayed put."

I check him out. He is actually fine not that he needs to know that.

"Your incision is alright but due to the stress you put on the newly placed stitches, I think its best you stay the full twenty four hours," I say and snap my gloves back off.

"Oh come on…"

"Have you spoken to the police yet?" I ask.

His face pales.

"No, not yet, I wanted to head down the police station later," he lies.

"No need, they should be here soon. Don't stress out over it,"

"But,"

"I will come by and check on you before you I discharge you tomorrow night,"

"I can request a discharge," Mr Smith says angrily.

"No, I'm afraid not, not if the police are involved," I reply.

"They shouldn't be involved, no one called them,"

"The hospital did. Any incidents that are classed as violent have to be reported."

His head slumps back onto the pillow.

"Now rest Mr Smith and be nice to the nurses. You should bear in mind we also report your behaviour to the police." I say crisply.

Mr Smith shuts the hell up and reaches for the TV remote.

"Good day to you Mr Smith." I say and head out of the cubicle.

The nurses all smile as I walk past but the one I want to in particular doesn't look up.

"Nurse Jones, walk with me. You need to fill me in on Mr Smith." I tell Holly.

Her shoulders sag but no one bats an eyelid as she trails after me.

She starts talking about Mr Smith, but my mind is elsewhere as I spot an on call room off a secluded corridor. As we reach it, I pull her inside with me.

"What the...?"

"Shush," I whisper shutting and locking the door.

"Nick." she moves backwards, her back pressing against the door.

Before I think about it, I press myself against her and my lips are on hers almost bruising hard.

She tastes of Holly, smells of Holly and it feels like home.

"Nick stop." she tries to push me back.

She didn't kiss me back. It dawns on me as I step back.

"I want you so bad Rag Doll,"

"You can't have me," she folds her arms around her body.

"Why not?"

"Do you want me to reel off the list?" she snaps.

No, I just want to stay inside this room with her.

"How much will it cost to become my mistress again?" I blurt out.

Her eyes narrow. Damn I should have worded that a hell of a lot better.

"Go to hell Nick,"

"Go on, give me a figure,"

"No amount of money could make me shag you again."

This was not going to plan.

"Holly, I want you back,"

"You have a girlfriend!" she cries out in disgust.

Well fiancé actually.

"I don't care. We were so discreet, she would never figure it out," I coax.

"Oh yeah, I remember a close call whilst I was shut in a wardrobe and watched her suck your dick!"

Yeah, she had to bring that up.

"Yeah well we can be discreet, I will come to you."

I am so clutching at straws here.

"No Nick, never happening. I am not some toy you can play with. Been there, done that and got hurt." her eyes brim with the pain I know I caused.

"You don't understand…"

"I understand Nick. You miss sex with me and you are willing to buy and bully your way back into my pants. You see me as some pathetic desperate slut who is willing to whore herself out to you on tap," she moves away from the door and gets in my face.

"You are a selfish jerk. Stay the hell away from me."
Holly spits out and spins on her heel. I catch her hand.
"Rag Doll, I need you…" I try once more.
"No you don't, you want me Nick. I should be flattered
but I am over that. The answer is no." she pulls her hand
out and carefully slips out of the door.
I sit on a bed and put my head in my hands. Well that
did not go as I wanted at all.

Chapter Twenty Four- Holly

I stomp away from the on call room, almost shaking in rage. Changing quickly I head home before he can get to me again. My entire body is humming with need, which only angers me further. How could my body and my mind be in such different places? He has ignored me for weeks, no worse than ignored; I have been invisible to him. I thought he was entirely over whatever shallow feelings he had for me. I wished I felt the same way but just one kiss has me reeling. I hate the affect he has on me. Like I am a rag roll, his rag doll to pull and push away whenever the hell he feels like it. If it wasn't for the baby, I am pretty sure I would have let him do whatever he wanted in that on call room, girlfriend or not. Now that is why Nick can treat me like a whore. I am fast becoming one if this is my attitude to his relationship. I finally get home and crash out into bed, before I phone him and beg him to take me back for free.

The night shift is especially busy, almost a farcical frenzy. Saturday nights are always busy with drunks, drugs, fights and car accidents. Tonight it seems like everyone was in party mode. I'm up to eyeballs in puke and blood, dealing with a sixteen year old drunken lad when Tom comes rushing over to me.

Tom and I have become good friends since our chat in the bar weeks ago. He is over his crush on me. We hung out many times as friends.

I glance up in surprise seeing his worried face and move away from the boy.

"Holly, I just went to check in on a patient. He is high as a fucking kite, he has been beaten up and he needs his stomach pumped before handed over to the police," he blurts out.

"Okay," I'm not following; it's not out of the norm tonight.

"He is asking for you." he whispers.

My blood runs to ice.

"What does he look like?"

"Short blonde hair, blue eyes, his name is Robert Jones."

My heart races so hard, the room spins.

"It's him isn't it? Your ex-husband?" Tom whispers again.

"He isn't my ex yet," I breathe.

"Right, you go nowhere near him. I will inform the police as soon as they get here."

I nod numbly, concentrating on breathing in and out. I want to leave, but would be selfish especially given how busy we are tonight. Robbie is going to be sedated before his stomach pumped. Matt will make sure that happens as soon as possible. As long as he can't get to me, I am safe. Besides he is in a public hospital and at the hands of the police. He will finally be put to justice. Part of me is relieved but mostly I am just shaking in fear as I continue my work, acting as if the man I am petrified of isn't under the same roof as me.

An hour later I go to the rest room for yet another toilet break. I wash my hands and glance into the mirror. I see him in it.

I have to be seeing things I tell myself as my head spins.

"Hollleee." Robbie slurs.

God he doesn't look good. Two and a half years have not been kind to him. He was so handsome once, now his skin looks papery and I can barely see the blue in his eyes any more, just a swirl of red and black.

My hands shake as I grip the sink. He steps closer to me. He stinks of sweat and booze.

"Came to see you baby, slipped the quack. I ain't having my stomach pumped"

I can see a nurse has taped up his eyebrow and his cheek. His lip is split and swollen. I wonder if Martin has finally caught up with him.

I need to play this smart. I need to get him into a public place.

"You're hurt Robbie, let me help you," I say brightly, despite I am shaking like a leaf.

My pager is in my pocket. There is an emergency button on it.

"Nope, they would see me. Police are hunting my ass."

My fingers slip into my pocket and I touch the pager.

"Don't fucking think about. Hand it over NOW!" Robbie barks at me.

I gulp and take out the pager, pressing the emergency button as I hand it over to him.

His face drops as he sees what I have done.

"I don't have a lot of time now. But I will find you soon Holly and you will stop the divorce proceedings." he hisses at me, standing even closer to me. I try to move back but the sink bites into me.

"How?"

"I know everything,"

"Why?"

"Because I love you." he says simply. He kisses me softly on the cheek, shocking the hell out of me.

Robbie looks back at me as he heads to the door.

"I won't let you go baby." he says simply, before slipping out.

My dizziness takes new heights as the room spins like I'm stupidly drunk. After all Robbie did to me, how could he still think he could love me?

I clench the side of sink. I can't breathe properly, it like the air can't get to my lungs. Spots dance before my eyes and my fingers slip from the sink.

Chapter Twenty Five- Nick

All hell has broken loose. Some druggie has apparently legged it before the police got here to arrest him. The police are here checking every nook and cranny in every floor, which has many patients on edge. Not helpful.
I sit with my coffee in the staff room trying to block out all the gossip and frantic panicking of a group of nurses. I should be worried, hell maybe even going to help search but I have another surgery in just under an hour. More to the point, I don't think I give enough of a shit.
 "She is resting now, the poor thing," I hear someone say.
"Phoebe is on her way down after she finishes some stitches."
Phoebe? I listen carefully.
"I just don't understand how such a sweetie like Holly, could be married to such a monster."
"Where is she?" I yell standing up.
"Who?"
"Holly, You are talking about Holly Jones right?"
She nods.
"Ward 11, room B" another voice says.

I sprint straight there.

I yank open the door and step inside to find Holly asleep in bed. The room is thankfully empty.

I sigh in relief as I see she appears to be unharmed. I take a seat and sit next to her.

That junkie they are all looking for, it was her ex-husband. I hadn't even been bothered to help the police find him. I didn't protect her in any way, shape or form. Yet again I let her down.

"I'm so sorry Rag Doll" I whisper and gently touch her face.

I pick up her charts to find out why she is here. I scan through the usual formalities when a word in biro stops my heart; *Pregnant.*

My hands shake as I continue to read that she is estimated at eight weeks. I count back, it could be mine. I could be having a baby. I concentrate on taking a few deep breaths. It may not be, she could have slept or even be sleeping with someone else by now. But somehow I just don't see Holly jumping into bed with someone straight away. Or maybe that's just not what I want to think.

I hear Phoebe's voice so I slip out the room quietly as she is approaching it.

"What are you doing Dr Willis?" Phoebe asks.

I have no idea if she knows or not. I hope not, Holly promised me. But let's face it I was an absolute prick and Phoebe is her best friend.

"Just checking in on one of ours," I say coolly before sauntering off. I am actually going to have to rush to get to surgery on time. Not like me at all.

After I finish up in surgery I head back to Holly's room. I find an empty bed, she's gone already.

I have to talk to her. I have to find out the truth about the baby. I don't know what I will do if it the baby is mine. I cannot be a father. I cannot have a baby with Holly.

I'm still reeling as I get home. I always used protection with Holly, didn't I? I don't know what actually is worse, that she is pregnant with my baby, or she is pregnant with someone else's baby. I head straight to my gym room and start on the punch bag with my ear phones in. I am engaged to Penny. Penny is the dream, this baby will ruin everything. If Penny finds out I got another girl pregnant she will end it and be hurt. I can't hurt her, she doesn't deserve it and she will be humiliated. She doesn't deserve that either.

Pissing Penny off would piss Lawrence off. He is a nasty bastard when he wants to be. He could make my position on the board dicey. If I piss Lawrence off that would also piss my father off who has got the power to postpone my position on the board. He actually would do that just to teach me a lesson. That's what my Daddy's lessons are like. Cruel and he uses power to control me, but it always works.

I have worked to damn long and too damn hard to let that happen. I am ready to move up and take a board position. I want it so bad I can taste it, I'm so close. She can't fuck this up for me. She won't fuck this up for me. Holly needs to go and get the hell away from me.

Feeling exhausted I slip off the gloves and head to bed. I need to talk to Holly when I wake up. Slipping in between the bed sheets I close my eyes.

My alarm bleeps at four pm but I am already awake; I'm unnerved and haunted by the dreams and images that featured in my head throughout my sleep. All I could see is Holly with a round belly. Images of a baby with Holly's beautiful features. There were even images of me holding the baby seeing love shining through my eyes.

If I wasn't determined before my broken sleep, I am now. It's not enough to pay Holly to leave town and never come back. I can't live knowing that my baby is out there and not be part of its life. I'd give in at some point and find them. Then there would be joint custody arrangements. Holly will always be part of my life, connected through our child. I can't share something that precious with her and not fall for her. Letting Holly go was agony and yet I crawled back to her like a bitch and begged her to come back to me. I would be with her now if she had said yes. She is a like an addiction I can't shake loose of. Adding a baby into the mix would be like feeding that addiction. What happens when I marry Penny and she moves on? The idea of her with another man makes a fire in my belly.

No, the baby has to go. It's the only way.

I go for a long jog to consolidate my thoughts.

When I get back I call Holly.

"Hello?" she answers groggily. I must have woken her up, with all her sexy wild bed hair, probably wearing a loose top and panties. Or even one of those unstylish baggy nighties.

I shake it off as my body starts responding to the images.

"It's Nick." I bark down the phone.

There is a pause, she clearly didn't look at her phone before taking the call.

"We need to talk. Can we meet up at mine or yours?" I continue before she hangs up on me.

"I have nothing to say to you,"

"Tough shit Rag Doll, I know about you being pregnant"

A very long pause follows.

"Wh-who told you?" she stammers.

"I read your chart this morning."

She sighs.

"Fine,"

"Good, meet me at mine?"

"No thank you, you come to me, I don't need to be stuffed in your wardrobe again," she says heatedly.

"Ok fine, I will be at yours…"

"Actually I have moved."

She reels off an address which is not far from here at all.

"See you soon."

I hang up and decide to walk to hers, making a stop on the way. My head is clear, my thoughts are composed. Asshole Nick mask is firmly on as I go up to her new apartment.

Her apartment is so much nicer than her old one. A two bedroomed place with a lovely big living room, it has its own kitchen and bathroom too. It's safe. I could sigh in relief. No more living in a crappy bedsit hounded by scum.

I face Holly finally. She is wearing a pair of pyjama bottoms with a vest top. Fuck she is isn't wearing a bra and her tits look gigantic.

I can't help but stare and Holly clearly notices and slips on a hoodie. Damn it! However, it will be easier to concentrate on the task at hand with them out of sight.

"Would you like a coffee?" she asks nervously.

"Please."

She busies herself in the kitchen and I watch her. She has a half-eaten cake on a cake stand. I smile as I think back to the cakes she made me. Little things like that are what I miss about her the most.

Being alone with her is harder than I thought. My hands are in fists as I physically restrain myself from pouncing on her and kissing every inch of her delicious skin. Holly comes back into the living room and sits on the armchair. Given no choice I sit on the two seated chair as she hands me my coffee.

My mind goes blank.

"Should you be drinking coffee?" I blurt out.

She rolls her eyes, like she always does. It's adorable.

"Decaf,"

"Right... well that's good,"

"Nick do you want?" she sighs.

"Are you really pregnant?"

"Yes,"

"Is it mine?"

"No." she says, her eyes widen. They always do when she lies.

"You are lying," I growl.

"No I am not,"

"You are,"

"No I am not. I met a guy in a club after we broke up, and I had a one night stand without protection. Very, very dumb and stupid... but I was wasted and..." she babbles on. Another sign she is lying. Babbling and nervous as if she is making it up on the spot and that is exactly what she is doing.

I place my coffee adown and kneel in front of her and my eyes lock with hers.

"You are lying, I know you Holly. Better than most people. So stop fucking lying to me and be straight with me" I say evenly.

She looks me straight in the eyes and deflates. She knows she has lost.

"Fine, yes. The baby is yours Nick, happy?" she snaps.

"Fuck off am I. I am with Penelope, in fact we got engaged."

She sinks back in the seat. Damn I have hurt her... again.

"Congratulations," she whispers.

"Shit, sorry Hol. I didn't mean to blurt it out like that,"

"Well at least I heard it from you, face to face,"

"So you see why I can't have a baby with you, right?" I ask gently.

"Yes of course, I never expected you to want this. I wasn't going to tell you, I didn't want you involved. I know this wasn't your plan,"

319

"Of course it wasn't. This was never supposed to happen." I shout.

"Well it you who didn't use a condom." she shouts back.

"What? How is this was my fault? Since when didn't I use protection?"

"The night you made love to me,"

I sit back on my heels. The night Sam died, the night we made love. Flashbacks are forming in front of my eyes. I was lost and caught up in the drunken moment. Yeah, that would explain why make I forgot.

"Well it takes two. You could have remembered." I argue back childishly.

She rolls her eyes again.

"Oh for fuck sake Nick," she grumbles.

"Yeah it happened. Let's just move forward on what to do about it,"

"Agreed."

We sip our coffees in silence.

"I won't ask you to play Daddy. Your name will be off the birth certificate. You are safe from anyone knowing it's yours Nick. I swear." Holly tells me.

I am not safe; I am never safe around her.

"I would know,"

"I won't ask for a thing. I don't want a thing from you,"

"Just get an abortion." I snap. The word rolls off my tongue roughly. It makes me feel sick just to say the word aloud.

Holly's eyes widen in horror.

"No."

"Yes Holly. It's the only way,"

"No it isn't. How is killing a baby the only way?" she yells.

"Holly listen please, I don't want to do this,"

"You don't have to do anything. Just forget about me, about the baby, carry on with your perfect life and stay out of mine,"

"I can't do that. You can't just give birth to part of me and expect me to forget about it,"

"Fine don't forget, just don't give a shit. It's what you do best," Holly replies coldly.

"If anyone figures out that the baby is mine, my life is over. My reputation will be destroyed, Penny will leave me, my seat on the board will be gone. Everything I have ever worked for and wanted will be down the pan because of a fuck up." I yell at her.

My life will be ruined, although I know having a child with Holly will ruin me more.

Her eyes narrow.

"So you are telling me to kill our baby for the sake of your reputation?"

"Yes." I wince as I say it. I sound like an evil cunt and I know it.

"Unbelievable!" she screams.

"I'm sorry but that's the way it goes."

Cracks are starting to form in my armour. I need to end this and get out fast.

"Nick please, I am begging you. Don't do this. I will disappear; you never have to see me again. But please, please don't make me give up this baby. I lost a baby before, I can't do it again." she says softly. I spin to see tears in her eyes.

She lost a baby. Knowing that makes the sickness in my stomach ten times worse.

"I swear, you will never see me again. I will pack up my things and move far, far away from the hospital, from this town. No one will ever know anything about it. Your reputation will stay intact. You and Penelope will get married and have children of your own and be happy

322

together. You will forget all about me and this baby. No one has to lose here." she begs.

I could never ever forget her or forget that I have a baby somewhere with her. I will lose any way you look at it. I gulp down the emotion weighing in my throat. I'm close to giving in and I can feel it.

"It's for the best Holly. With all the drama in your life do you actually think it is right to raise a baby in it? It's not fair. What happens when your lovely husband decides to find you again. What happens when Martin decides he wants to use you as a messenger again? Huh? Do you actually think you are fit to be a mother?" I roar at her, hating each and every word I say to her.

"You..."

"No Holly. How can you work the shifts you do when you are heavily pregnant? How are you going to support the two of you once you are off on maternity leave? How are you going to work after it's born with no one to help out? You have no family to help. You have no one, hell you sold yourself to me because you were that desperate. Is that the route you will take? Whore yourself out to feed it?" I continue attacking her with everything I have.

"You are an absolute bastard Nick Willis! I will protect my baby at all costs." she screams at me in agony.

I hurt her before, but I think I have broken her now as she buries her head into her hands.

I kneel back in front of her.

"Costs that wouldn't exist if you had better judgement of the men you fuck." I tell her quietly.

Holly looks up at me in disgust.

"You're right about that."

That hurts but it is so well deserved so I take it.

"I'm so sorry Holly for putting you in this position, but it is for the best."

I take the envelope out of my coat pocket and hand it to her.

She looks at it.

"What is this?"

"Ten grand in cash. It should cover the private clinic I booked for you on the way here. Your appointment is tomorrow at 9am. I made sure to book you off work for the next two days for your recovery. The rest is for your discretion and compensation. The clinic information, address and contact details are all in there as well." I reel off impassively.

I stand up and finish off my coffee.

"And if I refuse?" she asks quietly.

"I will end your career. I will go to the board and tell them all the dealings with Martin and your drug addicted husband. There are so many cases of medical supplies going missing, and I will make sure they look at you. All your dirty laundry will come out and no one will want you in any hospital in the country." I spit out.

Her face pales.

"You have no proof."

"I have proof of knowledge, and no one would question me and you know it."

She sits breathing hard. I just want to go over and hold her, soothe away the pain I have inflicted onto her. But that's it now. No going back after this.

"Goodbye Holly." I whisper.

I walk out and hold me head up high all the way home. Once my apartment door is closed I break down.

A red haze carries over me as furniture flies through the air; things are smashing all over my floor. I hear the splintering of wood, the tinkling of the glass but I don't see it. I don't feel it. I don't feel a thing except the anger coming over me in waves as I destroy my home. I have truly become a monster. I hate myself, and what's worse is that Holly hates me too. I could see in her eyes and why shouldn't she? I just asked her to terminate our baby. I am nothing but a murderous, lying bastard.

I go to work and continue surgeries adopting my usual cool persona. Then I go home and carefully clear away the wreckages and broken furniture. By then it is just past nine am, so I phone the clinic. They confirm that Holly has shown up for her appointment. She is there and she is doing what I told her to do, I don't know if its relief or sorrow I feel, probably a mixture of the two. To distract myself I order new items that I destroyed over the internet and then head to bed.

Three hours later I have a text from Holly. I wasn't exactly sleeping anyway and snatch my phone up.

HOLLY: *It is done. I never ever want to see you again. I hate you.*

I put down my phone with shaky hands. The red haze that is still alive in my belly lightens up again and tears swarm my eyes. I blink them back, and with that the red haze turns black.

Chapter Twenty Six- Holly (Four hours previously)

"Holly you can't let him bully you like this," Phoebe shouts at me as I am changing.

"What choice do I have?"

"Run away,"

"I can't just run away from him," I sigh, wishing life was that easy.

"So you are seriously going to just abort the baby you want so badly?"

"Yes I guess. What kind of life could I have given him or her anyway?"

Phoebe sinks onto my bed and pulls me down to sit next to her.

"One full of love and happiness." she tells me.

The river banks break as I start crying all over again.

"He will end my career and then how will I raise a baby?"

"What's the point of a career if you are dead inside? I know you Holly. He can take your career away or your baby. Which is more important?" Phoebe says holding me close.

"Oh god. What am I going to do?" I sob in her arms.

"We will figure it out together." she comforts me.

I get back up and finish getting dressed.

"Are you going to go through with it?" Phoebe asks in shock.

"I don't know, all I know is that I have to be at that appointment, Nick will call and check. " I reply and pull my hair back into a ponytail.

Phoebe nods and goes to her bedroom.

I think I hate Nick. How can I go from loving someone to hating them in a matter of seconds? The things he said to me will scar me forever. I thought he cared about me. I knew he never loved me but after the way he helped me, took care of me I thought he felt something, no matter how small. But I was lying to myself. The Nick I knew before I fell for him is the Nick I have always known. Nick is a cold, ruthless, selfish asshole who asked me to abort our baby for the sake of his precious lifestyle and reputation.

I have no idea what to do. If I go through with the abortion I'm pretty sure I will never recover from it. Yet on the other hand, how can I have a baby and support it? Am I even doing the right thing bringing a baby up in my dangerous world? Nick has planted so many seeds of doubt in me that I am no longer sure I will be doing the right thing by keeping it.

As I go to walk out of the door, Phoebe is flying out of her room fully changed.

"What are you doing?" I ask.

"Coming with you, either way I think you need me,"

I smile at her.

"Yes you know what? I really do."

The clinic was very posh, I felt dirty just by entering it without a suit on.

"Holly Jones." I say nervously, to the super model behind the desk.

She taps at the screen with perfectly polished nails.

"Yes Mrs Jones, do take a seat." She smiles warmly at me.

We sit on a big leather sofa, and Phoebe reaches for a pregnancy magazine.

"Oh isn't he just a cutie?" she cries shoving a picture of a baby underneath my face.

He was.

"You are not helping," I snap at her.

"Ladies would you care for drink? We have some sparkling water, herbal teas, juices," the lady trails on.

"Oh, an orange juice please," Phoebe replies.

"Same,"

"Sure ladies, I will be right back," the lady says and spins on her heel.

"I feel like we are in a spa or something," says Phoebe.

"Huh."

After waiting around for a few minutes and drinking deliciously fresh juice I am called in.

"Hello Holly, I am Dr Taylor," a female doctor announces as we walk in the door.

"Hi,"

"Your friend can sit there."

Phoebe sits in the chair Dr Taylor points to.

"So how far along are you?"

"About ten weeks," I reply.

"And you have come to terminate this pregnancy?" Dr Taylor asks. There is no judgment in her eyes as I feared. Then again she must get this a lot.

I nod.

I hear Phoebe gasp.

"Okay well you don't need a surgical procedure. We call this an EPT, Early Pregnancy Termination. It is quite straight forward. We inset a termination medicine vaginally which will then cause you to miscarry. We need to check you over first and ask some questions"

I begin going through my medical history with her, but my head isn't really there. I am going to bleed and lose the baby like last time. It won't be an operation where I go to sleep pregnant and wake up not.

"WAIT!" I shout out as Dr Taylor is taking my blood pressure.

Dr Taylor stops immediately.

"I can't do this," I cry out.

"Oh thank god," Phoebe rushes over to me.

"I can't terminate this pregnancy Dr Taylor, I don't want to, I never did," I say leaping off the bed.

Dr Taylor nods her head slowly.

"That's your choice Holly. Come back if you change your mind or need anything" she says kindly.

"Thank you" I say as I rush out the door.

"I changed my mind on the pregnancy, but if someone phones to check.." I begin to tell the receptionist.

"Doctor patient confidentiality Mrs Jones," The receptionist replies warmly.

"Thank you, what do I owe you?" I ask taking out the brown envelope.

"Ninety nine pounds and ninety nine pence. We will call it a consultation"

I pay and sprint out of there as fast as I can.

"Oh my god," I call out as I run to the bus stop.

"Good girl Hol," Phoebe says hugging me.

"Oh shit Phoeb, I am ruined. What the hell am I going to do now?"

"Let' get home, stick the kettle on and we can plan from there okay?"

"Okay"

We arrive home and I literally collapse on the sofa, whilst Phoebe makes us a drink.

"Nick is going to destroy me," I moan.

"Not if he doesn't know."

I sit up and take the cup of decaffeinated tea Phoebe hands to me.

"I can't lie to him Phoebe, he sees right through me"

"Okay, I have come up with a plan. It's drastic, but I think we can make it work," Phoebe says and sits down beside me.

"Shoot,"

"First of all you text Nick to say you went through with the abortion, then you tell him that you never want to see him again, how you won't ever forgive him and all that." she starts.

That would hurt him, but then again would it?

"Well that will be easy enough to do,"

"Thirdly, you quit the hospital."

I nod, I don't want to. But I can't be around Nick now. Goodbye maternity leave.

"What will I do for work?" I ask nervously.

"I'm getting to that. My Auntie Martha owns a pub in Eastmore,"

"Where is that?"

"It's a sleepy little town about half an hour away, anyway my cousin Becks has just divorced her husband and has moved back in with her. It's all complicated but Auntie Martha now has two girls to take care of whilst Becks is at night school. She really needs help with the pub, she asked me but I can't do it with our shifts, but you can," Phoebe exclaims.

"What pull pints and serve chips?"

"Yeah, it's not glam, it's boring, but it will do and earn you a crust,"

I take it in. It's a paid job, not some where Nick would ever show up or even know about. It could work.

"I guess I have the money Nick left me, I have nearly ten grand to cushion me," I say slowly.

"Exactly. You can live here and take the train to work every day. There is a direct train to Eastmore from here,"

"What if he sees me? I'm too close."

"Just be careful. I'll spread the word you have left so he doesn't comes looking for you."

I nod again, like he would any way. He will be too busy playing happy families with Penelope.

"It could work, if don't go wandering into town or anything, don't meet up with our lot,"

"Exactly."

I look up at my best friend with hope. I could keep the baby, my career won't be destroyed, I can go back to work, maybe in another hospital once the baby is born and I can get him or her into childcare. It could work.

"What do you think?" Phoebe asks.

I throw my arms around her.

"I love you so much." I gasp.

"I'll give Auntie Martha a call."

When she goes to call Martha, I text Nick. Each word cuts deep but it's not as bad as what he said to me. I will give up my job, my friends, anything to keep this baby.

Chapter Twenty Seven- Nick

"So this is the selection of cakes we have. I will let you look over it, and come back to take an order for the samples," Wendy the cake shop manager says, handing us a menu.

"Fantastic." Penny beams.

I flip open the menu style brochure and nose through the fancy wedding cakes.

Wow, that's a hell of a lot of cake.

"Oh Nick what a wonderful way to spend the afternoon,"

"Hum."

She chats about the various styles and flavours whilst I switch off.

That text from Holly has long been deleted, yet it is still imprinted in my brain. I never even knew she was leaving until Tom let it slip on her last day, when they all went out to 'Benny's' for a goodbye dinner just over four months ago. I wasn't invited, unsurprisingly. She has been gone five long months. I have tried to call her dozens of times but her phone is disconnected. She truly has vanished out of my life. It should have been a good thing, without Holly, things were supposed to go back to how they were before. But it's not like that. I work, I exercise, have sex with Penny, and go to brunches with our fathers. But it is like watching the same film over and over again, everything is exactly the same, yet everything feels different. I stay at Penny's most of the time now, even with new furniture I hate being at the apartment. I see the table I fucked Holly on, the bed we made love in, the spare bedroom which will always be her room and the kitchen she cooked me food on. She haunts every inch of the place.

"Nick, choose one," Penny says, clearing my thoughts.

"Choose what?"

"A cake of course," she laughs.

"Oh yeah sorry I was…"

"In your own world again,"

"Yeah,"

I study the list. I want chocolate cake, chocolate fudge cake. It won't be as good as Holly's though, none ever are.

"Um, the lemon cake looks nice"

"Oh yes I love lemon cake, let's try that one,"

"Sure,"

Wendy appears again out of nowhere.

"Which would you like to try?" Wendy asks.

"The Victorious Vanilla, the Luscious Lemon the Fabulous Fudge and I think the Stunning Strawberry please Wendy," Penelope says handing back the menus.

"Great selection guys, I will get them ready, would you like tea or champagne with it?"

"Champagne," I tell her.

"Got it," Wendy grins and walks off.

"We're both are on call," Penny mutters.

"One glass won't hurt,"

"No I suppose not."

We are getting married in three months time. It feels like we have been engaged forever. Time just stretches and lingers. The venue is all sorted, everything is ready. Penelope has sorted it all out, well with a huge amount of help from a wedding planner, on her Daddy's bill of course. She has done my head in with the whole thing. I want to marry her, I just don't want to help with any of the shit leading up to it. I got bullied into the cake tasting and only gave in because I was feeling guilty.

"So no one has turned down our invite, so all three hundred and sixty guests are coming," Penelope tells me happily.

"Great,"

"So it is just the cake and the presents left to go,"

"Great,"

"We need to decide where we are going to live though, I think I will phone the estate agents later and see what we can find,"

"Great, wait what?" I ask shocked.

"We need to a home to live in together." she says slowly like I'm six years old.

I sit up straight. Of course we need to buy a place together but that means giving up the apartment. I love that apartment, even if I am not there much these days.

"Move in with me, let's just get the wedding out of the way first, we can easily buy a house after," I breeze.

"Well these things can take time Nick, Don't worry about it. I will deal with it." she smiles. I should be mad that she is making all the decisions, I should have an input in where I goddam well live. But honestly, I can't be bothered to argue.

She will be in for a shock once I get back to being me again. I like to be in control, I like to be the trousers. I just need to get back to being me, that's all.

"Fine call the estate agents. It needs to be close to work, at least two bedrooms"

"Of course, we need a room for a baby."

Baby! Shit me. A hot pain shoots through my stomach at the word. It's the same pain I get when I see any baby at work, sometimes even when I see a pregnant woman. My baby would have been about seven months along by now. Holly would look like she swallowed a beach ball, with swollen feet. We would even know what the sex was by now.

"Excuse me," I go to stand as Wendy comes over with a tray.

"Here we go." she announces.

I sit back down. The cake slices look like pieces of art, but my stomach rolls.

"Ok here is your champagne and the cake samples, enjoy. Let me know which the winner is," Wendy tells us placing everything in front of us.

"Toast time." Penny squeals holding up her glass.

I force a smile on my face and raise my glass to hers.

"To us," she says.

"To us," I repeat and drink the fizz down.

"Nick you're supposed to sip it,"

"Sorry,"

"Okay, which first?"

"You choose,"

She beams at me. She always likes me saying that.

She selects the lemon, and puts a tiny piece on her fork. I sit and watch her and she tastes it, groaning like I'm fucking her.

"Oh baby, try it," she says forking up another piece and holds it to my lips.

I eat it but I can't taste a thing.

It continues like this, as she practically orgasms over every piece. The pieces are so fucking small I can't see how she actually tastes it.

"Last one, the Fantastic Fudge" she says grabbing the chocolate fudge cake. I look at it in horror as the sticky fudge icing is dived into.

"I didn't think you liked chocolate,"

"You love chocolate fudge cake, it's your favourite," she argues.

"Yeah but I didn't think you liked it,"

"This one is for you," she says and takes a bite.

"Oh that is heavenly." she moans.

I take a large forkful and swallow it. It is good, really good actually, but still doesn't top Holly's. Like all the others it just doesn't have as deep a chocolate flavour.

"Yum," I say, trying to be enthusiastic this time.

"Which one shall we go for?"

"Not the fudge cake," I say automatically.

"Why not?"

"It just doesn't seem right for a wedding," I shrug.

"Alright, which was your favourite?"

"Um I liked them all, you choose. I have to head off any how," I say and hand her my card.

"Oh," she pouts.

"Sorry Princess." I say kissing her head as I leave.

I am a bastard to her, she deserves so much better than me. Yet she takes it and comes back for more.

I don't need to leave at all, in fact it's only five pm and I still have three hours before I start my night shift. So I head back to my flat, grab my running gear and go for a long run. I run so much these days, physically I am in the best shape I have ever been but for once it is not about my vanity. I do it because it helps me to clear my head.

As usual my mind drifts to Holly. I wonder where she is and what she is doing with herself now. Is she still nursing? I checked every local hospital but she isn't there. I can't help but fear for her. She is alone in the world, she has no family, her friends are all here and with her husband clearly on the loose it is not safe for her. I don't know what I would do if something happened to her. She hates me but I don't hate her, far from it. I miss her even when we ended things, just seeing her at work was better than this. She calms me and without her all I feel is darkness.

I end up jogging down the street by the flat where Holly used to live with Phoebe like I do on occasion. I know she is gone, but it still just feels like I'm a little closer to her, somehow. I go to jog past it when I see a man in a hoodie by the complex door. I stop and take a good look at the man. It's not Martin. The man's hands are shaking as he discreetly tried to open the door using a card. It doesn't open to my relief. Could it be Robbie? I'm not sure, but after a few minutes he spins around angrily and drops something on the doorstep of the complex and quickly moves down the street, pulling his hoodie over his head, covering his face. I notice he is wearing a wedding band. As soon as he is out of sight I dash up the steps by the front of the complex and pick up a bunch of flowers off and an envelope with Holly's name on attached to it. I shouldn't have but the feeling in my gut made me open it carefully. I pulled out the little card.

"Holly, I love you, don't do this you will regret it. Hubby xxx"

Bile rises in my mouth as I slip the card back in the envelope and drop the flowers where I found them. Luckily she isn't here anymore so she would never find them. But Phoebe would. Something needs to be done about that monster, once and for all.

As soon as I get home I call the police station and asked for George Harris. George Harris is one of my closest associates, one I could call a friend but I don't keep in touch enough for that. His father is also a member of the board but he no longer attends the social stuff, as an officer he works more hours than me and that says something.

"Harris," his voice booms through the phone.

"Hey Georgie boy,"

"Fucking Nick Willis. Wow have you murdered some one?" he teases.

"Not yet, but I do need your help,"

"Shoot,"

"I need your discretion," I warn.

"Always bro, you know that,"

"Well have you heard of a druggie scum called Robbie Jones?"

"Yeah we have, we have a case on him, slippery son of a bitch," George says menacingly.

"Well I am friends with the woman married to him,"

"Holly Jones?"

"Yep,"

"You don't have friends. Hell I am the closest you have,"

"Fuck off. So I have just seen him trying to break into her old apartment,"

"22, Regent Drive?"

"That's the one,"

"For fuck sake, that poor woman," he gritted out.

"What do you know?" I ask quickly.

"Nah, I can't tell you that one mate. Let's just say he was an abusive fucker,"

"Fine well, I fear for her safety. I need you to get in touch with her and warn her about him. Make her press charges. She seems to be petrified of the police,"

"Not surprised, a lot of abusive victims are the same,"

"Can you help her? Please?"

"Of course I will, but I can only try. She is the one who has the power in this,"

"Mate I owe you one. Can we catch up and grab a beer sometime?"

"Sure. I will call you once I speak to her and we can go from there,"

"Cheers buddy,"

"See you later Nick."

We hang up and I feel relieved. I shouldn't have interfered but I can't let anything happen to her.

Chapter Twenty Eight- Holly

"So that is two pints of larger, three gin and tonics and one lemonade." I confirm to my regular punter.

He hands over a twenty, which I cash and hand him back the change.

"Want me to bring them over for you?" I ask.

He looks me up and down grinning.

"No thanks love, I can handle it." he teases and carries the tray of drinks away.

I can't blame him, I am huge! At nearly thirty weeks pregnant I can barely see my toes any more. Still despite all the drama that has happened he was worth it. My little boy was worth leaving my career and Nick behind.

Martha has been an absolute godsend. She is a fiery red head much like her niece but with a heart of gold. She has told me I can work at the pub as long as I want, and she even has a spare room for the nights when I am too exhausted to travel home. Her sister in law Susan is also a child minder who helps her with her grandchildren when she is busy with the pub. Martha has set me up for my boy to go to Susan's when I am ready to go back to work. I can even use her when I go back to nursing eventually.

It's all fallen into place thanks to Phoebe and her family.

I am just polishing some glasses when Martha comes in.

"Hello love, how are we doing?" she says warmly.

"Slow but steady." I reply.

It is always slow and steady. Phoebe wasn't lying when she says it was a sleepy town. It's quiet, quaint, and a bit boring to be honest. It's crazy to think that this pub is twenty miles away from where I live but it's like being in a different world. It's refreshing but lonely.

"Great, you head on off now, the train is in fifteen minutes," Martha shoos me out from behind the bar.

"Okay thank you. Table ten is waiting on two pie and mash and Table three is waiting on their desserts," I inform her.

"Gotcha now, now scoot."

I smile at Martha and grab my things. The walk to the train station is literally five minutes so I get there is good time and sit waiting for the train.

It's been nearly five months since I last set eyes on Nick. I feel the pain in my chest when I think about our last encounter. I try to focus on the anger. It's easier than thinking about the other times: the times we are almost a couple, the times when I thought I could see affection in his eyes. I can't always block it out but I try hard to.

I get on the train and begin the twenty two minute ride home. I need to get home and have a long bath. It may be my last before my son is born. It takes a hell of a lot of manoeuvring to get out the tub these days. Hopefully the divorce papers will have come as well. Everything is finalised without Robbie and now I am just awaiting the papers to legally confirm it. The lawyer phoned a couple of days ago to say they were on their way.

The train pulls into Bridgeton station and I get up to exit the train. I pull my coat hood up over my head as usual. I have never bumped into any one from the hospital. (I doubt any one people commute from Eastmore and the times are different from the major train lines) but I got this baggy coat just in case. I can't be too careful. Between Nick and Robbie I feel that all I ever do is hide. Robbie has been sending flowers to the hospital, Phoebe has been telling me. Even Martin has shown his face a couple of times asking for me. I hate to think about what the staff think of me. Tom apparently even threatened to call the police if Martin came back asking for me again. I seem to be safe in Eastmore but it's the commute that is the tricky part.

I arrive home just before seven pm. Phoebe is off today and has promised to have something half edible on the table by seven. I step through the door but I can't smell any food.

"Phoebs?" I call out.

"Living room," she replies, her voice sounds off.

I walk into the living room, to see her sat with a man in a checked shirt.

"Hi," I say carefully.

"Holly isn't it? Come take a seat" the man says, holding his hand out to me formally.

Panic starts to bubble as I sit down. Phoebe is worried; giving that she is fidgeting like a loony.

"I am P.C Harris" he says and shows me his badge.

The panic swirls in my gut.

"What is all this about?" I ask politely.

"We are concerned about your husband Mr Robert Jones."

I have been questioned by the police many times, but I have never been much help. I refused to help them when we were married out of fear, and out of fear I haven't got involved since.

"I don't know where he is," I reply clipped.

"I am aware of that. I have been talking to your friend Phoebe here, who says that he has harassing you."

I glance at Phoebe, she looks back guilty.

"I'm so sorry Holly. But I panicked look at this." she says and hands me a crumpled bunch of carnations. I read the card and put it back on the table with shaking hands. He must be referring to the divorce. I didn't think he even knew about it being finalised, given that no one could contact him. More importantly he knows where we live. Shit!

"He knows where we live now Holly," Phoebe echoes my thoughts.

"I'm so sorry," I whisper to her.

"Well I am here today to enforce a restraining order for your protection. That may not stop him given that he has no known address, but we will send it to his parents." P.C. Harris informs me.

"How will it work then?"

"If he comes within one mile of you, any officer can arrest him on the spot,"

"Do you know about him P.C. Harris?" I ask quietly. Surely if he did he would know that Robbie hasn't been caught for assaulting me or his other offences.

"I do. We have a case against him. I also know what he did to you," he says softly.

"Then what makes you think that this will in any way help me?"

"I am not sure. All I know is that we want to protect you, and with your divorce, we are worried he may go over the edge,"

"Over the edge," I repeat numbly.

"Wait. The divorce is not yet been legalised," Phoebe says.

"I phoned your lawyer, everything is finalised. He has sent your divorce papers, they should be here any day."

Phoebe gasps and grabs a large envelope from the kitchen.

"Looks like that's them," I gasp.

"We also have an alarm system, which you should carry with you at all times. If he finds you, you can activate it which silently goes to our headquarters" P.C Harris continues.

"What about Martin?"

"The same will apply to him too. However I think he will keep clear once he gets the restraining order,"

"I don't know if I should do that. You must understand P.C. Harris, these men have threatened to kill me if I go to the police," I protest.

"Holly stop it! He knows where we live, he could attack you at any moment. Just do it." Phoebe shouts at me.

Stunned, I face her, tears are rolling down her cheeks. She is petrified and it is entirely my fault. They could hurt her to get to me. I am putting her in danger.

"Fine." I reply.

As much as I didn't think any of this would work, I needed to try and protect her and my baby.

"Good girl Holly. I know this must be scary and you have been too intimidated to come to us before but you are doing the right thing," Officer Harris tells me.

An hour later P.C. Harris has everything he needs from me, my statement of my encounter in the hospital, our marriage, when I saw him in the club, the abuse in our marriage. He also questioned Phoebe on the flowers and Martin at the hospital. It's exhausting, and emotional.

"May I suggest that you two stay elsewhere for a while, just until things calm down?" he asks us as he stands up to leave.

"Yes, we can do that," Phoebe answers.

"Holly, can I ask a last question?" he asks me.

I nod.

"Is the baby his?"

"No, no he is not Robbie's" I cry out.

"I am so sorry to ask but if anything happens to you, it's assault against you and the baby. We need to know whether it's towards his baby as well," he says sadly.

"I understand,"

"Is the father someone you can go to?"

I shake my head in shame. No I can't go back to Nick and beg him to protect me and the child that he thinks I aborted. Let alone hiding out from his skinny fiancé.

"Okay, well let me know where you are staying so I can send everything through to you," he replies and walks towards the door.

"We will do," Phoebe says.

"Good night Holly, Phoebe," he says warmly and leaves.

Phoebe fans herself with her hand.

"Gosh he was hot." she gasps.

355

He was actually.

"So we are in the middle of a drama with my now ex-husband, we need to find a safe house and are being grilled by the police, and you still have time to check out an policeman?" I laugh.

"Yeah, maybe not appropriate huh?"

I shake my head smiling.

"So let's pack a bag and head back to Eastmore," she tells me.

"Eastmore?"

"Yeah, Auntie Martha has loads of places we can crash,"

I sigh.

"I don't want anyone else to be in Robbie's pathway,"

"Well we won't stay at the pub then, Auntie Martha rents loads of places out, I am sure we can rent a place from her for a month or two,"

"But this is our home," I protest. I love it here, a place that I am proud to call my home.

"Yeah well, little man will be here soon and he needs his own room."

I look down at my tummy. She is right, I even feel him nudging me as if to agree with her. He likes to be part of our conversations.

"Fine." I breathe out and head to pack a few things.

"Of course I can find you somewhere, my darlings," Martha says bringing us both a cup of tea.

We are back in the pub just before closing time. It's deserted except for Mac and Steve who always stay until they finish their last pint after last orders.

"Thank you so much Martha," I say gratefully.

"Yeah thank you Auntie M," Phoebe smiles.

"You can stay at mine tonight, then tomorrow you can have a look at the cottage just down the road. It's beautiful, three bedroomed, and has a lovely garden for little one to run in," Martha tells us.

"Well I don't think we will be there for that long,"

"Well it's worth a thought," Martha clucks.

"It's just temporary until things are sorted." I insist. I haven't told her the whole story, just an overview, a deranged ex-husband who is stalking me. Kind of hits all the points.

"Okay my loves, you can move in tomorrow for as long as you want. The last tenants moved out three weeks ago, I was just about to put it back on the market,"

"Perfect," Phoebe chirps.

"This is so kind of you,"

"Well you still have to pay a bit of rent, and it needs repainting, if you fancy it?"

"No problems." I smile at Martha. She may be Phoebe's aunt, but after mere months with her she is fast becoming a step in one for me too.

The cottage is perfect. I love it instantly. Best of all it is fully furnished. I went and brought some essentials we needed whilst Phoebe grabbed lighter stuff from the flat before or after work. I finally read the divorce papers and discovered that I was back to being Holly Turner. The grin going ear to ear on my face was going to take a while to shift.

Chapter 29- Nick

Battling with someone who doesn't want to be saved is harder surgery. Lots of surgeons don't believe it, but I do. I had been battling for hours with a teenage girl who tried to commit suicide. Every time I think I have mended part of her broken body another part fails. Jumping in front of a car in the middle of a duel carriageway was one thing. Slicing both her wrists before that was another. I have a big team with me today and finally we managed to fix her physically. Mentally on the other hand, I don't know. I don't know if there is much we can do. I have Sharon, our child psychologist, ready to be paged when the girl wakes up. That surgery has pushed me to work through the morning. It's gone eleven and I am supposed to be going out to brunch with Penny and the fathers soon.

"Joy." I mutter sarcastically and head to change.

I take my phone out to find George has called me and left me a voicemail.

"Hey bud, just giving you an update on the situation you asked me to look into. Um not going to give details but call me back and we can meet up, I'm free until two." George says through the voicemail.

Penny or Holly, even with her gone it still feels like a choice between the two of them.

I call George back.

"P.C. George Harris speaking,"

"Dr Nicholas Willis calling," I mock.

"See you got my voicemail. Want to go grab a coffee somewhere?"

"Sure baby but I never put out first time though," I tease.

"Oh fuck off Willis. See you at Starbucks off Regent Street, half an hour?" George asks.

"Great." I reply and he hangs up.

Why Regent Street? That's close to Holly's old flat. It could be coincidence given I don't live far away from there either, but I don't like it.

Next I need to find Penny, so I change and hurry down to Paediatrics. Penny is barking orders at a poor student.

"So next time I say every five minutes, I mean it, not seven okay?" she snaps at a petrified male student.

"Yes Dr Sinclaire," he almost sprints away.

"Hey." I say coming up to her.

The frown vanishes and her dazzling smile appears.

"Hey you." she flirts and walks to her office.

I follow.

The door closes and she presses me up against the door, kissing me hungrily.

I break it off after a second.

"Sorry princess, I have another surgery in twenty, I can't make brunch," I explain.

Penny's smile vanishes.

"Oh,"

"I'm really sorry. Can you do brunch without me? They like you better anyhow,"

"Yeah sure, can you come back to mine once you're done?" she asks.

"Of course. I'll make it up to you"

"Okay, right I need to leave now anyway, just worried about leaving idiots here."

I pull her in for a hug.

"I am sorry." I really am but more for lying to her, than missing a stupid brunch.

"I know,"

"Thank you for being understanding,"

"It's my job," she smiles sadly.

It clearly bothers her more than she is letting on but I slip out of the office.

I get to Starbucks with a minute to spare and find George in a booth at the empty part of the café.

I head over to him grinning.

"Hey Georgie boy,"

"Hey Nick the prick," we shake hands almost formally, before he pulls me into a bear hug.

"Man, how have you been? I got your wedding invite," George says warmly.

"All good mate, all good. You better be coming,"

"Course, the toad and the princess wedding," he mocks.

"A damn good looking toad,"

"True, but beauty is only skin deep."

I laugh and sit down.

"You need to order your coffee at the counter," George laughs.

I meet the eyes of a young girl behind the counter and smile at her. She comes straight over.

"Hi, can you get you something?" she asks me.

"A cappuccino please honey,"

"No problems, I will bring it right over."

George sits there, his mouth open.

"You are such a prick," he mutters.

I wink at him.

"So what is going down with Holly?" I change the subject.

"Ok well you know it's all classified,"

"Just spill it, I may have helped you get Robbie Jones,"

"True, Ok well Holly has taken the restriction order against him and Martin Smith." George starts.

A smile widens on my face.

"Really? That's fantastic!"

"Yeah maybe," George frowns.

"What? Why is that not a good thing?"

"Well Robbie needs to know that he has a restriction order, to be aware of it,"

"What the fuck does that mean?"

The waitress brings me my coffee, but I'm no longer interested in teasing George.

"Thank you love," I say handing her the change.

She leaves a little disappointed.

"He has no address, he is ghost. He has a very low profile. He knows if we find him, he will be going down for a real long time," George mutters.

"I know he is drug using loser and he hurt Holly, but what else have you got on him?" I ask curiously.

"He has allegations of abusing, dealing, theft and now I have some new information, which could lead to an attempted murder charge"

"Fuck. Who did he try to kill?"

His eyes narrow, which tell me the answer.

"Holly? What did he do to her?" I whisper.

George sighs.

"We were after him three years ago. He had been spotted selling dodgy cocaine at the local college, he was in a fix with Martin Smith and Smith was after blood. Anyhow he obviously found out we were tracking him and disappeared. The next evening two of my guys spotted him going back to his house and by the time we had back up sorted, Holly Jones supposing fell from the bedroom window and onto the pavement. One of the guys ran after Robbie but lost him as he disappeared. He is brilliant at escaping. The other went to Holly. She lost their baby and was in hospital for a couple of weeks with her injuries. She insisted she fell. Its bull but now we have her on our side; I am hoping she will press charges of attempted murder, as that's what it really was" George informs me.

My heart is breaking for her. She went through all that. I know she lost a baby, but she should never have lost it like that. My stomach is in knots, I made her abort ours after what she has lost. The guilt literally feels like a weight on the back of my neck.

"Poor Rag Doll." I mutter sadly.

George gives me a curious look.

"Can you be straight with me?" he asks.

"Sure,"

"What was your relationship with her?"

I take a moment to drink my coffee. Should I lie to him?

"We worked together, and she was an exceptional nurse. I saw that cunt at the hospital and I know she doesn't have family or anything. I care about her, I want her to come back to work. She is the only nurse I trust to do as I ask." I lie. Well partly lie. What I am saying is true, just omitting our very, very sexual affair.

He studies me for a moment.

"If you say so,"

"So why are we here?" I ask him.

"I am observing Holly's building. The creep knows her address as you discovered. He has been spotted on CT camera a few times. He is getting lazy or desperate,"

"Why is he still after Holly?"

"Dude is seriously fucked up in the head, given all the flowers at the hospital and her home, my guess is that he wants her back or he wants her dead. Possible both,"

I take a deep breath. I didn't even know about his flowers at work.

"What's the plan then?"

"The plan is that we wait. He is losing his shit with everything going on. Holly has a buzzer on her that will alert the police should he confront her. Then we get him and slap everything we possibly can on the dick," George tells me.

"What's going on?"

George opens his mouth then shuts it.

"That's Holly's business, I don't mind telling you work related stuff, but I can't tell personal shit,"

"Oh okay," I say deflated.

"Sorry, but this woman is the key to putting Robbie behind bars. I won't break her confidentiality. If you wanna know, ask her yourself," George shrugs.

"Yeah of course,"

"Right then, I have to get back to work. We should get a beer together soon. Miss hanging out with you man," I say sliding out of the booth.

"Yeah we should. We can try and sync days off,"

"May take a while," I laugh.

We shake hands warmly then I leave him to do his job.

I head back home and go straight to the punch bag. I could have picked anyone, anyone to be my mistress and I picked her. The broken, fragile doll I played with and hurt all over again. Shame roars through me as I take it out on the bag.

A couple of hours later I head to Penelope's house freshly showered, changed and much calmer. She is sitting at the dining room table with brochures everywhere.

"Hey," I greet.

"Hi Nick," she doesn't even look up from the brochures.

"What you got there?"

"House brochures,"

I take in a deep breath. She doesn't waste time.

"Already?"

"Well I had brunch with our fathers, I told them about us looking for a house and your Dad recommended great estate agent." she explains.

"Oh,"

I sit down next to her.

"Have a look with me? We can sort out viewing on Saturday. I booked you off work already."

"Why would you do that?" I ask horrified.

"Because it's my day off, and you always work Saturdays,"

"Yeah because we are so busy, it's the busiest day of the week." I snap.

She looks up at me surprised.

"I didn't think you would mind,"

"Well I do. Who gives you the right to rearrange me schedule?"

Penny looks up and I can see she is about to cry. Damn.

"I'm sorry Nick... I didn't think." she says and the tears fall.

Damn again.

I sigh and put my arms around her.

"Sorry I didn't mean to snap," I say holding her.

"I'm just so stressed out over the wedding and looking for a house as well as my own job and you just don't help at all." she cries.

No. No I really don't.

"I'm no good at this stuff Pen,"

"And you think I am? I have never done any of this before. I am trying to do make a life for us, and I don't think you want it."

"What no, of course I do. I'm sorry, I will come with you on Saturday," I tell her.

"Are you having an affair?" she blurts out.

"What? Fuck no, what makes you say that?"

"You weren't at the hospital this afternoon, and you keep disappearing on me." she explains.

Now she is checking up on me? Fuck me; I thought she was supposed to be the easy one.

"I just didn't want to go to brunch," I half lie.

"So where did you go and why lie to me?"

"I don't know, you wanted to go and I hate it. You know me and my father don't get on well these days. I just sit there feeling like a spare part,"

"Where did you go?"

"Out running, had a coffee, worked out,"

"So you are not having an affair or sleeping with anyone other than me?" Penny asks sitting up straight.

"No I am not. Why would I?"

"I wouldn't have put it past you a few months ago," she snorts delicately.

"Penny I promised you that if we got together I would be a changed man. And I am," I tell her truthfully.

"Good because I swear to god Nick, you humiliate me like that and I will have your balls and your chair on the board," she says lightly, but looking in her eyes, I know she means it.

"If I am that stupid to cheat on you, I will hand them both to you wholeheartedly." I laugh falsely.

She climbs onto my lap and starts unbuttoning my shirt.

"In that case, let's go have our first make up sex." she says slipping her hand over my bare chest.

Was that even a fight?

"Sure." I say and stand up, wrapping her legs around my waist.

Guilt rips at me all over again. She is accusing me of an affair when little does she know I am cheating on her, every time we have sex. It's never her I am fucking.

Chapter Thirty- Holly

I ring the bell to signal last call.

Immediately the last four punters get up despite still having a mostly full pint's on the table. I smile as they approach and order another round but unlike usual I am grumpy beneath the smile. I'm shattered. My son however isn't as he is kicking around like he has a football in my uterus with him. My back and feet are aching as I have been stocking up all night due to the slow stream of customers in here. I just want to lock up and go home, back to my nice comfy bed and sleep until my boy decides to make an appearance. No scrap that, after my boy makes an appearance would be better.

I clean down the surfaces and place the beer nozzles in soda water. Finally it is time to ring the final bell.

"That's it now boys, drink up." I order to my four regulars who are engrossed in conversation. They acknowledge me but don't take another sip of their beers.

I have actually finished all the cashing up and swept the entire floor by the time they finally leave.

"Night Holly love," Johnny says as he heads out the door.

"Night Johnny. Drive home safely," I reply and lock the doors behind them.

I mop all the sticky floors and sigh with relief as the longest shift ever has finally finished. I can work a double shift in the hospital but it never feels as long as a shift here. It's so slow and boring, the hours just drag on and on. The hospital has such a fast paced, exciting environment that I crave badly these days. I will be back as soon as I can.

Martha comes out with our bags and coats.

"Well that's another boring day over with," she sighs.

"It will pick up again soon,"

"Not with all those chain pubs opening up here."

Possibly not, but I don't wish to tell her that.

"We have quality, local produce not some boil in the bag rubbish." I press.

Martha smiles wearily at me and hands me my things.

"Gosh I can't wait for my bed tonight." I mutter.

The baby kicks me suddenly, and I grasp the local table.

Martha chuckles and places her hand over my tummy, where he is kicking. He kicks at her hand.

"Kiddo, go to sleep," I wince.

"Let's get you home, and you should have a warm cup of milk," Martha tells me kindly.

"Sounds good."

Martha drives me home, although it is only ten minutes away. I feel bad, but she insists with everything going on. I am so grateful for this woman.

"Night Martha, thank you," I say as she pulls up the cottage.

"Night sweetheart, see you tomorrow,"

I open the front door and step inside, turning on the lights as I go. Then lock the door back up.

I go to change into my pyjamas as my milk and honey warms up in the microwave. My bedroom is such a comfort to me, as I see the bassinet that I purchased last week and the little blue fleecy blanket folded perfectly inside. He even has a little teddy bear that Phoebe brought him.

"Ten and a half weeks to go little man," I mutter to him.

A breeze hits me. I look up surprised to find my window open.

I frown; I haven't opened it at all today.

My heart speeds up as I glance around.

Phoebe is on a night shift and would never leave a window open before heading out.

I go to my handbag and reach inside for my phone and alarm, when I feel a gloved hand around my mouth.

"Don't move." a gravely male voice I don't recognise says.

I press the button on my alarm, luckily it's silent.

The man has a white cloth in his hand, it's pressing in my mouth, and it must have some kind of sleeping drug on it, as I feel my body turn heavy, my eyelids battling against me to close.

I press my hand against my belly as I sway and my eyelids close.

My head is pulsing as I wake up groggily. I feel sick. The room is spinning. Then I feel vibrations underneath me and it hits me. My eyes snap open instantly. I am moving, and I'm travelling. The wide and dark walls make me believe I am in some kind of van. It's hard to see as it is dark but a sliver of light from the front of the van makes me able to see dim shadows.

I can't move my arms at all. but I think I'm tied up, rope is digging into my wrists.

374

"What's going on?" I shout at the front of the van. The driver and the passenger shadows don't turn around. With a sigh I sit uncomfortably for what seems hours until the van finally stops. I have processed a few things. One this could be the work of Robbie. It would make complete sense, but hired thugs? It seems upmarket and smart for him. Possibly Martin, who is a lot smarter, and could possibly pull this off. My frightened brain also makes me think of Nick, if he knew about the baby and my deceit. This appears to be a professional job and Nick is everything that makes a professional. Yet deep down as much as Nick is a complete wanker with a mean streak I couldn't seriously think he would want to harm me.

The other thing I have figured out is that I pressed the alarm in time but it is nowhere on my body. It is still in my handbag at home. So it may not be any help now but at least the police know something is wrong. The last thing I have figured out, which isn't helpful, is that I am in my huge, maternity, purple pyjamas.

 A man who looks like Hulk opens the van doors.

"It's dark, we are alone so don't try anything. I don't want to hurt you" he warns and lifts me out of the van. It's the same man from the cottage. His hand for a second time clamps over my mouth.

My feet hit the ground, as I realise that we are in some kind of farm yard. Pens surrounded us yet there are no animals to be seen or heard. A dark building looms up ahead which Hulk heads towards, one of firm hands on my shoulders, the other still on my mouth as he pushed me to follow.

 We go into the building and enter a kitchen. It looks cosy almost with an old fashioned oven and wooden surfaces. Hulk opens what looks like a basement door and leads me down the steps carefully.

The cosiness ends there. The white lighting is stark and there are tables littered with drug paraphernalia and little bags of white powder.

My stomach sinks as Hulk pushes me roughly on a battered chair facing him and the steps I just walked down.

"One Holly Turner." he yells out to no one.

I hear a door open, but I can't see it and slams shut.

"Holly JONES!" a voice roars.

My skin crawls. I knew who it would be; I don't know why I questioned it.

I can feel him coming closer and I hear several other footsteps coming up behind me.

I look down, not wanting to face him. I see his shoes first, fancy brown leather shoes. Not dirty battered trainers any more then.

"Holly." he whispers.

I refuse to look up.

My hair tugs back, forcing me to look into Robbie's blue eyes, red where the white is supposed to be.

"Hello Wifey."

My wife." Robbie says gleefully.

I could say something, I'm desperate to in fact but his eyes have me frozen in fear.

He strokes the top of my head like I'm a dog.

"Oh baby. It's so good to see you." he continues, pressing his lips to my head. My skin prickles instantly as I feel his salvia on my face.

I hear throat clearing, and look behind him. There are several high men all staring at me.

"Boss can I have my payment?" Hulk asks, eyeing up the table.

"So rude, interrupting our reunion." Robbie mutters to me.

He straightens back up and turns around.

"Oh the table Sid, oh and boys piss off with him for a little bit."

Hulk picks up a few bags of the white powder and the men follow him like dogs after a bitch on heat up the stairs.

"Where were we?"

Robbie tilts my chin up and starts to attack my mouth with rough kisses, I don't return the kisses. In fact I'm scared if I open my mouth I will vomit everywhere. My bladder is now stinging, My third trimester half hour wee schedule has majorly disrupted.

"Robbie, please can I go to the bathroom?"

"Sure I will take you," he unties my legs allowing me to stand.

"SHIT you're pregnant!!" Robbie screams.

I look down at my enormous stomach and back at him surprised. How did he not know that? How did he not see that?

"Yes,"

"FUCKING HELL!" he screams, tugging at hips short hair.

I don't know what to say or whether I should apologise so I just stay put.

"Where's the bathroom?" I ask.

He points to a door to the side where I go and use the toilet. There isn't even a window or anywhere to wash my hands so I return slowly back to where he is.

"Sit." Robbie snaps, pointing to my chair.

Emotional Robbie has gone, now is angry Robbie whom I fear the most of all his personalities.

I sit nod shut my eyes.

A loud smack echoes around the room. I hear it before I feel his fist leave my cheek bone.

"You disobey me and now you are having an affair? You dirty slut!"

I hold back my cries as he hits me a second time.

"There is no affair .We have not been together for nearly three years. We are divorced," I say quietly through my bloody nose.

"No, no no!" he cries out.

"Robbie what is this all about? Why have you been after me?" I ask tiredly.

He stares at me in disgust.

"This is about revenge. It's about taking back what is mine," he snarls.

"I am no longer yours,"

"Martin will pay. He will pay for everything he has done to exile me, to make me leave my precious wife. I am more powerful than he will ever be now," he continues ranting, ignoring me completely.

"This is between you two. Why drag me into it?"

"You have also wronged me," he grips my chin tightly. "You have divorced me after everything I have done for you. You have been having an affair, some dirty shit has been fucking my woman and now you are having his child. Not mine." he yells, spit spraying my face,

Anger curls in my stomach. After everything he did to me, continues to do to me and yet he still thinks I am to blame? I knew he had a few screws loose when we were together but now I think he has lost touch with reality altogether!

"There is no affair, we are not together and are no longer part of my life," I inform him.

"Liar, you belong to me!" he yells back at me.

I look into his eyes. The pupils are so large you can barely see the blue; they're black and red; the eyes of a monster.

"Let me go please," I beg, part of him somewhere loved me deep down, beneath the drugs.

He moves away and begins pacing the room.

"LADS!" he calls suddenly.

The guys slink back into the room, buzzing.

"Go fetch Martin. I'll stay with my wife."

They nod and walk back out of the room.

The way they obey him makes me realise he really has changed for the worst. He isn't just some little drug dealer any more. He has employees. He has got big somehow.

 He heads to the table and takes out a huge white bag. I've seen little packages in my time, but this bag alone had to be worth thousands of pounds. He lines up, and I look away in disgust.

"So you are some big time drug dealer now?" I ask.

"Yep, I am rich and loving it,"

"So you didn't think to help your poor wife out whilst she was being beaten and robbed for your debt?"

"Martin hurt you?" he asks in alarm.

"Frequently. He used to take my wages to pay for your debt,"

Robbie stands up.

"That fucker will die. I will slice his fucking throat out for touching you."

Despite what he did to me, I was still stunned to hear the violence in his voice. He meant it.

"Robbie don't. He isn't worth it,"

"Oh he is, he really is worth it. I am invincible. No pigs have ever found me. I have made myself better, stronger and wealthier than ever before. I will fix everything baby. Starting with that." he said and points to my stomach.

My chest is thumping so hard, my head spins.

"What?" I blurt.

"That is standing in the way of us," he points again at my stomach.

"My baby?"

"Your bastard, but don't worry. I will take care of it, of you, of everything. I love you, despite everything you have done. I forgive you" Robbie says kissing my face between his words.

"Please Robbie, I beg you. I will do anything you want, but please don't hurt my baby," I cry out, tears spilling down my face.

"Once it's gone, we can start afresh. We can get re married, Move away from this shit hole, go to Cuba to live a life in paradise." he say dreamily, unaware that I am crying.

"It's going to be perfect, you in a bikini, sipping cocktails in our Villa's swimming pool." he continues.

I cry harder.

"Just you and me. What do you say?"

"I would rather die." I spit out.

Robbie stares at me in shock.

"What did you say?"

"I said I would rather die. You killed our baby and what will you do to this one?" I ask.

Robbie runs his knife gently on my stomach.

"Kill it too. I do not share." he whispers.

I scream then.

"I hate you. You touch my baby and I swear I will beg you to kill me."

Robbie's eyes sharpen.

"You would rather die than be with me?"

"Yes."

He takes a gun out the left pocket and lifts it to my head. "Who am I to deny my wife?"

Robbie yanks my head back and kisses my mouth. I can taste my own blood on his lips as his tongue try to part my lips, despite me trying not to let him, he pushes through kissing me sloppily.

When he finally pulls away I feel nauseated, still able to taste him. I'm so overwhelmed I hear the gun shot noise, before I feel it.

I can't help but scream hysterically as my thigh bursts open. Blood explodes from my thigh like a bottle of shaken up coke.

"Shut the fuck up,"

"You shot me!" I cry out in horror.

Robbie looks at his gun stupidly.

I retch.

"Oh for fucks' sake." A plastic bag is thrust under my nose as I throw up noisily into it.

When I finally finish throwing up everything in my body, I look up at him. He has the gun still in his hand; he looks completely and utterly insane.

"There, there baby." he coos and hands my lukewarm beer. I gulp it down, washing away the sick and the flavour of him.

"Have you completely lost it altogether Robbie? What do you want? Do you us to play happy families or do you want to kill me?" I gasp. My leg feel like it is on fire, the burn of it is sheer agony.

Robbie beams at me, disturbingly and squeezes my uninjured thigh.

Tears blur my eyes as I see my unflattering pyjama bottoms are stained crimson down one side, blood spilling out over the floor.

"Please Robbie stop," I beg.

"It's me or that bastard inside you."

Nick was right all along. I should never have tried to bring a life into this world. My world is with psychos' like Robbie in it. It is too dangerous to be responsible for another life. I have let my son down. I should have had an abortion, it would be kinder. Even if there is a chance I could survive this, I could never survive loosing him.

I raise my head up and look Robbie straight in the eyes. "Him, I love my baby more than I ever loved you, more than you could ever love anyone."

I barely hear him screaming in rage. It washes over me as I think about the son I will never meet. Somewhere in the distance I see the gun is dropped and he grabs a large knife from the table. I can't even feel the pain of the knife as he slices through me over and over again. Black dots swarm my vision, everything is dimming. Mummy loves you baby, and I am so sorry, so incredibly sorry.

"You fucking bitch, I love you so damn much" I hear faintly before the welcome darkness ascends over me.

Chapter Thirty One- George

George's work phone rings as he is in bed, Danielle's legs wrapping around his like a cobra's.

Groggily, he reaches for it.

"Alarm code 183 activated." Derek our D.C.I. shouts over the phone.

George tries to break free from her as he thinks of whose alarm it belongs to.

Alarm 183- Holly Turner's alarm!

"We you need a team of about twenty, I'll get the cars ready and text you the location asap" Derek barks through the phone.

"See you in a few," George replies.

"Off again?" Danielle's swollen lips pout.

George throws back the duvet and changes into his crumpled uniform. He couldn't even face her.

"Yep," he replies, grabbing his gear.

"Bye then," she yells as he slams the bedroom door shut.

By the time he got to his car, he has the location.

Eastmore, clever girl no one would think she would be there. Problem is that it is over twenty minutes away.

George grabs his siren and activates it.

The sound of it fills his ears as he zooms through the streets.

Eighteen minutes later George pulls up at a quiet cottage to find the front door locked.

Without hesitation he bursts through the door and follows the alarm's location through his phone.

George finds a bedroom and realises its Holly's by the sight of the bassinet next to her bed.

The alarm location is pinging crazily as he steps through the room.

Her handbag is by her bed open.

Hunting through he finds the alarm.

"They gone?" Steve, a junior P.C. asks as he enters the room.

"Yeah, they have gone." George sighs.

Holly is in trouble and he doesn't have a clue where she or Robbie is.

"Go question the neighbours," he barks to Steve.

Come on think, think, think George he mutters to himself as he scans the room.

A cute teddy bear peeks out from the bassinet alongside perfectly folded blue blankets.

It is going to be a boy, he thinks stupidly.

"A woman said she saw a dark blue Volvo park up by the cottage at four pm" someone tells him.

"Plates?"

"She didn't think to write them down,"

"Fucking hell" George yells.

"Right lets split up. I will lead a team by Martin Smith's usual hangouts see if we can get any answers. I need Clive to lead a team questioning here, and the rest stand by 999 emergency calls."

The separate teams head out.

It is over two hours later parked in a cramped car by Martin Smith's apartment when a dark blue Volvo parks up.

Frank is already writing down the plate, which is obviously fake given the Volvo must be over twenty years old and the plate is this year's.

A bunch of our usual suspects get out, Robbie's boys.

"Are we going in?" Kyle asks.

"Not yet. Stick a tracker on the car,"

Kyle pulls a hoodie over his uniform and discreetly walks across the road.

"You don't think the girl is in there?"

"No, she will be with Jones."

Robbie won't let her out of his sight. His cronies are in there, which means Robbie is finally making his move, with Holly to witness it.

Fuck, she doesn't know half of what he done since he left. Rumours have it that he travelled to America and smuggled in hundreds of thousands of pounds in heroin and crack. How the hell he managed it and get it in this country George has no idea. Robbie got smart somewhere down the line. Someone like him getting brains is a lethal combination. His only weakness though is Holly. He can't seem to let her go. If he forgot about her, and immigrated he could be leading a very comfortable life somewhere.

George thought Nick was an idiot until he finally met her. Hell, now he can see why Robbie can't leave and why Nick is so wound up about them. Nick is clearly in love with the girl, despite his 'good nurse' bullshit. She is something special, innocence and sweetness just surrounds her like a halo. He can't quite see how his fiancé fits into the mix, but that's his issue. George only wants to protect her and bring that abusive, sick bastard to justice.

The doors open and they spot Martin and his gimps being dragged into the car.

"Follow that car." George says to the other two drivers on the intercom.

After a good hour or so everyone pulls up at an old farm house.

From the outside it looks like a normal place but they all know the shit goes down in the basement.

They have back up; about twenty more officers are arriving and ready to go.

George counts down as they surround the back door of the basement. A team is waiting inside and another on the outskirts of the building.

"Go!"

George bursts into pandemonium. Robbie's lads have knives up to every one of Martin's boys as their eyes are on Martin. Robbie has Martin on his knees, a gun pointing into his face.

"POLICE!" George and hit team shouts.

George's eyes are on a very angry Robbie.

"Mr Jones, put down your weapon, you are under arrest." he hears someone say.

Robbie smirks and pulls the trigger, showering George with brain and blood.

"Fucker, put the weapon down." George roars.

Another gun shot rings out.

"No, bastard, no."

He watches as a member of his team falls helplessly to the side.

Suddenly everyone is loose and attacking every on of all sides.

Gun fires are being echoed from all over the place like a machine gun.

George heads behind Robbie and knocks the gun from his grasp after he puts three bullets in one of Martin's boys.

"Got you fucker." he hisses.

Robbie's eyes fill with rage.

"Fuck you," He spits out.

"You are under arrest" George begins, taking out his handcuffs.

Suddenly, silver glints in his eyes.

"No!" George yells trying to grab him but Robbie slices his own throat in front of him.

Coward.

George watches Robbie's blood cascading down his body like a volcanic eruption.

Robbie falls in a heap at his feet.

The fucker is dead, but a bitter pill swirls in his gut. He should have been brought to justice and paid for his crimes.

His team start to lead the remaining handcuffed crew members from either side away, whilst George and several of his team search for Holly.

It takes no time, just heading through the little door in the basement and there they found her unconscious and tied to a chair.

The floor around her was crimson and pooling around her.

"Ambulance," Carl shouts into the phone.

George can't take his eyes off her as his team rushes to help.

She is going to die, her and the child.

Chapter Thirty Two- Nick

"This time next month we will be husband and wife,"
Penny squeals down the phone to me.

"Yep,"

"Aren't you excited, even a little bit?"

I can actually hear pout through the phone.

"Of course I'm just..."

"Grumpy, tired, the usual I know,"

"Sorry,"

"You know what Nick, after chasing me for years upon
years, I honestly thought you would ecstatic about this,"
Penny snaps.

She has been snapping a hell of a lot these days. I can't
say I blame her, even saints have limits.

"Look Penny, are you sure this is what you want?" I ask
seriously. I don't make her happy. She tries so hard to
be everything she thinks I need her to be. But it's not
enough.

"Of course I do, I get a handsome husband, a better
position on the board. With our joint vote alone,
we could make miracles happen." she replies brightly.

I sigh. Yeah that does sound good. I get the same but with a beautiful, incredibly smart woman.

"Don't you want that too Nick?" she adds.

"Yes, yes I really do,"

"Good then stop being so analytical and grumpy."

My pager buzzes.

"Brutal stabbing, Ambulance on route, OR 2 ASAP"

"Gotta go Penny," I say quickly.

"But...."

I hang up rudely, In my line of work there is always an emergency, so there is no excuse but I just don't want to finish this conversation.

I walk briskly but I see a flash and find Tom running past like a sprinter.

"Mate what's the rush?" I yell ahead.

Tom spins around, looking distraught.

I catch up with him.

"What's wrong?"

"It's Holly." he yells.

My heart stops.

"What?"

"I overheard ambulance control. They identified the Brutal stabbing victim as Holly Turner. It's her, it's Holly," he cries out.

"Holly's last name is Jones." I correct.

Damn, so much for pretending I barely know that woman.

"Not since her divorce, her maiden name is Turner,"

"Holly." I whisper as I race with Tom to the door.

The ambulance arrives an eternity later. Two paramedics jump out and get the stretcher.

"HOLLY!" I hear Phoebe scream from somewhere.

"Female. late twenties, multiple stab wounds to chest, abdomen, arms and neck. Gunshot wound to the right thigh, heavily pregnant, foetus is in distress." the paramedics reel off to the staff.

Pregnant.

Stab wounds.

Gunshot wound.

Pregnant.

"Willis get over to OR 2 now!" someone roars.

Everyone is staring at me and I realise I am frozen to the floor. The stretcher and my team are already gone.

I need to save her.

I run to the emergency room to wash up. I can see her through the glass for the first time in months. Her perfect face is swollen and grey. But her lips are cyanosed. She is dying.

"Team, this is Holly, one of our own, we have to save her at all costs," I shout, snapping on my gloves.

"Chase up that ultra sound," Dr Sahri shouts, the paediatrician doctor on board.

We start to work the minute we undo the bandages the paramedics used to dress her wounds, blood cascades down her body.

"Baby is alive but the heart beat is far too faint, I think the amniotic sack has been compromised. We need to perform a C section," Dr Sahri informs us.

"She is losing way too much blood, we can't risk performing a C-section," Sam yells.

"We need to try to save the baby, if the mother has a high risk of fatality." Dr Sahri replies to me.

I can't speak. Everyone is looking at me but I am just opening my mouth like a goldfish, nothing is coming out.

"Do it." Tom cuts in authoritatively.

Usually I am the one to make that call, in-between priority surgeries.

"Nick deal with the neck" I hear Tom say after lots of white noise.

Immediately my gloved hands are covered in Holly's blood. By the time I have begun to stitch up the vital wound on her neck, I hear someone shout that the baby is out. I can't think of that as Tom is stitching up her thigh, Liam and Luke are working on the puncture on her left lung.

"Baby born par two, at roughly thirty weeks."

Thank god.

We work endlessly on Holly. It has been hours, she is being stitched up fast, but her body is not recovering quick enough. Even with the bags of blood we are putting into her, she has lost far too much blood, too fast.

The monitors suddenly bleep aggressively.

"She is in cardiac arrest."

I should wait for Neilson the cardiac specialist, but I grab the defibrillators and shock her heart.

"Come on Rag Doll," I yell.

It doesn't work.

I shock her again.

"Come on."

I throw the defibrillators and begin to pump her heart manually.

"Holly please, please." I am begging her now, my tears dripping over my hands as the pumping continues.

The monitors suddenly stop their bleeping.

"NO!" I hear someone scream. I think it's me.

Then a single bleep is heard. I hold my breath, thankfully another beep follows.

Her heart is working again. I sigh in relief, I've done It.

I drop back and watch as her vitals come back slowly, weakly, but they are there.

"That's its baby," I whisper, stroking her hair.

"We will finish up here boss," Sam says gently.

"It's okay,"

A hand is placed on my shoulder firmly. I look up to see Luke.

"No, Leave. Now." he tells me firmly.

Shaking, I glance around. Everyone is staring at me in shock.

Not knowing what to say or do I turn around, ripping off my gloves and leave the OR.

I still can't leave her though, my feet freeze by the window as I continue to watch them finish up on Holly. I can't stop it. I can't stop crying, not quietly either. No. Dr Willis is crying uncontrollably in front of all of the hospital staff on the ward.

I lost her. I nearly lost her.

"NICK!" a voice shouts next to me.

I look to find Phoebe standing next to me distraught.

"Hol..." her voice breaks.

"She's alive, we saved her." I breathe out. Whether her body and her mind will recover is a different matter.

"Oh thank god." she mutters and throws her arms around me.

I put my arms around her and hold her tightly. I have no idea why, but we both needed it. Phoebe cries in my arms, as I continue to watch my team finish putting Holly back together again. From the looks of the equipment they are bringing in, they are going to put her in an induced coma, for her recovery. The lack of the oxygen from the blood loss may have affected her brain.

"The baby?" Phoebe whispers.

"I don't know. It was born by C-Section." I say automatically.

Holly's baby! MY baby!

"Fuck" I yell and sprint towards the Neonatal Unit with Phoebe at my heels.

"Holly's baby?" I ask Patty in reception.

Patty looks up in surprise.

"He is alive, He is ten weeks premature. He is in an incubator and considering the trauma he is stable for now Dr Willis."

He. I have a son.

"Can I see him?" I ask her.

She looks at me confused.

"You will need to change and clean up, this is a very premature baby." she tuts.

Of course I am still in blood coated scrubs. Holly's blood. I still have my god dam scrub cap.

Sprinting back male scrub room, I have the quickest shower in history and return in clean scrubs less than ten minutes later. Patty shows me the little room where he is being kept.

Phoebe, the cheeky mare is already sitting down next to his incubator watching a blanket.

Stepping closer I peer inside the blanket and see his tiny, unnatural tiny form. He is so thin I can see his blood vessels through his purple skin. But he is here, alive, despite his traumatic, premature entry into this world. My child is here and he is the most beautiful thing I have ever seen in my life.

"He will be okay, he is stubborn like his father." Phoebe whispers.

I look to find her staring straight at me. I knew he had to be mine but seeing Phoebe just made it seem real.

"How much does he weigh?" I ask, looking back at him.

"One pound, eight ounces."

Shit.

"He is going to be just fine," Phoebe whispers and traces her fingers down the incubator.

"Will he?"

"He has to be." she tells me simply.

As I suspected Holly has been placed in an induced coma to allow her body and brain to deal with the stress of the operations. But I don't go to her, I stay with my son all night. One of his parents needs to be here, fighting for him. It's frightening that he doesn't move at all, he doesn't stir. The monitors bleeping, reassures me that he is alive.

I have some serious explaining to do to my team and to the hospital but I hide out here with him. Every hour I am I am in here is changing me. I can't even tear my eyes away from him for more than a moment or two.

"Dr Willis, Dr Sinclaire will be here to do a full examination on baby Turner in ten minutes." a nurse tells me cautiously.

Of course Penny will be here, this is her bloody unit.

"Thank you. I need to freshen up. Can you stay with him?"

"Sure."

The Nurse takes over as I head back to the scrub room. I am due in surgery tonight, but I won't be able to work. I grab much needed coffee and freshen up before walking back to the unit. I don't know what to say to Penny, or how to explain any of this. This was everything I wanted to avoid. It's going to be a disaster. By now I am sure the hospital rumour mill will be running into overdrive. I don't know what is going to happen, but one thing I am certain of. I cannot and will not abandon my son. I cannot pretend he is not here, fighting to adapt into a world he wasn't ready for. Holly isn't here to fight for him right now, but I am.

I head in and take back over from the nurse
eagerly. How is that I missed him?

I hear the tapping of Penny's heels before she even
enters the room.

"So it's true then? Patty and of course all my staff
informed me that you had been here all night."

I don't even look at her.

"I won't leave him."

She sits next to me.

"I need to examine him. Would you like to help?"

I nod gratefully.

"Go scrub up. Get a mask, cap and gloves on."

I do as she tells me.

As I return, she opens the incubator. She expertly and
gently picks him up, with his thermal blanket on.

"Hold him, whilst I do his checks." Penny instructs.

I hold my arms out to receive him. I am utterly petrified.
He is the tiniest human I have ever seen.

"Support his head and keep your hands on the blanket
at all times. It's too cold for him without it."

I do, he is so light I can barely feel him in my arms. It's
like I am not even holding anything.

Penny is checking him over, but he is all I can
see. Tubes are all over him, one going into his mouth, I
watch his little mouth pucker up. It's the first time I have
ever seen him move. Then to my amazement his eyes
open the smallest fraction. I know he can't see me yet,
but his unfocused half gaze is on me.
I burst into tears.
"Nick!" Penny shrills. Alarmed, she takes him from me.
My hands are still open as I look down to find him gone.
"No, don't take him." I shout at her.
Penny looks at him and then at me, but says nothing as
she puts him back into the incubator. She listens to his
tiny chest, and does various tests on him, checking
every part of him and taking a blood test.
"Good set of lungs on him, his vitals are much better
than I hoped for. If they continue to carry on like this, I
think he is going to make it and have no long term
complications," Penny says writing down some notes
onto his chart.
He is strong and he going to be alright.
"Thank you."
She spins around looking every inch the professional I
have always respected her for.

"Right well I have some more checks to do. Can we meet up for a coffee in an hour?" Penny asks.

"Well I need..."

"You need to explain some things to me, and here is neither the time nor place," she cuts in.

"Okay,"

"Good, let's go to 'Benny's', I think you have caused enough drama here."

Penny takes her charts with her and walks out the door.

An hour later I sit in Benny's waiting for her. Phoebe is on compassionate leave and is taking over with the little guy for me.

Penny marches straight up to me; her professional exterior has been left at the hospital along with her white jacket.

"Is he yours?" she demands.

"Yes,"

"Are you sure?"

"Yes."

Penny slumps into the booth opposite me.

"Penny..." I start.

She holds her manicured hand up.

"Don't Nick. Let me see if I have figured this out. You have been sleeping with Holly Jones, you have gotten her pregnant and now you are a father,"

"It was over before we got engaged,"

"But you were sleeping with her whilst we were dating?"

I nod shamefully.

She sips the Earl Grey I brought her.

"I get that, I actually do, sowing your wild oats etc. before committing to me. It's not as if I said you couldn't. I expected you would so I am not mad about it," she says to me shocking the fuck out of me. I look at her face, she is completely calm. If she loved me, really loved me she wouldn't be calm, she would be hurt, angry, heartbroken.

"It's this baby thing. How could you have been so stupid not to have wrapped it up? Oh dear lord! The scandal!" she moans.

Again, it is all about the image, what others think of her. I think of Holly and all she has had to deal with everything that has been done to her and how she continues to fight. Penny is worried about a scandal? There are so many bigger things in the world than the public image.

"How could you be so selfish Nick? Do you have any idea what people will think of us now? You're a father and it's not my baby. I will have a stepson," she says in disgust.

"You don't really love me do you?" I ask quietly.

Her head snaps up.

"Of course I do. I admit it's not the kind of love in silly films or in novels, but I respect you, I admire you and I care about you. You're amazing in bed and I'm attracted to you. Isn't that enough?" she reels off but I can see the doubt in her eyes.

"I feel the same about you but it's not enough for me any longer. It's not enough to marry you,"

"It's the little boy, baby Turner isn't it? The way you looked at him, the way you reacted to him. Nick I have never seen you like that in all the time I have known you."

"I paid for him to be aborted. I paid Holly to get rid of him. How could I have done that?" I blurt out.

Penny gasps.

"You asked Holly to abort her baby? Did she want to?"

"No, she begged me not to make her. She told me she didn't want anything from me that she wouldn't tell anyone the baby is mine, but I refused."

Penny puts her hand over mine and I feel my insides ache again. The guilt that has been eating me alive ever since, is coming to a head as I break down for the second time in two days.

"You did it to protect me and our future. I can't agree with it, but I understand why," she says softly.

"I can't marry you Penny."

Her face falls but I tug her and she comes to me, folding her onto my lap.

"Oh god. We are supposed to be getting married in a month and now you're backing out!" she cries into my lap.

"I will take the heat. I will be the villain, and it's well deserved," I mutter to her and kiss her hair.

"I think you are amazing Penelope, you deserve more, you deserve a man who loves you with every fibre of his being, a man who puts you first and to be his everything."

"But me and you, we are perfect, we were supposed to be together." she wails.

"Are we? Or is this what our fathers wanted us to think, what we have been brainwashed to think?" I ask. I had thought about it long and hard last night.

"Maybe."

Penny stops crying and cuddles into me silently. I think she is thinking the same thing. Ever summer and Christmas we have been thrown together since we were kids. I was groomed to want women like her; rich, strong, medical background. We went to the same medical university together for goodness sake. Our fathers have always wanted us to be a couple, for the same reason we wanted to be, for a stronger vote on the board.

"How did you get so smart? This lovely dovey stuff isn't you. It's not just the baby is it?" Penny asks after a while.

"I operated on Holly last night, she was failing and I snapped. I broke down on the table and was sent out by my team."

"Shit." she sniffs. Penny knows me, she gets me. I am as cold as an iceberg in theatre. You have to be to be good at shutting it off or you won't survive.

"You love Holly."

I don't know what to say.

"I have fucked up so badly. I don't I can love, I pushed her away treated her like shit. I wanted that baby aborted not only because I wanted to marry you, but because I couldn't have him without her in my life. She hates me, and you should too." I cry out.

Penny listens and lets me rest my head on her shoulder. "You don't know how to love, neither do I. Our fathers royally fucked up teaching us what love is. But we can learn from this, we can be better, complete people." she whispers to me. The hope in her eyes gives me strength.

"You are one intelligent woman Penelope Sinclaire,"

"I saw the way you looked at that baby Nicholas Willis, and that has given me hope that I can feel like that too one day. I will be learning from you,"

"I don't know how to be a father. I don't know how to get Holly to not only forgive me but to love me."

"Becoming a father comes naturally. You just need to love him and care for him, as for Holly? I can't help you there."

I sigh in frustration.

"You know we kept thinking we need to be married to change this hospital. But we are like family, family is strength. We can change this hospital side by side without the romance," I tell her.

"Yeah, one in two marriages ends in divorce these days any way. We don't need marriage, we need this to be family." she smiles.

I smile back for the first time in a long time.

Penny slides out of the booth and off my lap.

"Oh and I will hold you to it, by the way," she grins as she stands up.

"What?"

"You being the villain, you can explain this to everyone. You're the asshole, I am the innocent victim," she laughs.

"I'll play the asshole. I happen to be exceptionally good at it."

As I head back to Holly's room I find George and his crew standing outside.

"George,"

"Nick, mate, I can't believe she pulled through," George gasps pulling me in for a hug.

"You heard?"

"No, I was there."

The hug he gave me was nothing as I squeezed him back with everything I had.

"Thank you, thank fuck for you," I mutter.

"Is the baby okay?" George asks, panic in his eyes.

"Yes. He is tiny but yeah, he is here"

George looks at me strangely.

"Can I meet him?" he asks.

"Of course, you saved his life,"

"Well it was a team effort but I will come another time, when I'm clean and not shattered. I'll bring a teddy or something," he shrugs, suddenly looking exhausted.

"Sure, I would love you to meet my son." I say proudly, it sounds so alien yet beautiful on my tongue.

George smirks.

"I knew it was yours fucker. What a shit hot mess you're in."

"How did you know?"

"Mate, I've seen her."

I laugh as George walks away from me.

Chapter Thirty Two- Holly

"Come on sweetheart." a faint voice echoes through the darkness.

Its foggy everywhere. There is a constant thunder in my head.

"Wake up Holly." the voice tells me again. This time it is clearer and louder.

My eyelids move and I push them open. The light is blinding and my eyes snap shut again.

"That's it sweetheart. Now you come back to us,"

I open my eyes again, slower this time. The bright, strip of lights suggests I am in a hospital. I take in the IV drip and the monitors next to me.

Why am I here?

Images of Robbie form in my mind.

My hands move to my stomach. It is empty.

"Baby!" I gasp.

A cup appears in front of me with a straw.

"Drink this." the voice says again. It's a woman's voice. One I think I recognise.

I obey and suck the straw greedily. The cool liquid coats my dry, sore throat. I glance at the woman. It's Linda,

one of the nurses I used to work with. Am I in my
hospital then?

"Linda?"

"Hey Holly," she smiles at me.

"Linda, where is my baby? What happened? Please tell
me he didn't…" I break off, unable to ask the rest. Tears
fill my eyes. He isn't here. I didn't protect him. Is he
dead because of my stupid past?

"He is okay. He was born, I promise you he is alright,
calm down." Linda tells me, stroking my face.

I take a deep breath and let her news soothe me. He
made it.

"Oh thank god,"

"Yeah him, Dr Sahri and of course Dr Willis and his
team,"

Nick. Nick saved him.

"Speaking of whom," Linda winks as the door opens.

I blink and Nick is standing before me.

"Holly," he sighs in relief.

"Thank you," I breathe out.

I haven't seen Nick in months. He looks exhausted, dark
stubble shadowing his face.

"You saved him; he wouldn't be here if it wasn't for you. Have you seen him?" I ask. My heart is thumping in excitement.

Nick nods. A smile spreads across his face.

"What is he like?"

"Perfect. He is getting stronger every day," Nick replies, and grips my fingers.

"I want to see him,"

"Soon. We need to make sure you are recovering first."

I glance down at my gown and gasp in horror.

Bandages, gauzes and dressings are covering most of my body.

I see Robbie, his face bunched up, the bloody knife in his hand.

"Holly, you are safe now I swear," Nick says faintly.

"What happened?" I ask again, the images still visible.

The door opens again and a flurry of nurse comes in with a couple of doctors.

"We will talk about that later" Nick tells me as he steps out of the way.

I breathe in and out deeply as I then become the patient.

I open my eyes and find its night time. I must have fallen to sleep as the last thing I remember is one of the doctors from Neurology talking to me. Chocolates, fruit and cards have appeared from somewhere. My body is aching and my head is pounding.

I don't think I could cope with any more, after hearing my long list of injuries. Honestly, it is as if I have been in a major car accident or jumped off a building.

My right thigh bone has been broken in three places by the bullet. I needed pins in temporary on to secure it, but will need surgery further on. My left lung has been punctured and needed major surgery. I have four broken ribs, a broken cheekbone and a broken nose of course. Furthermore my abdomen, arms, chest and neck required a serious number of stitches. Oh and I need a further operation on my neck due to nerve damage. But I made it and more importantly, so did my baby.

"Don't cry." I hear Nick say softly.

I didn't realise I was.

I glance to my left and see Nick is sitting in the visitor chair by my bed.

"What are you doing here?" I ask surprised.

"I haven't been anywhere else, just here and to Neonatal to see our baby."

He rubs his face tiredly.

"How long have I been out?"

"Five days, just to let your body heal."

Five days! Five days that my son has been alive, not knowing who or where his mother is.

"He has been alone for five days." I cry out.

Nick takes my hand.

"He has had me and Phoebe. He has been in good hands, just waiting for you."

I see softness in his eyes as he talks about him.

"Nick, I can't apologise for our son, but I am sorry, so sorry for the trouble I have caused,"

"Don't apologise for anything Hol, he is worth it."

Nick kisses my hand gently, sending a jolt through me.

"I'm the one who needs to apologise. I am sorry, none of this would have happened if it wasn't for me. I let you move away, to isolate yourself so he could find you. He nearly killed you and our boy. I could have prevented it if it wasn't for my bullshit that drove you away" he says, his voice breaking.

"No Nick, please don't blame yourself. My past was bound to get to me eventually. You were right; I had no right to try to bring a child into this. I don't blame you," I whisper.

"Holly I…"

"I am thankful. You saved me. You helped bring our son into this world safely. You protected me and you helped me way before he was even born. Do not feel guilty, please."

My eyes are closing before I even finish speaking.

"Rest Rag Doll,"

"I want to see my son," I cry out snapping my eyes open again.

"If you get a good night's sleep and your observation goes well in the morning. I will take you to see him." Nick says firmly.

"Then tell me what happened to Robbie. How did I get here?" I ask.

"No, I will tell you another time,"

"But…"

"You need to rest." he snaps.

I am losing the fight with my body, and him.

"Fine." I grumble as my eyelids force down.

I feel his lips against my head as I slip under.

The next morning when I wake up, and Nick has gone. Linda wake me up with breakfast, which I can't manage, my throat hurts too much, but I drink some milk after she nags me. I want a shower to clean up, but Linda tells me she would be bathing me later, much to my embarrassment. So I settle for a clean robe and Linda helps me to brush my teeth. She won't let me use a mirror. Apparently it will be unsettling and it isn't a good idea for me just now. The doctors come and do their checks and then Linda and another nurse I haven't met before lift me into a wheelchair. This is what I used to do, as much as I thought I understood how degrading it was for a patient, but I actually I don't think I did.

Just before eleven Nick comes through my door. I don't know if he stayed with me last night on that chair or if he found an on call room to crash in, but he definitely hadn't left the hospital. It looks like he is still wearing the same clothes as yesterday, looking to be honest completely and utterly un-Nick. His shirt is crumpled and untucked from his equally creased trousers. His hair doesn't look like he has brushed it in days, and is product free and sticking out in every direction. His stubble has grown and got darker overnight. My mouth dries up as I look at him. He is totally gorgeous, even more than usual, roughing it up.

"Coffee," he hands me a take away cup.

"Thank you,"

"Drink it fast, he seems to know you're coming, he has moved his head three times already," Nick says happily. I smile at that. I need to read up on premature babies later. He won't be like a normal baby, wriggling and alert yet, he probably has never cried or been fed normally either. But he will progress quickly I have missed a lot of changes already.

I drink my coffee impatiently. Warmth runs through me as I discover Nick remembers how I like my coffee.

"Let's go." I almost shout out.

The journey to the unit seems to take forever, but finally I am wheeled into a small room.

"Holly!" Phoebe cries out. She rushes over to me from the incubator and hugs me tenderly.

"I know it's not me you want to see right now, but I'll pop to yours for lunch. Bring you something yummy." she whispers in my ear.

I love Phoebe, but she is right. My eyes are glued to the see through box. A tiny figure is curled up inside.

I wheel myself so my nose is pressed up to the side of the incubator. A tiny little body is there, his features are so beautiful. Even premature I can see Nick in him. He is perfect.

Big fat tears roll down my cheeks as I stare at him.

Tubes and drips are everywhere, almost camouflaging him, but here he is.

His miniature head rolls and he is facing me. His eyes open. He is looking at me. I know he can't see me, but it's as if he knows where I am and who I am.

I hear Nick gasp but I ignore him.

"I love you," I say softly, my fingers touching the plastic where his face is on the other side.

"Shall I get him out?" I hear a voice behind me say.

I nod, unable to look away from him.

I watch a pair of hands expertly untangle him from his web of tubes and cover him with a specialised blanket. He doesn't move at all as he is lifted from his incubator and into my arms.

I try not to shake as this weightless baby tucks up against me. His eyes remain open.

"Hey you," I breathe.

"Did you see the way he turned his head to face her?" I hear Nick say proudly.

"I did. It is such good news. You would be amazed at the progress he will make now reunited with his mummy," the woman answers.

I turn at the woman's voice to find Penelope standing with Nick closely.

"Dr Sinclaire,"

"Hi Holly. I'm so relived to find you are making a full recovery," Penelope says brightly.

"Thank you for taking care of my son,"

"It's my job, and let's face it, who couldn't love this little guy?" she comes over to look at the baby.

"He is miraculous."

"Handsome, strong and stubborn just like his daddy." Penelope says looking at Nick fondly.

I am so confused. She knows the baby is Nick's and yet they are all cosy and perfect together. Shouldn't it be uncomfortable, the man, the mistress and the fiancé in the same room together? What has Nick told her? Or worse, what have they planned?

"I am so sorry Dr Sinclaire." I mutter. I am actually very

sorry for my part in this. I have affected her future as well now. Yet here she is, taking care of my son when I have not been able too. She is a better woman than me. I have always respected her as a doctor, but now my respect has grown for her as a person.

"He has a good set of lungs on him. They are growing well, taking fluids, responding. If he continues like this over the next few weeks I think he is going to be absolutely fine," Penelope informs me.

"Thank heavens."

Penelope comes closer to me.

"Time to go to sleep now handsome." she coos to him. I let her take him out of my arms and watches as she places him carefully back in the incubator.

Despite his tiny weight, my arms feel desperately empty.

"We had better go too," Nick tells me.

"No," I plead.

"Come on, you need to recover too."

I turn to the incubator sadly.

"Can I come back later?"

"You can come whenever you want Holly." Penelope says kindly.

Nick wheels me back to my room in silence.

He watches me as Martha and Annie put me into the bed like a child.

"So what name did you have in mind for him?" he asks.

"Sam." I reply

I didn't know I had decided on a name until it came out of my mouth.

I had a few names I adored in mind, but once I saw him, it was the only name that would suit him. Sam: the warrior. Just like my patient Sam who was a warrior to the very end. He was a precious star who meant to so much to both to Nick and I. The night we lost him, he was the reason Nick bared his soul to me. The night he let me in, the night we made love and conceived our son. It was also the night that I realised I was in love with Nick.

"Sam. That's perfect Hol" Nick whispers.

I look at him, and see realisation in his eyes. He understands the reason for the name.

He looks back at me. For a moment, I think I forget to breathe.

"So we should discuss his full name," he breaks off.

The door opens, perfectly timed with Phoebe's hip, as she carries the most enormous tray overflowing with food.

"Lunchtime lady time to catch up," she announces happily, placing the tray on the bed table.

"How much?" I ask laughing.

"Well most of this is for me but I got you some soup: carrot and coriander," Phoebe winks as she hands me a take away container and a spoon.

She knows me so well. When feeling low it is soup, always soup for me.

"Thank you."

Nick clears his throat.

"I'll step out then but can I come back in an hour or so?"

"Nope. I am her assigned nurse this afternoon and we have work to do," Phoebe replies.

"But.."

"No but Willis, you hogged her to yourself all day yesterday. My turn now," she glares.

"Okay, okay," Nick laughs.

They seem to have become friends in the short time I was out.

Nick leaves us alone. I love Phoebe. I do not want to start the arguments over Sam yet. I saw the way he looked at Sam, the love was written on his face. He wants him.

"So I am assigned to be your nurse today and after lunch we are going to have a shower," Phoebe tells me sharply.

"I can wash myself,"

Phoebe glares at me.

"No, you can't, so suck it up."

I want to cry at the indignity of having Phoebe and Linda wash me in the shower. I have to sit on the wash chair, whilst they scrub blood and goodness knows what else off my skin. Luckily for me I think they know not to treat me like a patient. They don't ask if the water is alright or chit-chat to me. They just get it done quickly not making eye contact with me.

"Babe, we need to cut your hair," Phoebe whispers to me whilst rinsing the shampoo out of my hair.

"What? Why?"

Linda's eyes well up as she looks at my head.

"Bastard!" Linda yells suddenly.

I put my hand to the back of head and notice large chunks of my hair are missing.

Phoebe pulls her face into a tight line.

"Why would he cut it?" she asks.

I don't remember him doing this. It must have been after I passed out.

"He loved my hair."

Both women looked at me.

"He loved my hair. He always threatened to chop it all off, he said no man would look at me twice without my hair. He said there was nothing else to look at," I continue miserably.

"Well I am glad the bastard is dead and burning in hell for all I care," Phoebe shouts.

"He's dead?" I cry.

Both woman look alarmed.

"Let's get you out of the shower." Linda says, turning the water off.

Phoebe wraps me into a towel and they lift me into the wheelchair.

"Phoebe, tell me what happened." I scream.

"I didn't know she didn't...." Phoebe pales.

"Well she does now. You better explain," Linda replies sharply.

They both put me on the bed and I turn to Phoebe.

"Tell me what happened."

Phoebe sinks to the chair by the bed.

"This shouldn't be coming from me. I thought Nick would have told you…"

"Phoebe, talk to me NOW,"

"George Harris and his team tracked you down. When they got to that farm house there was bloodshed. Martin's guys against Robbie's guys, anyway the police managed to get Robbie but he…"

"He what?"

"He stabbed himself," Phoebe finished.

"He killed himself rather than be arrested?"

"Apparently. They say that Robbie killed Martin in front of them, he would have been locked up for the rest of his life,"

"So he took the coward's way out." I mutter angrily.

Linda nods.

"You can take comfort in knowing that he won't ever be coming back." she says, taking my hand.

I don't know what to feel. A mixture of emotions is running through me all at once. I'm angry, and yet sad, relieved and also broken hearted. How is that even possible?

I loved him once, we were man and wife. I hate him now and all the shit he has done to me. But I didn't want him to die.

He deserved to be locked up for eternity, to pay for and reflect on what he did. Yet Robbie has again managed to escape justice. The perfect escape, he will never have to think about the sins he committed. If there is a hell, I hope to god he is in there.

"Thank you for telling me." I say thickly.

Phoebe hugs me.

"I'm sorry to be the one to tell you, I honestly thought you knew already,"

"I'm glad it was you."

After my hair is cut, I feel cold.

"It really suits you. Would you like to see?" Phoebe asks lifting the mirror back up.

I don't want to see myself again. I don't want to see my short hair and bashed in face. I squeeze my eyes shut.

431

"No thank you, I think I need to sleep." I mumble.

Phoebe hugs me tight and she and Linda leave me too it.

As the door closes I lie on the bed and feel the tears I had kept at bay come to the surface. I shouldn't be feeling like this. I am alive and so is Sam. So why does it feel that Robbie has once again destroyed my life? I have never classed myself as pretty, but seeing the disfigured, scarred face staring back at me in the mirror was unbearable. I can't believe Nick hasn't looked at me in sheer disgust. It must be his professional attitude being pushed to its limits. He sees me as a patient and not as the woman who was once his mistress. No one looked had ever looked at me the way Nick did. The way he acted like I was the sexiest, most beautiful woman on the planet when we were involved is a feeling I will cherish.

"Holly?" his voice slips through the door.

Great I am now a blubbering, ugly wreck and he is witnessing it.

"Sorry," I mumble. Luckily my head is facing the other way to him.

"Are you alright?"

"Yeah just sleepy,"

"Oh, not up for a chat then?" Nick says. I can feel him closing in to the bed.

"No."

To my dismay he sits down in the seat next to me.

"Okay, well you can listen whilst I talk then." he sighs heavily.

I move my head so I am not being rude, but I don't look him in the eyes.

"I have some news about Robbie," he starts.

"I know he is dead. Phoebe just filled me in," I reply.

"Right."

A thick silence coats the room.

"I am so sorry,"

"Don't be, you didn't kill him."

"Not about him. I am sorry I didn't protect you and Sam from this. None of this would have happened if it wasn't for me,"

"How can you say that? Robbie is, was, my problem not yours,"

"You left because of me. I drove you away and he nearly killed you and our son,"

"I made the decision to move away, you didn't make me,"

"I did. When you went against the abortion you had no choice but to leave, thanks to my threats and bullshit blackmail." he yells brokenly.

I look up in shock, to find Nick with tears in his eyes. It pulls at me. I honestly thought I hated this man when he tried to force me into ending the pregnancy. I didn't think I could ever forgive him nor would I want to. I was wrong.

"It is not your fault, please don't blame yourself. You were right, I endangered our child, and he could have been killed because of my past."

"No, thanks to you he is alive. If you had obeyed me then he wouldn't have been here at all. You going against me was the best thing you could have ever done,"

"I won't apologise for him Nick," I tell him truthfully.

"I don't ever want you to apologise for him, he is just... everything. I was such an idiot, now that he is here he has changed everything, he has changed me."

Overwhelmed by his words, I just nod stupidly. He gets it.

"How does Penelope feel about all of this?" I ask. As much as I don't want to share Sam, I will have to face reality that she will be Sam's Step Mother. I respect her though, and what better person to be a Step Mum than a paediatrician?

A nurse comes in then interrupting us.

"Sorry Holly, just giving you your meds before you go to sleep. You need rest. Tomorrow you are scheduled for your nerve operation," she tuts at Nick disapprovingly.

"Oh okay."

Nick moves back.

"Dr Willis, Dr Willis Senior and Dr Lawrence Sinclaire are waiting for you for Dr Sinclaire's office." she informs him.

I see Nicks face drop.

"Okay. Can you inform him that I will be up momentarily?" he asks.

The nurse scowls at being used as a messenger, but leaves.

"Go on Nick, I better rest any way" I go to roll on my side. It's how I feel most comfortable when I sleep, but a sharp sting makes me gasp. Of course I can't sleep on my leg, the stitches are stinging by my weight on them.

"Oh Rag Doll, come here," Nick groans and lifts me carefully off the bed.

"Get off me." I protest.

Nicks looks at me confused, but continues to hold me whilst putting a pillow on the bed length wards. He gently puts me back down, propping my leg against the pillow, but I can lie on my side without putting any weight on it. Instantly it makes me feel like I can sleep.

"Thank you," I whisper.

"You always sleep on your side, all huddled up." he replies fondly.

I can't help but smile, he knows how I sleep, and he remembers it.

"Good night Nick,"

"Night." he stokes my hair softly, it's soothing and I feel myself lured into sleep.

Chapter Thirty Three- Nick

Crap.

I haven't spoken to my father since Holly was brought in. I know he knows, judging by the not so pleasant voicemails he has left on my phone. I am about to face one very angry man.

I glance at the mirror, I look like hell. Days and days of stubble covers my face, my hair looks like something is living in it and I can't remember the last time I showered.

"Daddy." I hear Penelope pleading. I head that way hearing Lawrence cursing me.

"He has conducted himself shamelessly. He is just another prick who can't keep his dick in his pants,"

"Oh come on now Lawrence, he is just another bloke like us," my father replies weakly.

"No, he is the stupid one to think he can cheat on my daughter!" Lawrence yells back, just as I head into Penny's office.

They silence as they take in my appearance.

"Bloody hell Nick," Lawrence stands back.

"Good evening father. Lawrence, can we stop the insults and spreading more rumours in our workplace?" I ask coolly.

"Now looks here, young man," Lawrence blurts, red in the face.

"I understand you are angry at me, but I think Penny has suffered more than enough. She doesn't need to have yet more gossip about her from this uproar. We are after all in her office, her team is working close by." I argue.

Lawrence looks at Penny shamefully and shuts up.

"Son is it true?" father asks.

"Let's discuss this over dinner shall we? I haven't eaten properly in days; let's get out of here, where we can talk freely?"

"Good idea Nick, I have finished work anyway," Penny says kindly.

"Yes, but please change your appearance before you do?" my father asks.

"Of course. Why don't you three head to The Hilton and I'll quickly shower and change before meeting you there?"

An hour later, I am sat in The Hilton, drinking wine and eating steak. The atmosphere is distinctly frosty.

"So, you have been sleeping with another woman behind my daughters back?" Lawrence booms.

"Yes, but I ended it before we got engaged,"

"That makes it alright?"

"Father, in his defence, we were only dating. I didn't tell him we were exclusive." Penny says defensively.

I smile at her gratefully.

"And you believe this is acceptable?" Lawrence asks her.

"I didn't think it was unacceptable." she says quietly.

Lawrence looks at her in disgust.

"My dear where is your pride? Your self-respect?" he asks shocked.

"I knew what Nick was like; he is a total womaniser,"

"Like father like son," my father sniggers.

"I told Nick to get it all out of his system before we settled down. If not, I know he would have cheated on me whilst we were married. He was completely faithful to me after we got engaged." Penelope tells everyone.

"But now you have broken off the engagement?" my father asks her.

"Yes Michael, it was going to cause a scandal with the baby,"

"BABY?" Lawrence yells.

My father's jaw drop open. Obviously Penny hadn't told them everything.

"What did you tell your father?" I whisper to her.

"That we have broken off the engagement, due to your infidelity. It's not my place to tell them about the baby or his mother." she whispers back.

She would be correct. It is my job to tell my father that he has a grandson.

"Yes congratulations Dad, you have a grandson." I announce.

My father blinks then reaches for his tumbler of whiskey.

"A baby? Is this some kind of joke?" he snaps, after draining the contents.

"No, His name is Sam."

"Oh I love that," Penny says happily.

"Why are you so happy Penelope? You have been with a cheating bastard that has the stupidity to not cover up," Lawrence barks.

"I think that it may have been a blessing in disguise," she tells Lawrence.

"How is that so? You two are perfect for each other," my father asks.

"Yes, perfect in everything that doesn't matter. We are not in love, we can't make each other happy," Penny tells everyone.

"We care about each other greatly, but not enough to be married." I finish.

Both men look a strange shade of purple.

"Love? This isn't about love," my father yells.

"It's about being a team, about the numbers on the board. It's what we raised you to do. You owe us." Lawrence shouted.

"Now wait just a minute, are you saying that you don't care about our happiness, just about the power of the board?" I ask.

Lawrence's face goes red and my father's pales.

"No, it's not that," my father says quickly, but Penny and I have both seen it. I think we always knew it, but seeing it on their faces strikes us anyway. Penny looks like she is going to cry.

I put my arms around her gently as she leans on me for support.

"Well, you know what, we are still going to be team, and we are still going to have the power. Because Penny and I are a team, we always will be. We don't need to be married to each other to think the same," I tell them.

"I guess," father shrugs.

"Both of you need to understand that this is our life that you are trying to control. Ours, not yours and I think we both deserve a chance to love properly and to be happy." I add.

My father snorts, as a waiter comes by with a bottle of whiskey.

"Shall I pour sir?" the waiter asks.

"No, just leave the bottle," he replies.

"What the hell do you know about love boy? Love makes you weak,"

"It made you weak,"

"How dare you!"

"I do dare. All your advice on love is absolute bullshit. I fucked everything up because I was scared to love. I nearly married Penny because I knew I could never love her like that," I challenge him.

442

"You're a fool, a disgrace," my father says shaking.

"No you are and you too," I add to Lawrence. "

Penny is one of the best people I know, and she deserves to be loved with everything a man can offer, that's what you, as a father, should want for her."

"You have made a fool out of all of us." Lawrence yells back. I have hit him though, where it hurts. Honestly, I know he is a selfish prick, but he loves Penelope more than anything.

"I have and I apologise for the scandal. But we won't back down on this," I add holding Penny's hand.

"Fine. I have had enough of this," Lawrence stands up, draining his drink.

"I will drive you home Daddy." Penelope says standing up as well.

I lean over to kiss Penny's cheek. She has been so brave tonight and so wonderful to defend me like she has, after all I put her through.

"Show Michael the baby. Nothing warms someone like a new born" she whispers in me ear.

I smile and wave her and a slightly drunken Lawrence off.

"So you are disappointed in me then?" I ask my father.

"Disgustingly so,"

I signal for the bill.

"So I take it you don't want to meet your grandson?"

He looks at me then for a long time.

"Of course I do,"

"He is in the Neonatal Unit, back at the hospital" I smile.

"Why? Is he hurt? What happened?"

"He was born ten weeks premature. But he is fine, he is fighter like us,"

"Where's his mother?"

"She was admitted, she is on ward 8, after a brutal assault. That's what brought the baby on,"

"Is she going to be alright?"

"I hope so. She is through the worst of it,"

"Well then, let's go and meet my grandson." my father hides a smile and pays the bill.

"Oh my heavens, look at you." my father gushes looking at Sam, cradling him expertly in his large arms.

Somehow my father has transformed into this gooey, emotional blubber of a man in the presence of Sam. I have to admit it is proper freaking me out but pleasing me at the same time. It is strange but heart-warming.

444

"He looks like you," my father continues.

Maybe, I honestly can't see how something that beautiful can look like me.

"I think he looks like Holly,"

"Holly is the mother?"

"Yes."

"Holly, Is she the mistress you spoke of so long ago?"

"Yes,"

"Did she know you were going to marry Penelope? Did she know she was just a mistress?"

"Yes, I made a deal with her. She was trouble with some drug dealer..."

"She's into drugs?" my father says in disgust.

"Oh god no. Her ex-husband was an evil, abusive bastard. He skipped town and left Holly to the drug dealers." I explain.

"What a coward,"

"Anyway I got Holly to agree to be my mistress if I paid off her husband's debts to the dealer. The bastards hurt her, took her every penny. She was desperate and I swooped in so I could have her, she wouldn't agree be with me."

"Are you saying she turned you down son?" he asks in disbelief.

"Yeah," I laugh.

"Wow, impressive,"

"Not good for my ego, so I paid ten grand for her,"

"Clever,"

"Yeah, as bad as my motives were, it was one of the best decisions I ever made,"

"So what are you going to do about it?"

"Sam? He is mine and I want to be a father, an active one in his life," I answer heatedly.

"No I mean about his mother,"

"Holly, she is his mother and she will also be an active part of his life,"

"That's not what I am getting at,"

"And then what? We will work out an arrangement. I have to thank my lucky stars that she will even allow me to see him now. When she feeling better she may decide she doesn't want me in his life at all," I mutter.

"Well..."

"I screwed up. I didn't even want a kid and now I can't live without him,"

"What about her?"

"She hates me,"

"Do you hate her?"

"No! How could I? She is the most caring, strongest, most wonderful person I have ever met."

"Do you love her?"

That stops me in my tracks. That's the second time I have been asked that now. Do I love her? Before the pregnancy I knew my feelings for her were out of control. She has been in my every thought for longer than I care to admit. Now I won't and can't seem to leave her side. She has brought our baby into this world but not without sacrifices and heart ache. In doing so she has yet again created emotions in me I never thought were possible. Holly has given me something that has filled a void I never knew I needed filling, twice.

"I don't know, I don't know how to love." I whisper.

 I feel like a scared little boy. I have pushed these feelings aside, concentrating on Sam and on Holly's recovery. I haven't wanted to face them.

My father sighs heavily.

"She will ruin you,"

"She already had ruined me, I can't go back to the man I was before. I have all these feelings," I explain uncomfortably.

"Then you are in love."

I am in love with Holly. Hearing it from his mouth confirms it. I am in love with her and have been for a long time.

I nod stiffly.

This is where I disappoint my father, this is where our relationship changes.

"So what are you going to do about it?" I hear him ask, putting Sam back into his incubator.

"She loved me once, she told me herself. After all I have put her through I don't think she loves me anymore,"

"Only one way to find out." he shrugs putting on his coat.

I stare at Sam through the plastic.

"And if she doesn't?" I ask without looking at him.

"Then you brush it off, hide your pain and try to make it work for your son." I feel his hand clamp on my shoulder.

I spin around.

"I am going against everything you ever taught me,"

"Yeah well, I am a bitter, cynical and hateful man. It's no doubt my fault you made the choices you made." he tells me guiltily.

He goes to leave.

"You can come and see Sam any time you want." I call out.

A smile reaches across his face, a genuine gut wrenching smile. It has been years since I have seen him smile like that.

"Thank you son."

I smile as he leaves.

It has taken me a couple of weeks to get my head together, accept the truth of my feelings for her and plan my next steps. I haven't been around her as much as I should have, but when I'm there I just want to blurt everything out and it's not fair. I need to know myself and know I am not going to screw it up as usual. Holly had her nerve operation. Fred, the neurologist assures me everything was successful. She also has had the operation to fix her broken thigh bone. Everything is going to be fine now. The road to recovery is well underway. Physically she is fixed. It now leaves the psychotherapy, cosmetic and physiotherapy to go now. It won't be long until she is discharged and she can go home. That's the problem; I want her to be in my home with me. Thankfully I have been granted me paternity leave and not that I have worked since Holly was brought in. Sam is by far the most visited person in the entire hospital, all my co-workers and Holly's have come to bring gifts to our son. He will be discharged in a few more weeks, but he is strong and changing every day, looking healthier. I love the fact that he looks at me now. He can hear me enter the room and he just rolls his head to my direction. He does the same with Holly and annoyingly Phoebe.

I am going home after visiting hours now too, as I am on leave I have to follow the rules like everyone else. Well mostly, but I try my best. Entering the hospital I am congratulated and greeted as I head to Holly's room. Today is the day I lay it all out there.

"Good morning Rag Doll," I smile as I go in, holding take away cups of coffee in my hands.

"Morning." she is neutral as usual. Her face is healing up well. Her cheek bone will take time, but her nose is no longer swollen and the bruises are starting to fade.

"I need to talk to you and I know you don't have any visits until gone two today," I open up with.

"Okay," she says slowly. I can see a flash of panic in her eyes. What does that mean?

"So I guess you know that Penelope and I are no longer getting married,"

"I heard. I am sorry for my part in that Nick," she replies guiltily.

"I'm not, she isn't either," I shrug.

"You said this would happen if I kept the baby, she wouldn't marry you. It's my fault,"

"Yep it is," I grin.

"I have ruined you." she cries.

I smile harder. She does care and she doesn't hate me. This is good.

"Don't smile that smug grin at me like you're not angry at me," she snaps, noticing my face.

"You have not ruined me, we called off the wedding because we are not in love with each other,"

"You have never been in love with each other, that wasn't the reason for your engagement,"

"No I didn't think it did matter, but now it does,"

"Why?"

"Because I am in love with you," I whisper and take her hand.

I look at her, her hazel eyes filled with shock. That's right Rag Doll, I actually said it.

She doesn't say anything for a cool minute.

"No you don't," she whispers back and takes her hand out of mine.

"I do," I say defensively.

"No you don't Nick. Don't fuck with me," she spits out.

Shit, this was not how I wanted it to go. When I practised it, she would tell me she loved me too and we would kiss and maybe even have sex in the hospital bed...

"I am not fucking with you Holly,"

"Don't lie to me Nick, just don't okay,?"

"Holly…"

"Listen, we can make parenthood work without us being romantically involved. I can see you love Sam, I won't stop you from seeing him,"

"I do love you. I've loved you for such a long time. I loved you when you said you loved me all those months ago. I just couldn't face it. I didn't understand what I was feeling. When I saw you brought into the hospital, I lost my shit in theatre. I couldn't lose you Holly, you and Sam mean everything to me." I tell her slowly, choking up a little like a pansy.

Holly stares at me coldly. She doesn't believe me, or worse she doesn't care.

"You chose Penelope over me, remember, when you made me hide whilst she came in and blew you?" she says in disgust.

Shame fills me all over again. That really was low.

"I know I did. It was such a shitty thing to do. It wasn't that I wanted her, it was because I wanted you too much. I didn't want to face what I felt for you, so I pushed you away like the selfish coward I was,"

"Well you certainly did that,"

"Penny was the safe option. I knew she could never hurt me like you could. You could hurt me, you could destroy me Holly. That's love for you," I cry out, trying to make myself heard.

"No, that's guilt Nick," Holly shouts back.

"Rag Doll..." I try to sound calm.

"Don't call me that Nick, I am not your rag doll. I stopped being yours when you told me to abort Sam. You couldn't possibly have loved me if you could have even asked me to do that." she yells.

I hang my head in disgust. Yeah I guess she does hate me. I really can't blame her for refusing me. She does not believe me. So now I get to feel the burn my father warned me about. And shit does it burn.

Chapter Thirty Four- Holly

December 17th has finally arrived!

I am finally being released from hospital today after six weeks and two days in hospital. The only down side is that Sam won't be home for another few weeks, roughly six to seven weeks Penny has informed me depending on his weight. He is doing amazingly well, no set backs or problems. He is just still far too below the weight he should be and not strong enough to be off the oxygen. Apparently it is all very normal and we should be overjoyed that there are no complications currently.

I am grateful and blessed. It just feels wrong to be apart from him. I have been with him as much as I can be, in between the follow up consultations and therapy. Now I have to come during visiting hours like everyone else.

I finished packing over an hour ago and changed into real clothes. Well a long dress much to my dislike (trousers are really hard to do solo) and a thick cardigan. That took ages, but it's done and now I am currently re-reading a mystery novel Phoebe brought up for me.

Finally Phoebe opens my door and steps in.

"Are you ready to go?" she asks, not looking at me.

"Waiting on discharge papers," I grumble.

"Oh, well I can go get us some coffee."

I study her and she is still not looking at me.

"What's up chick?" I ask.

"Nothing," she says brightly.

"Bull,"

Phoebe flushes a bit.

"Right, coffee." she mutters and before I can say anything she scarpers out the door.

What was that all about?

With a huff I get back on my bed carefully. Those physiotherapy sessions are helping so much in my movements since the operation. My right leg is just so weak now. I couldn't even stand on it for more than a minute the first couple of days. Now I can manage very short trips. The rest is crutches or the wheelchair. But I will get there eventually.

The cosmetic surgery can't be performed for at least six months on most of my body so I am still one frightful thing to look at but the psychotherapy is helping me deal with that. My daily visits are going down to three times a week, which scares me. Considering when I was first

456

told I was going, I hated the very thought of it. It has soon become my lifeline. Dr Melanie Travis my consultant is my new god. She can bring me out of the dark thoughts, the nightmares and fears and help me refocus on the tasks ahead. Get better, be a healthy mother to Sam, move on.

The door reopens and Nick comes in.

"Guess what I've got?" he says holding my papers.

"Yay," I cheer as he comes closer to the bed.

"Let's get you home." he whispers.

I can smell his aftershave which makes my skin prickle. I thought things would be awkward after he told me he loved me. I thought he would stop coming to see me. But that hasn't been the case; Nick is around whenever he can be now he is back to work. He works his shifts, sees Sam and then crashes in my room every day or night. In fact Linda has made him up a bed on the other side of the room. He even used my shower, toilet and my wardrobe. It's as if that conversation didn't happen, or in his head it went a hell of lot differently. Those days are over now though, we will be going our separate ways now I'm heading back to the flat I lived in with Phoebe. He will be back in his lonely, cold apartment.

I meant what I said to him though. He doesn't love me. He is talking out of guilt. He has realised his mistakes and now wants penance for his wrong doings. You can't force a family together and I would rather raise Sam separate than together unhappily. Nick was not meant to play happy families. We still need to sort out arrangements but he refuses to make any plans until Sam is out of hospital and safe. I accept that.

We get on well as friends.

"Phoebe is getting coffee but she has been gone ages,"

"Alright well let's head out slowly. We can pass the canteen on the way."

I sit up and swing my legs to bed edge. Nick goes to help, but my hand stops him. I need to be more independent. Soon Sam will be home and I need to be completely mobile.

I get up slowly and move to the wheelchair. Baby steps but it still pleases me.

"Wheel on Willis,"

Nick pushes me though the ward, stopping constantly so I can thank everyone and get hugs from my friends and my carers these last six weeks. I was embarrassed that my former co-workers know what happened to me, and see me now, with all the stitches but Melanie soon knocked that negativity out of me.

Next we go to say goodbye to Sam. He turns his head to face me as we draw up close. I love that. It's as if he can sense me.

Fear clutches me as I look at his gorgeous little face. I don't want to leave him. He has lost his lanugo now and his hair is growing. It's so dark I am sure he will look a lot like Nick.

"I don't want to leave you baby boy," I choke out.

I feel Nick's hand on my shoulder. It comforts me knowing he is there for us.

"I know Hol, it's not fair but you are still going to come and see him every day,"

"It's not the same, we won't be under the same roof or anything,"

"He will have me, Phoebe, Penny, everyone that loves him. At least two of us will be under the same roof as him at all times."

That does reassure me. He won't be alone. He will be safe.

"I will be coming to see you every day." I tell Sam. He stares at me with his dark blue eyes as if he understands every word I am saying.

I feel Nick wheel me away but my eyes are glued to the person who is my everything.

"There you are." Nick shouts to Phoebe who is carrying three coffee cups in one of those paper trays.

"Sorry, I got caught up," she blurts out.

"No problems," I smile at her. She is acting strangely today. Maybe she is nervous about having to care for me in the flat by herself. I would be if the shoe was on the other foot.

The taxi ride is slow and tedious. My leg needs to stretch out.

The taxi driver takes a left, heading towards the ring roads, rather than downtown.

"Nick, he is going the wrong way." I grumble.

Phoebe glances at Nick nervously.

My stomach sinks. Where the hell are they taking me? As the minutes trickle of uncomfortable silence, I realise we are not going back to our flat. But as we go through the ring roads and head out into the country lanes panic seeps in. I know I haven't been myself, but who would be after that attack? They wouldn't lock me up in some psychiatric ward... would they? Nick, I can see him, the sly sneaky bastard. I can see him pulling the wool over my eyes but Phoebe?

"I am not mentally disturbed," I yell out in alarm.

"What?" both Nick and Phoebe gasp.

"Look, I know I am not Miss Sunshine, news flash I never have been. I am not traumatized or delusional. I just want to go home not some mental institute!"

The country lane turns into a drive and we pull up to a large detached house in the middle of nowhere.

"You are not going to an institute Holly," Phoebe giggles.

"Then why are we here? Why aren't we going home? Where are we actually?" I bark out.

Nick opens the door and fusses with the wheelchair in the boot.

"Phoebe!" I snap.

"Just wait." she whispers.

I get out of the car and get into the chair warily.

"Merry Christmas." Nick cheers.

I roll my eyes. As much as I have to be grateful for, I am not up for carol singing when my son is spending his first Christmas in hospital.

"This is your new home." Nick informs me, confused by the eye rolling clearly.

I gasp as it dawns on me.

"I brought it outright three weeks ago, no chain or anything. It's all ready for you"

Okay guilt is one thing, but a guilt buying an at least five hundred thousand pound house is just insanity.

I can't even make a sarcastic comment as he opens the door and wheels me around the downstairs of this enormous house.

In one word it's a dream. The sort of home you see on the television. It has a huge back garden, modern but elegant décor, a wonderful spacious kitchen and a beautiful living room. There is even a laundry room, an office and a playroom. It's surreal and way too much to take in.

Nick is talking eagerly about everything, but it's just a hum in the background. Buying his child a house, a big gesture yes, but this? This is outrageous.

"Let's go upstairs and you can see Sam's room" Phoebe squeals like a child.

"Wait." I croak out.

Nick kneels in front of me.

"Do you like it?" he asks.

"What's not to like? It's a poor girl's wildest dream," I mutter.

"But?"

"But this is all just so over the top it's stupid Nick"

Nicks face drops and I know I have hurt him. I should have just kept quiet.

"I'm sorry, I don't mean to sound ungrateful,"

"Let's help you upstairs." Nick says neutrally and they carry the wheelchair upstairs.

There are four bedrooms, two with en-suite bathrooms, and a family bathroom.

I am pushed into one and gasp I delight. It's Sam's room, fully decorated and complete with furniture. It's painted in a jungle theme, full of animal stickers and green trees. His cot is more the size of double bed, plenty of room for cuddles. Then I see the toy boxes with more toys than I could imagine possible overflowing everywhere. It's everything and more than I could wish for my son. He has everything and anything he could possibly want. Even his wardrobes are brimming with adorable outfits.

"Oh my gosh Nick, this is just mind blowing,"

"It will be complete when he is here," he replies.

"Yes,"

"Right I will go make some coffee and leave you to arrange everything else." Phoebe says quietly to us. She heads downstairs.

"What else do we need to arrange?"

"Sleeping arrangements,"

That spins me. He wants to live with us? Of course, he brought this dream house and expects to live in it to. It's more than fair. But living with him?

"You want to play happy families? Mum, Dad and baby all under the same roof?" I ask.

"Yep, well I don't want to play it. I want to be a happy family."

He wheels me into the next room which has a huge four posted bed in the middle, his and hers end tables and a beautiful dressing table complete with mirrors next to the wall long built in wardrobe.

"Shit." I gasp. It had to be bloody perfect didn't it?

I stand out of the wheelchair and lay on the softest bed in history.

"Do you like it?" Nick hovers over me.

"It's alright I suppose," I joke.

"Please say yes? I love you." he begs.

He loves me. His eyes tell me he does, but how can he love me now? He didn't love me before, why should he now?

"I don't know if I believe you Nick. Honestly all of this is just overwhelming and generous. But then you always have been over generous. I need time." I say slowly. Do I love him? I did once very much, parts of me knows I love him still but after all the hurt, can I trust him not to hurt me again? Right now I don't know.

He lies down next to me. I can feel the heat of his body close to mine. Not quite touching me though.

"Ok, at least this time you're not yelling at me."

I snort at that, yes I was a real bitch the last time he told me he loved me.

"I just don't understand what's changed Nick,"

"Nothing has changed. I have loved you for such a long time. I just know it. Now I do and I won't give up Rag Doll, you said you loved me once." he tells me earnestly.

I can't say anything. If I do the dams will burst.

After a minute he sits up.

"I have the room across the hall, Phoebe has the room next to you."

"But..."

"I figured with us both here whilst you recover and when Sam comes back, it will be easier on you,"

"What happens if I don't want to be with you?"

"Then you keep this house and I will move back into my apartment. But let's not think about that, as it won't be happening." he winks.

I huff in frustration. He can still be the arrogant prick we all know.

"Thank you so much Nick, for this dream home,"

"You're welcome." he sits up to get off the bed. I move to sit up too, when he spins around and kisses me. The world blurs as his lips press on mine. He tastes like heaven. I want to deepen the kiss, but he pulls away before I part my lips.

"Let's go and have coffee." he jumps up, holding his hand out for me.

I allow him to help me, feeling dizzy and I know it has nothing to do with my injuries.

Chapter Thirty Five- Nick

The weeks fly by with Christmas and New Year being the busiest times of the year for us at the hospital. All the parties and drunk drivers, and of course family fights has been the reason why the hospital beds are overflowing.

Holly is recovering well. She no longer has the wheelchair at all and is walking around independently or with crutches for bigger trips. She seems to be more herself each week and is having consultations now for cosmetic surgery for her scarring. Not that it bothers me in terms of her appearance. She has always been so beautiful, scars or no scars they don't change that. But it matters to her confidence and it will bring her one step closer to me. So I am on board for that.

That woman has me in awe. If I hadn't loved her already, I would have fallen in love with her now. Her determination and courage to get back to her herself again is inspiring. Many would have given up or fallen into the dark hole of depression. Not her. She isn't exactly shouting out her successes but that steely determined look in her eyes turns me to mush.

I change into my jeans and go to Sam. It's just gone nine now, and he has his bottle at nine twenty so I head over there. I like to give it to him whenever I can. He is so alert now and likes to touch my fingers whilst I feed him. That's his new accomplishment; his ability to touch and explore with his hands and feet, its adorable.

I head in there when I find Penny with him.

"Hey Pen." I beam at her. She is holding Sam, who seems to have grown bigger overnight again.

"Morning, look at you. Such a handsome little chap like your Daddy." she coos to him.

I laugh and take him off her. He doesn't need the specialised equipment any more, but he still needs his oxygen tanks and drips.

"Good morning my boy," I talk to Sam. I see his recognition in his eyes. He knows his daddy now. Or at least that's what I believe.

"I have some good news," she says to me.

"Yeah?"

"Sam has gained another three ounces this week,"

I look at her excitedly.

"Does this mean he can come home?"

"Yes, I think we can discharge him next week. He has two ounces to go to make four pounds," she informs me.

"Oh mate, get drinking!" I cry out, putting the milk bottle in his mouth.

Sam drinks eagerly.

"I'm so happy for you," Penny says and hugs me.

Our friendship is getting stronger week by week. She is happy and even been on a couple of dates recently.

"I can't wait to tell Holly,"

"Tell me what?" I hear her voice coming into the room. She is wearing jeans and a hoodie, looking so much like her old self I could laugh. They are baggy and ugly but she looks stunning to me, always.

"Sam has two ounces left to go before he can be discharged. It could be next week," I tell her.

"Oh my gosh!" she gasps and walks independently to him.

I hand him over instantly and she cuddles him.

"I love you so much Samuel Nicholas Wills," she whispers. Yep we have decided on the full name a week ago. It makes me fill with pride for him to have my name. I wish she would say 'I love you' to me. But seeing her like this is enough.

"He has gained another three this week," Penny tells her.

"Oh this is just amazing news." Holly.

They also seem to be bonding over Sam. I think one day in the future they will become firm friends.

"Where have you been?" I ask her. I should know this; I have her schedule of consultants and therapy but this one I didn't know about.

"Another cosmetic consultant, they had a cancellation and called earlier,"

"Right, all okay?"

"Yep, I have healed enough so they are booking me in for my cheek and neck, should be in the next few months. The rest of the scars aren't ready," she replies smiling.

"That's fantastic news, what an amazing day, shall we celebrate?" I ask taking her hand.

"Sure"

"Why don't we go out for dinner?" I ask.

"Um no, I don't…" she hesitates.

I instantly kick myself. She is still so self-conscious about her appearance. I don't notice it, but others do. She won't go anywhere except the hospital and home.

"Sorry, I wasn't thinking. How about a takeaway then?
Just us, Phoebe is on nights,"

"Yeah that sounds nice,"

"Okay right then my little man, time to go, bulk it up," I
say taking him off Holly and back into Penny's arms.

I kiss his little hand whilst Holly kisses his head tenderly.

"I hate saying goodbye," Holly says sadly as she gets in
my car.

"I know, it won't be for much longer though,"

"How was work?"

"It wasn't a good shift. We had a high speed collision car
crash, three out of the four didn't make it and the fourth
may be paralysed, her spine was fractured badly. We
saved her, but whether or not she will want to be saved
when she wakes up is a different matter,"

"I miss it,"

"Miss what?"

"Working."

I know she does. She quizzes me on my shift regularly,
wanting to know every detail.

"Maybe you can come back one day,"

"Maybe I will, but not for a long time yet. Sam is going to need me," she replies.

"Yeah well maybe I could go part time and you could go part time, we can work it out together."

Her face clouds over. Yep, I am talking as if we are a couple again.

She nods her head and stares out the window. Clearly subject closed.

"So what are you going today?" I ask.

"Um not much, I have to go to the physiotherapy later this afternoon so I can pop and see Sam again later tonight. That's it."

"Well I am going to sleep so you're doing more than me," I joke.

"True."

Finally I pull up at home. I have to pinch myself at times to remind myself that this is actually our home. I brought it with the intention of making it our family home. I just pray Holly comes round to me, I don't want to lose it, even without Sam, it feels more like a home than my apartment ever has been.

It was my father's idea to buy this place. He heard about it from a friend, it hadn't even been put on the market yet. We literally exchanged hands in one friendly meeting over coffee. Yet another valuable piece of advice I had off him. The best by far was not to give up on Holly.

"Be as cunning, as ruthless and as determined you can be. If she loved you once, chances are she either still loves you or she will love you again. You already won, just stick to your guns." he instructed, sounding like some kind of sports coach.

I am. She knows how I feel; now it's up to her. She gives me even a slight inch, I will grab it with both hands.

Chapter Thirty Six- Holly

The sweat pours off me as I jog on the treadmill. Forty seconds, forty one seconds the screen tells me.

"Don't push it Holly, you can stop anytime you want," Sally warns.

I continue to push through the burning pain in my leg. I have to get better; I could jog for at least thirty minutes before getting tired before the incident. I will get to one minute.

Fifty eight… fifty nine…

I slam the button to stop the machine and allow the machine to roll me off it, before collapsing the deep foam mats on the floor.

"That was brilliant Holly." Sally hugs me on the floor.

I breathe in and out hard. I did it!

"I am so proud of you." she carries on, helping me back up.

I have been working so hard, but today I just needed to push myself. Sam is coming home soon. I have my first cosmetic surgery booked and I can finally start looking like me again. I look in the mirror and despite the bruises and swellings have gone, the scars from across my nose and cheek are there. The hollowness of my face, the sickly shade of my face and the big bags under my eyes just make me feel like I'm a different person. I lost a lot of weight and strength through the surgeries and induced coma. I just want to feel normal. 'Emotional Hurdles' Melanie calls them in therapy. I need to get over one to be able to reach the next one. I know where I want to be. I want to be happy and normal and do simple things like play football with Sam and chase him around the house. Nick features heavily in that too. I want to look like the woman he desires again. I want him to not treat me like a fragile china doll and be roughly fucked on the kitchen table again.

Heat pools through me at the thought.

I want him so badly I could just throw myself at him sometimes.

I know what he game he is playing when he walks into my room in a towel or when he squeezes past me unnecessarily in the kitchen. He even fell asleep the other night on the sofa whilst we were watching a film. He spooned me and when I tried to move, he pushed his erection further into my bottom. He knows how to push my buttons and weaken me.

But it's not just lust. He has been at my side every step of the way. I don't think I could have come this far without his praise and encouragement. I don't love him like I did. Ever since that kiss the day he brought me home, I have known I love him more. The glimmers of the amazing man I knew were in there when I was his mistress now shine through. He is happy and not afraid to show his feelings towards me or our son. I need to tell him how I feel but I want to be fixed first.

I get home by taxi just past six o' clock. Phoebe is in the kitchen with coffee.

"Hey," I greet her.

"You look sweaty,"

"I managed one minute jogging," I tell her happily.

"That's amazing,"

I beam at her despite the ache in my legs and chest.

"What are you and Nick up to tonight?" Phoebe asks, with a knowing look on her face.

"Just getting a takeaway"

"Are you going to shower first?"

I laugh.

"I've got an hour before I need to move, do you want some help?" she offers kindly.

"Nope I've got it."

I get tired way to easily still, much to my frustration.

"Come on, can I at least sit with you?"

"Okay, thank you." I give in, as my right leg twinges.

I refuse to let Phoebe undress me, she has done far too much of that already. I get into the shower without looking at my reflection. I don't want to see it all; the scars on my neck and thigh are so ugly and savage. But it's the ones on my stomach that I can't bear. Every time I see them, I see Robbie. His crazy eyes as he tells me he is going to kill my baby. How Sam came out unscathed is baffling to everyone. There is a strong chance he is going to be my only baby, but that will be a hurdle further down the line.

I try to reach for the razor to shave my legs and my leg buckles.

"Argh," I cry out, steading myself.

"You okay?" Phoebe is at the shower door.

"I'd better sit down."

I sit down carefully on the shower floor.

"Can you shave my legs?" I ask embarrassed.

"Of course," she picks up the razor and the gel and starts shaving my legs.

"They don't need much, why are you doing it again?" she asks with a smile.

"Just do it please?"

"Anything else you need help with?" she teases.

"No thank you,"

"Okay, shout when you want out."

She closes the shower door and heads off out the bathroom whilst I shave the other bits myself sitting down. I know she knows how Nick and I are dancing around each other, but she is winding me up.

I call out to her and she stands by, ready to help in case I slip with wet feet. That has happened a lot. I don't fall thankfully and wrap a towel around myself.

"I got you some clothes out",

"Oh thank you."

I look at the bed to see my usual hoodie and jeans combo gone. Instead are some very pretty lilac pyjamas with a matching dressing gown.

"Phoebe?"

"It's a present from me, do you like it?"

"They are beautiful thank you,"

"You can wear them tonight. Try them on; with the amount of weight you've lost I hope they fit"

I slip them on. They feel lovely and so soft. A little loose but I love them.

"Oh you look so pretty, can I do your hair and makeup before I leave?"

"Why would I be doing my hair and makeup when I'm not going anywhere?"

"Because you want to impress Nick and you want makeup to boost your confidence, so that when he starts declaring his shit again, you can make up and have make-up sex?" she teases.

I smile, she is far too involved in our lives, but I am grateful.

"Well in that case, yes please."

I thought I would continue to hate my new short hair but actually since I have been to the hairdressers and they have layered it all up it actually looks nice. Phoebe blow dries it so it falls nicely just below my shoulders and puts some make up on my cheek and neck to help camouflage the scarring. I put on some mascara, blush and coloured lip balm. Don't want to overdo it or look ridiculous.

"You look gorgeous," Phoebe compliments me.

"Thank you so much,"

I actually look alright.

"Right, I really need to go, have a wonderful night,"

"Nothing will come of it," I protest.

Phoebe looks back from the door.

"It could if you let it."

"So what would do you fancy? Chinese? Curry? Pizza? Chippie?" Nick says pulling out the stack of menus out of the draw. I mentally make a note to start cooking properly again. We have been living off snacks, convenience food, take-away's and Phoebe's cooking. She has many talents my wonderful friend, but cooking isn't one of them. I think the best meal we had in here was when I made scrambled eggs on toast.

"Whatever you want," I reply.

Nick selects the Chinese menu and begins rooting through.

"Do you want anything in particular?" he asks.

"You choose."

Half an hour later we have a banquet of various take away containers on the coffee table, Nick always orders a huge selection, fancying a little bit of this, and some of that. I am stuck by a sense of de-ja-vu of the night Nick invited me into his flat to discuss me becoming his mistress. How far have we come from then? So much has changed, so much has happened. But in a sense it's kind of ironically similar. He wants something from me and he has persuaded me to put my doubts aside and agree to it.

Problem is how do I make him know that I have agreed to it?

"Do you want to watch a film?" He asks.

"Um sure,"

"You look so pretty in those PJ's, lilac really suits you." he compliments.

I feel myself blush and Im sure he can see it, even with the dim lighting.

"Thank you. They are a present from Phoebe."

He nods and gets the remote, flicking through Netflicks.

"What are you in the mood for?"

You!

"You choose, I'm easy," I breeze

"You are anything but easy." he snorts and selects something with Will Smith I think? I can't be sure as he stands up and stretches showing off his abs in loose tracksuit bottoms and a white vest top. He is without a doubt the hottest man alive. He picks up all the half empty containers and heads into the kitchen.

 I stand up and carry the plates in. I need to think about how to bring this up. Damn it I have never seduced a man before and I already know he is interested. Why is this so hard?

I am thinking so hard, I don't see where I am going and trip over the step leading into the kitchen.

I cry out in shock as the plates skid across the kitchen, with me following it.

"Oh shit! Holly." Nick jumps and lifts me off the floor.

I could cry in embarrassment. I have been doing so well, and now I have tripped twice today.

"I'm fine,"

"No you're not. You should have left me bring the rest of the plates in." He tuts and places me on the sofa.

Now I feel like the pathetic all over again.

He runs his hand over my pyjama legs.

"I can't feel much through the silk, can I have a look?" he asks cautiously.

"I don't have any knickers on," I protest.

"You have a long dressing gown."

I let him slip off my pyjama bottoms and the air hits me. He doesn't look whilst I make sure I'm properly covered and then runs his hands over the harsh lines of my stitches.

I panic as his hands hit the ugly lines. I don't want to see the look of disgust on his face, or the pity. But as his eyes meet mine, they show me something I didn't expect. They are flared with need.

"You look fine, the muscles have locked a little bit." he explains and starts rubbing my thigh in strong but delicious touches.

I can feel his hands circling my skin and every hair stands on end. I do feel discomfort in my thigh but not pain, just frustration as his finger grazes my skin.

"How does that feel?" He asks, completely focused.

"Good,"

"Is this the right spot? Do I need to go higher or lower on the bone?"

"Higher I think." I say before thinking.

His hands rise higher up my thigh. I concentrate on acting normally despite the dampness he is so close to.

"Is this high enough?"

No.

"Um…"

I shift so he looks at me. I am crap with words and declarations. He was even worse than me once.

"A bit higher please" I say looking at him. I hope he understands what I mean.

His eyes flare again as his hands trail to the very top of my thigh. His thumb is so close to touching me, I'm shaking.

His fingers circle in slow lazy movements, his thumb teasing me.

"Just say what you want Holly." he whispers huskily.

Unable to resist any longer, I reach up and pull his face closer to mine.

"You." I breathe.

I press my lips against his gently. Nick stares at me for a second then cups the back of my head and smashed his mouth against mine. I feel his heat as he presses his weight carefully against mine. My body is in overdrive as I grip his back, deepening the kiss.

"Are you sure?" he whispers.

I nod and help him remove his vest so his mouth watering torso is on display. As soon as the vest is off he is back on me kissing me, like his life depends on it. Nick unties my robe sash. My body freezes up. He is going to see me.

"Oh Holly, how I have wanted this." he moans and I feel the dressing gown getting pushed to the shoulders, only leaving my pyjama top on.

I try to fight the panic as I put my hands back on Nick's warm sexy body, but as he rains kisses down my neck he mouth touches the scar on my neck and I jolt away.

"Hol?"

I bunch myself up into a ball. Tears of frustration and embarrassment fill my eyes.

"I'm sorry, I want this so much," I blurt out.

"It's alright," Nick says and puts his arms around my bunched up shoulders.

"No it's not alright. I want to be with you," I groan.

He smiles and kisses the top of my head.

"Come with me," he says, standing up.

I stand up and tie my robe back up.

"Where are we going?"

"To bed."

I let him lead me up the stairs to my room. He switches the lights off, leaving the room black.

His arms go around me and he swings me round. His mouth claims mine once more. He slips off my robe again.

I let it slide to the floor this time and let him lower me onto the bed. My top goes along with his tracksuit bottoms.

"I love you too Holly, I love every inch of you, scarred or unscarred. It makes you who you are," he says, kissing the scar on my neck.

"This is what I stitched up when I fought to keep you alive,"

I didn't know that.

His mouth lowers to my collarbone and down my chest.

"You are still the sexiest, most beautiful, amazing woman in the world to me." Nick continues, kissing every scar on my body.

I feel tears on my cheeks, but I don't want him to stop.

"Make love to me Nick," I ask him finally.

He enters me, stretches me and I instantly feel the delicious burn.

As he makes love to me tenderly and so sweetly, I feel another piece of me return. It feels like I'm finally home.

The next few days are blurred, very blurred. I don't think I get out of bed much to be honest. Nick wears me out in every tingling way. Today though is the day I have been waiting for, the day Sam comes home. Nick is out getting the last few things Sam may need like extra small nappies and the specialised formula they have been giving him at the hospital. He still needs his oxygen tanks and will do for many months to follow. But our boy will be here, in our home with us. He will have his Mummy and Daddy here with him, a real family. Not forgetting Auntie Phoebe who is beaming like a Cheshire cat at mine and Nick's reunion.

I doubt whether sexual intercourse is some kind of medicine but I am stronger and happier than I have been in many, many months. I have been baking and cooking whilst waiting for Nick get back from town. The lasagne is ready to go into the oven tonight. Now I am finishing frosting the chocolate fudge cake. It's a surprise for Nick but I can't wait for Sam to be sitting at

the table in the kitchen eating cake with us in the years
to come.

"Hol," I hear Nick yell shutting the front door.

"In the kitchen,"

He comes in with armfuls of bags.

"What's all this?" I laugh.

"I went a bit overboard,"

"I can see that."

Nick spots the cake behind me.

"Cake?" he squeals like a child.

"It's time to celebrate,"

"Oh I am one lucky bastard," he says, going over it to.

"Not now, we can have some after we bring our baby
home,"

Nicks face drops a bit.

"I may have another reason to celebrate, if it is can we
have cake now please?" He gives me his begging eyes,
which are really hard to refuse.

"Nothing can be better than having Sam here,"

"No" Nick fumbles with his coat pocket. "But this could
be a second best."

I freeze as he goes down on one knee in front of me.

"Nick.." I gasp.

"Marry me Rag Doll?" he asks softly.

"Nick, we have only just got back together…" I start shocked.

"Yes, but we have been in love with each other for over a year now. We just realised it at different times. You are the only one for me Holly, you have made me the kind of man I always wanted to be and never knew how to be. I want you to be my wife,"

I melt.

"Well I suppose I better say yes then." I grin.

Nick picks me up and kisses me so hard I think I can see stars when he finally puts me down.

"All of this for chocolate fudge cake?"

Nick laughs and reaches for the cake.

"Yep, let's wrap a piece up to go. We have a son to pick up."

EPILOGUE

Nick (Two Years Later)

"Well I think you look spiffing son," I tell Sam as he pulls at his waistcoat.

"No want on," Sam moans.

"I know dude, but we both have to."

I pull Sam up and hold his hand as we walk to the walk in wardrobe which has a floor length mirror.

"See, we are the same." I tell him as we both look at the reflection in the mirror.

We really are as well, although he is by far the better looking Willis. He takes after me though in looks, with our dark hair and eyes, his skin is a lot lighter than mine but my father swears he is the spitting image of me. Holly does too. But so much of her I see in him, the way he smiles is identical to hers and is so many of his expressions are hers. His calm and quiet inquisitive nature matches hers. Personality wise he is Holly.

My amazing little mini me, who has had to endure so much in his short life, so many consultations and minor surgeries but he is always smiling. He is catching up fast and once he is fully caught up I think he is going to fly.

491

He started walking a few weeks ago, and is picking up words daily. Premature babies often are a bit behind others their age but his mind is just amazing. Mentally, Sam is a very clever boy and loves nothing more than playing with his train track or listening to one of his many favourite story books.

"Mummy?" Sam asks tugging at my hand.

I smile at his little face, so much hope in those eyes.

Yeah, I totally get it, I want her too.

"Let's head downstairs and wait for her."

His arms go up and I pick him up. I shouldn't really, everyone says he needs to walk everywhere now, but I don't care today.

Voices fill the garden as we head down to the marquee.

"There he is," my father announces as we walk through the crowd.

"Gan-dad." Sam squeals.

I put Sam down and he quickly walks over to my father. That man is a completely different man to the one he was before Sam. It seems Sam has brought my father back. This is the father I must have had once before he got burnt by my mother. It is surreal but in glimpses I remember moments of clarity. Like the way he always bends his knees when talking to Sam, so they are on the same level. Or the way that he strokes Sam's hair when he is upset. Just like he used to do with me so many years ago, I had forgotten until now.

"Ready Nicholas?" he asks me.

"I have been ready for over two years now,"

"Ah but now she feels ready, this is the time."

Holly has been in and out the hospital many times over the last two years since her incident. She refused to marry me until she was herself again, mentally and physically. So when she was discharged as a patient four months ago it was time. Now here we are on our wedding day.

"Nick, it's time," the minister says quietly.

I nod and head up to the makeshift altar in the marquee. Nothing flashy, something simple they are Holly's words. I hope I have done her proud having it here in our back garden. A big marquee is our church with about fifty people attending. The only decorations are woodland flowers.

Excitement bursts through me as the music starts playing for Holly.

I am one lucky asshole. I never thought I could feel this, let alone want to. Holly has changed everything. I found her, even if at the start it was a shady business deal. I am glad it happened in a way, it brought her to me. She somehow saw through me, through the bullshit I believed was myself. Holly made me into the man I was too scared to want to be.

I take in a deep breath when Holly appears at the entrance.

There is my Rag Doll.

Although she looks far from it today, but I couldn't care less if she was in those baggy jeans and hoodie, she is so beautiful it is overwhelming. She has let her hair grow again and it is curled today in ringlets down her back with flowers adorning her head. Her dress is so simple, plain and hanging to her ankles, not showing off what I know is her sensational figure. Just elegant and stunning like her.

Sam squeals and breaks out of my father's arms and rushes to her.

A few people stand up, but she laughs and holds his hand. She walks up the altar with him.

My perfect family, one I love with everything I have.

"Dearly beloved" the minister announces.

THE END

Acknowledgments

The first thank you has to be to you. Whoever has chosen to read this and took a chance on a new author like me. Thank you so much. I hope you enjoyed it as much as I enjoyed writing it.

Thank you to all my family and friends who have supported me throughout my first novel Fusion. It has been an emotional ride to gain confidence and crippling worries over grammatical errors.

Thank you to my father who was the first person to buy Fusion and being so proud of me, despite the awkward phone calls about the sexual nature in my book! I'm sure after he has read Enemies with Benefits there will be even more shocks in store for him. Sorry!

Thank you to mum for pushing me, nagging me and forcing me to make a career for myself. Without her I doubted I would have passed my GCSE's let alone go to University to study Creative Writing. Thank you for

496

helping me become who I am today and for your endless support, encouragement and love.

Another thank you has to be to my sister Natalie Gill for reading, re reading and reading my manuscripts a million times over. Going over each and every line, word by word, you are not only an amazing sister, but my best friend. Thank you.

Thank you to my wonderful friend and college Louise Marks first of all for reading Fusion, but for taking Enemies with Benefits and helping me toothcomb it. Your expert advice and grammatical eye has been an absolute blessing. The attention to detail is mind blowing. I won't forget getting my folder back and seeing so many 'pink for thinks' (as we say in school). You are simply a legend Mrs Marks! Thank you.

Thank you to my daughters as always, Bella and Evie you are my absolute world. You both make me so proud and so happy. I love you both with everything I have, my beautiful, little treasures.

Thank you to my partner, Spencer. Spencer, your patience with me has been incredible. Once the children are asleep, you don't bat an eye lid when the laptop cranks open and I know you most nights you must feel like you are on your own, when I am mentally taken away into my characters world. Thank you for your support and patience. I love you.

Printed in Great Britain
by Amazon